Additional praise for
Portofino . . .

"Charming."

—*Boston Sunday Globe*

"Calvin's observations reveal the ironies of a family that speaks in biblical phrases but faces all-too-human foibles . . . Under Mr. Schaeffer's graceful rendering, this is a story of sympathetic characters, a deft feat considering some of their narrow views."

—*Washington Times*

"Delightful . . . a wickedly funny story."

—*Chattanooga Times*

"Wonderfully lucid and witty . . . *Portofino* walks a beautifully balanced line between the serious and the humorous, poking gentle fun at the foibles of religious zealotry without disparaging the deep dedication behind it. Hilariously funny at times."

—*Anniston Star*

"A wry coming-of-age tale . . . splendid laugh-out-loud moments."

—*Kirkus Reviews*

"Richly ironic and satirical. At times it borders on hilarious . . . wickedly charming."

—*Milwaukee Journal*

"A rich brew of cross-cultural comedy . . . enlivened by discoveries and misapprehensions, family squabbles and healings and the dizzy sensibility of a boy whose world opens up in all kinds of poignant and hilarious ways . . . Schaeffer makes this utterly unpredictable family—besides the parents, there are Calvin's two sharply drawn older sisters—both painful and appealing."

—*Los Angeles Times*

continued on next page…

Praise for
Saving Grandma

"*Saving Grandma* is the sequel to *Portofino*, which introduced us to young Calvin, his parents and two older sisters. Although *Saving Grandma* has been carefully designed as a stand-alone story, you might as well buy *Portofino* while you're at it, because once you hear the irresistible voice of Calvin, you'll want to read both . . . Frank Schaeffer has a strange and singular story to tell, and he tells it with happy assurance. It's impossible not to love it."

—*Rocky Mountain News*

"Raucous."

—*Entertainment Weekly*

"A triumph! Not since Huck Finn has American literature been graced with a character as irresistible as Calvin Dort Becker . . . Mr. Schaeffer's gifts as a novelist are more than merely comic: *Saving Grandma* has a deeper river flowing through it as well, one that is sensual and loving and full of true grace. This is a wonderful book!"

—Andre Dubus III,
Pushcart Prize–winning author of *Bluesman*

"The same humor and warmth that distinguished *Portofino* . . . great insight . . . *Portofino* will soon be made into a movie, and one can hope the same will happen to the present work."

—*Library Journal*

"[A] sweet-natured, comic tale."

—*Kirkus Reviews*

"Funny . . . poignant . . . Schaeffer manages to be both irreverent and sympathetic toward the foibles of this hilariously holier-than-thou family . . . What's wonderful about this loopy coming-of-age story is Schaeffer's sensitivity in showing Calvin's need to break from a family he both despises and loves."

—*St. Paul Pioneer Press*

"Clever, humorous, and satisfying."

—*Booklist*

"Schaeffer's greatest feat is transforming Calvin from a rotten little kid into a character so compelling that I felt as if he were pulling me through the pages . . . On a par with Calvin's metamorphosis is Schaeffer's near-perfect touch with the details of religion. Somehow he manages to integrate the most serious issues of religious practice, even explaining their relevance to a less-informed reader, without losing the flow of the novel."

—*St. Petersburg Times*

"Irreverent, amusing . . . Schaeffer's slapstick jokes and often tender evocations of youth make for an uneasy but entertaining cross between *Portnoy's Complaint* and TV's *The Wonder Years*."

—*Publishers Weekly*

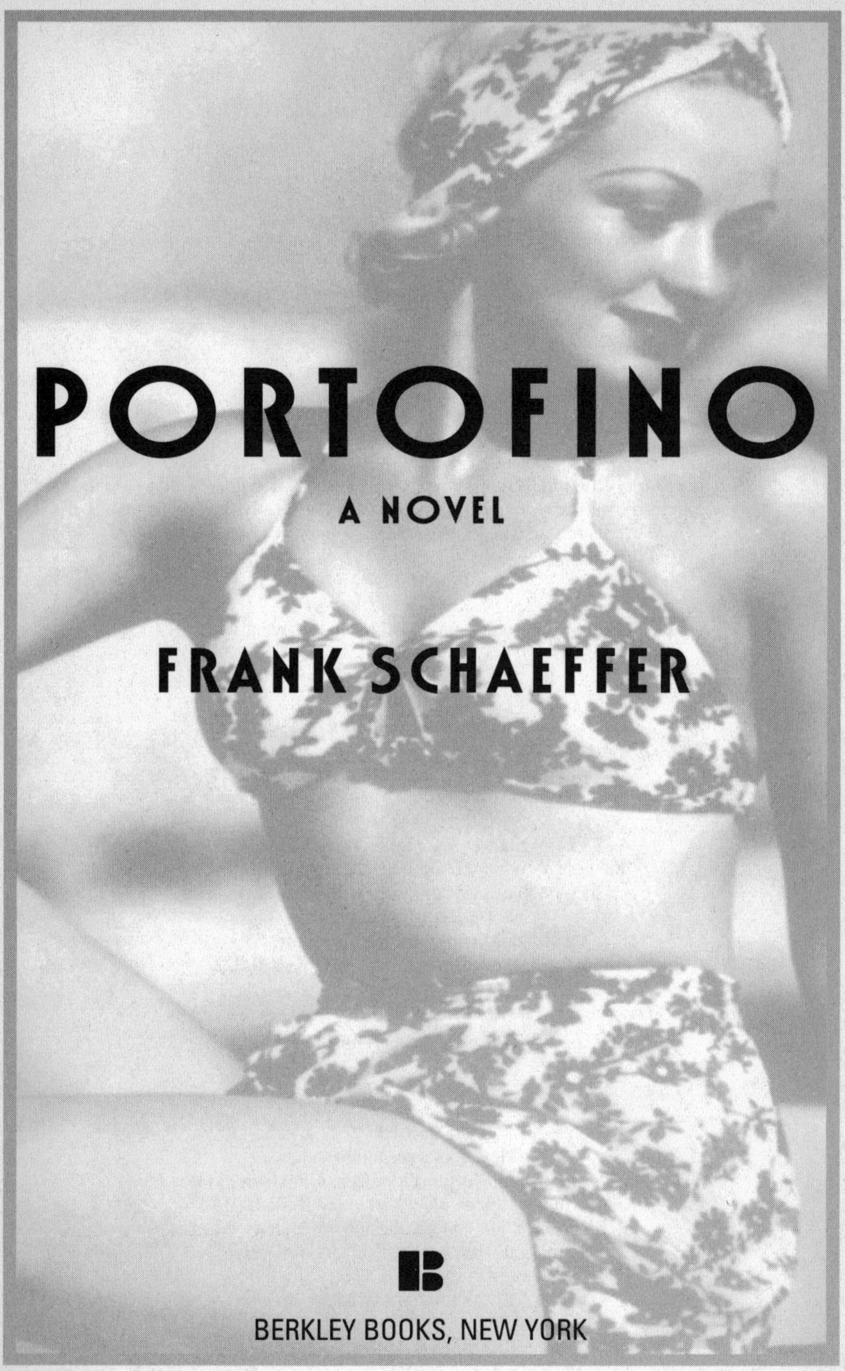

PORTOFINO

A NOVEL

FRANK SCHAEFFER

BERKLEY BOOKS, NEW YORK

This is a work of fiction. Names, characters, places, and incidents either are the product of the author's imagination or are used fictitiously. Any resemblance to events or persons, living or dead, is entirely coincidental.

PORTOFINO

A Berkley Book / published by arrangement with the author

PRINTING HISTORY
Macmillan edition published 1992
Berkley mass market edition / September 1996
Berkley trade paperback edition / January 1999

The Penguin Putnam Inc. World Wide Web site address is
http://www.penguinputnam.com

ISBN: 0-425-16694-5

BERKLEY®
Berkley Books are published by
The Berkley Publishing Group, a member of Penguin Putnam Inc.,
375 Hudson Street, New York, New York 10014.
BERKLEY and the "B" design are trademarks
belonging to Berkley Publishing Corporation.

PRINTED IN THE UNITED STATES OF AMERICA

10 9 8 7 6 5 4 3 2 1

To my wife

REGINA

PORTOFINO

A NOVEL

1962

1

THE FIRST GLIMPSE of the Mediterranean was always turquoise. "A turquoise bracelet studded with diamonds," my sister Janet said. I had two sisters. Janet, my angry fifteen-year-old sister, and Rachael, who was meek and thirteen.

Janet liked to clasp her hands in front of her and say things poetically, like about the Mediterranean being a bracelet. That afternoon the bracelet was framed between the dingy apartment buildings that line the railroad tracks behind the city of Genoa, Italy. Genoa was the place you changed trains in on the way to Santa Margherita.

Santa Margherita was where the summer vacation really began. The smells were right. Gardenia, ferrous oxide from the rusted train tracks, and a hint of urine. Not ammonia-rich, real, stinking, French-style urine, but the subtle Italian variety: a faint apology for the need to relieve oneself in a corner by the ivy-covered wall next to the fountain at the end of the platform.

If we had been rich we would have taken a horse and carriage all the way from the station to the Pensione Biea in Paraggi. We took the blue diesel bus instead.

Mom sat in the one unoccupied seat. The girls and I straddled the luggage. Dad stood staring out the back window. He was still in one of his Moods because Mom had almost made us miss our connection in Milano. She did that every year. She always needed to get something important she had forgotten to pack for the vacation. So she would rush out of the station and cross the road to the shops opposite to get what she needed.

Every year Dad said the same thing. "If the train leaves before you get back we'll just go without you!"

We children would sit, hearts pounding, praying for Mom. "Dear Jesus, please get Mom back in time. And if she's late please speak to Dad's heart so he won't leave her at the station."

God answered our prayers. Mom would make it back, but God would not go so far as to make Dad forgive her for making us all nervous wrecks and for risking spoiling "the few precious days of vacation I need so badly!" as Dad said.

Dad knew his rights. He had a highly developed sense of personal grievance. He believed that Mom was in a conspiracy to destroy his life and give him ulcers. He even blamed her for his toothaches. He believed she was in league with bus conductors and train engineers the world over to see how close she could come to making us all miss our travel connections. And how she could prove to Dad that the Lord was more on her side than on his, since the buses and trains were always just late enough so that we made them in spite of her having taken a long bath or gone shopping when he *told* her there was no time and she had to hurry or we'd miss the train-bus-boat, whatever.

There *was* no time according to the schedule. But for Mom schedules were irrelevant because angels from heaven always made the buses, trains, or boats late so we could catch them.

We knew this was a miracle and that Mom was more spiritual than Dad because the buses and trains that were late were usually late in Switzerland—that clockwork state run by chronographic fascists—yet when Mom needed a little more time to, for instance, finish shaving her legs, even Swiss trains *did not run on time*!

So we never doubted the existence of God, and Dad never got to see Mom miss a train and get taught the lesson she so richly deserved to learn. You can't fight God.

When we got off the bus in Paraggi I ran on ahead to the Pensione Biea. Dad called after me, "You *can't* choose your own room. You have to wait until we get there."

Rachael and I were probably going to get the Outside Room again. You had to leave the main part of the pensione to get to the Outside Room. It was a room that had been added on and had its own staircase and entrance. It also had no water pressure in the shower, and no toilet. The room was higher than the water tank, so when you turned on the shower tap it made a sucking noise, then spit at you. For some reason the bidet worked though, so we had clean bottoms and feet. Also I could run water in the bidet after I peed in it at night. Once I thought of doing the other thing, what we called ''Big'' rather than ''Little.'' (''Little'' was to pee so you can guess what ''Big'' was.) But I knew it would not go down the bidet drain and I'd be punished.

Because we were a family of born-again, Bible-believing, fundamentalist Reformed Christians who Stood on the Word, we had euphemistic names for everything embarrassing. My mom would whisper to my sisters that she could not swim that day because she was ''Off the Roof.'' Mom had a whole parallel universe of phrases that turned almost everything imaginable into either a moral lesson or de-fanged its passion and left it—sex for instance, or ovaries or wombs, whatever—as harmless as a faded Victorian lavender-scented postcard. ''Greetings from Montreux!'' ''I'm Off the Roof today,'' ''She has a Female Problem,'' ''Did you go both Big and Little?'' ''Is your Little Thing sore?'' ''You should wash under the little protective flap of skin God created to keep your Little Thing clean.''

When my ''Little Thing'' was ''naughty,'' it would stand up. It was part of ''God's beautiful gift that you must save to unwrap at Christmas—Marriage,'' as Mom would say.

But this was 1962. My ''Little Thing'' wasn't connected to my brain yet, and would go up and down for no particular reason. I was ten years old.

When Bible-believing fundamentalist Reformed Protestants go on vacation in Roman Catholic Italy, surrounded by unbelievers, they must witness to the truth.

When everyone else in the Pensione Biea was being served their antipasto at the evening meal, *we* had our heads bowed while Mother said grace.

When Mother prayed we *really* ''bore witness to

the light that was in us.'' She would pray as long in the pensione as she did at home. I would stare at three slices of tuna fish, three slices of salami, four olives, and a large round of mortadella while Mom prayed. I tried not to look up to see if Jennifer Bazlinton, the ten-year-old English girl at the next table, was watching us, though I knew she was. I was mortified. I tried not to think of how different we were, even though I knew we had to be since we had been ''called out from among the raging heathen to be a light unto the nations.'' I counted the pieces of green pistachio nut in my mortadella. There were five. I counted the pieces of the black peppercorn in my three slices of salami; there were two in one, three in another, and only half a piece in the last one.

''Dear Heavenly Father, we just come before Thee to thank Thee for providing the funds for our vacation''—the oil from my olives was draining off them, beginning to puddle—''. . . and we come into Thy wonderful presence to worship and thank Thee for this day.''

There was a nice Roman Catholic Italian family who were at the corner table. I had seen them say grace and they just crossed themselves *with their eyes open*. Their dad said something over the food, one sentence. They didn't seem embarrassed. But our prayers needed to be long so that we might not hide our lamp under a bushel, so that we wouldn't get to heaven and find that we had been ashamed of the Lord and that because of this He would say we had denied Him before men so He would deny us before the Father.

''We just praise and glorify Thy Holy Name, Lord, and we just ask that You will make our weaknesses perfect in Your strength.''

The dark green oil from the marinated olives was beginning to stain the mortadella slice at the edge. The worst thing that could happen was about to happen. So I began to pray too.

In my heart I said, "Please, oh please, don't let Lucrezia come to our table to ask if we want wine with dinner while Mom is praying!"

Lucrezia was the owner's daughter. When she cleaned the rooms with her mother they both wore blue housecoats over their day clothes. At night she was the pensione's waitress. She wore a white apron over her black pleated skirt. Her starched apron strings hung down to the hemline behind. Lucrezia wore her silver crucifix outside of her white blouse when she served us our dinner. It made her look *very* Roman Catholic.

Lucrezia was standing at our table. "*Vino? Rosso—? Bianco—?*" she said.

"Please, Lord!" I prayed.

Mom kept right on praying.

"*Vino*?"

Couldn't she see we were praying? Would Mom interrupt the prayer and look up?

"We thank Thee for this food and we pray for those who live and work in this pensione that they might come to know Thee as their personal Savior . . ."

"*Vino*?"

Mom opened her eyes, looked up sorrowfully, blinked as her eyes adjusted to the light, then smiled ruefully at Lucrezia. Poor girl, she didn't know the Lord. In fact, here we were praying, and she didn't even wait until we were done. Probably she didn't even notice. I guess she thought we were staring at our food while Mom talked to herself with her eyes shut. We had pity for Lucrezia and all the unsaved Italians. Roman Catholics thought they knew the Lord, but they worshiped Mary, not Jesus; they did not trust Him as their personal Savior but tried to merit salvation by works. I knew they were lost, but, just the same, I wished we didn't have to pray in front of them.

"*Vino*?" Lucrezia was starting to really wonder what was going on. She tried English. "Wine? Red . . . White . . . Yes?" She smiled. Mom smiled too. Mom's smile was full of compassion.

"No, Lucrezia, no, we won't be having any *alcohol* to drink."

"No wine."

"No, thank you, we're Christians, just some water please."

"*Acqua minerale*?"

"No, just natural water . . . *acqua naturale*."

It was Lucrezia's turn to look sorrowful and to smile wistfully. Mom took her smile to be an expression of longing to know the Truth. I knew Lucrezia just felt sorry for people who drank tepid tap water at dinner when a hundred and fifty lira would buy a bottle of Chianti or Orvieto.

When Lucrezia walked away, we bowed our heads to finish our interrupted prayer. "And, Lord, we pray for dear little Lucrezia. We pray that You will give one of us an opportunity to share Your love with her and an opportunity to witness to her. In Jesus' precious name we pray. Amen."

A fly was struggling on its back in the oil on my plate. Its feet kicked, it had smeared the pattern of its wings onto the glaze of the thick white dinner plate.

Jennifer was staring at our table. Then she said something to her mother and giggled.

2

• • • • •

I COULD SMELL the pine tree outside our window at the pensione. I checked for mosquito bites. Only one on my elbow. Rachael was still asleep. The white lace curtain hissed against the white wall as it fluttered, curled, then uncurled in the morning breeze. I could hear the grind of a diesel engine as a bus stopped, a Vespa accelerated around it, its flat horn sounded twice. The bus was leaving. I smelled the diesel fumes, then heard the voice of the Banini (beach attendant), who'd just arrived, call out "*Buon giorno*!" to somebody.

I sat bolt upright. This was the first day of our vacation. I was allowed to go out early by myself! I slept naked in Italy. No pajamas needed. In fact, I slept under just one sheet. Rachael wore a nightgown because she needed to be modest. Her womanhood was flowering, as Mom put it. But nothing was flowering on me, so I could be naked and cool during the night.

I pulled on my swimming trunks and closed the door behind me. I went down the outside stairs. There were two pine nuts lying on the steps from the tree above. I stopped to pick them up. The black powder on their hard thick shell cases, thicker than the white nut inside, dusted off on my fingers. There was a loose brick sitting in the garden. I always used that same brick each year we came on vacation to crush pine nuts. When I was little I used to smash them too hard; the thick shell would get all mashed up with the squashed nut, and you had to sort of suck the nut off every fragment of shell. You never got a big enough piece to really taste the nut. Now I tapped the nut lightly, just hard enough to crack the shell but not pulverize it. I squatted over the path, cracked my pine nut, looked briefly to see if there were any more after I ate it, then ran across the road to the beach.

The Banini swam out to a rowboat tied to a buoy in the bay, then rowed it over to where the other boats were moored. When he had made a "train" of boats, five in all, he would stand facing forward in the first one and row it to shore, pulling the others. Then he would drag the boats up onto the sandy beach and turn them over, so children would not play in them and get sand in them, and he would stick the oars next to them in the sand. On one oar he hung a hand-lettered cardboard sign, "For Renting. 1 Hours—*Lire* 250. ½ hours—*Lire* 150."

As the sun came up over the hill that fell steeply into the little bay at Paraggi, its hot white light turned our bay from dark green to turquoise. I could hear the creak of the oarlocks under the water as I swam out to meet the Banini. He smiled. A missing lower tooth made him look older than he was. "Youa back een a Paraggi? And youa seesters and mama back too?"

I nodded. He motioned with his chin for me to climb into the boat. I struggled to hoist myself over the high prow of the rowboat. The Banini laughed at my effort, then proffered a sinewy brown arm to help me. My hand scrabbled, wet and slippery on his hard, dry forearm. He pretended to let me fall back into the water, I made a grab for the side of the boat; as I slid backward, he caught my wrist and lifted me in one quick swoop into the boat. Dripping, I sat for a couple of seconds in the warm sun. Then I crawled from the front boat he was rowing into the one behind it, then onto the last one in the "train." There I looked about me at the familiar skyline.

Tall cypresses spiked the top of the hills. Here and there a villa broke the roll of the mountain. Where pine trees stopped, the gray smoke of the olive groves began and ran mistily down in shadows almost to the water. On the point sat the "Castle," a nineteenth-century villa, magnificent and frescoed, built like a Norman tower with some Renaissance remembrance in its colors, the size of its windows, and its fieldstone foundation made of huge, rough-hewn blocks. It was a fabulous building. People said that J. Paul Getty owned it.

On the beach the Banini's assistant was putting out the neat rows of red-and-white-striped deck chairs. Each with its own umbrella, ashtray, and side table. The deck chairs' rental cost was added to the pensione bill at the end of your vacation. We only rented one. This was so Mom could sit comfortably while she read aloud to us. The rest of us would lie on towels. The English family, the Bazlintons, rented a chair for each of them, even Jennifer. But they wasted their chairs. Jennifer was never in hers; her father went and stood talking at the espresso-pizza bar above the beach. Mrs. Bazlinton did not even come out to the beach until about twelve noon and left early each day to go shopping. When she was on the beach, she wore a two-piece bathing suit! Our mom always wore a one-piece bathing suit. It had a little ruffle, like the beginning of a skirt around it, so that no one would get the idea that our mom was immodest, let alone a loose or worldly woman.

The boat I was in bumped gently into the one in front of it. I hopped out into the water. It was only up to my waist. I helped untie the other boats and pull them up onto the beach. When the Banini turned the boats over I had to watch out for my feet as the edge of the hull crunched down into the sand. The year before I had not been fast enough and almost broke my foot under the hard varnished oak rim of the rowboat. Dad had said that to not be careful was irresponsible. I had risked spoiling everyone's vacation. If my foot had been broken, we would have all had to go back to Switzerland since Italian medicine was no good. He also said that I should be careful of these Italians. "They don't have the same sense of responsibility as we do," he said.

The Banini had been very sorry about the accident. As my foot swelled up, he had carried me up to the pensione and apologized profusely to my mother. Fortunately, she had the foresight to come equipped. She put a cool witch hazel pack on my foot, and in seconds it stopped swelling. She had also prayed that the Lord would "reach out and touch Calvin's foot with His healing hand." And He did, so the vacation wasn't spoiled. Not by me, anyway.

The sun was getting hot now. Because this was our

first day at the beach, Mom wanted me to wear a T-shirt from 10 A.M. until 3 P.M., the hottest part of the day, so I wouldn't burn and spoil the vacation.

That night she laid cold towels on my sunburned back. She said she didn't think it would blister too badly. She wanted to know why I did this every year. Dad said he felt sorry for me, but that since I had not listened to Mom, what did I expect? After it peeled it stopped being sore.

Janet was the first of the family down to the beach that day. She got to sit in our deck chair until Mom arrived. She had just started shaving her legs that spring. For some reason she got angry with me when I asked her about it. I had found her razor in the soap dish at home after she had her bath. I had asked her why there was a razor in the soap dish since Mom had not had a bath that day and Dad kept his razor in his toilet bag in the cupboard; Janet had snatched the razor away from me.

''Don't you know what the word 'private' means?'' she'd asked. She had stalked down the hall and slammed the door to her room.

''When girls get to a certain age,'' Mom told me, ''God begins to work a wonderful change in their bodies. One thing that happens is that they begin to grow a little extra hair on their legs. European women don't mind having that little bit of extra hair on their legs and under their arms. But American girls like nice smooth legs, and we find underarm hair unseemly. So we shave our legs and under our arms too when we bathe. Janet has just started doing this because she is becoming a woman. When we go through certain physical changes, at first we are a little shy about them. So you mustn't say anything about it anymore.''

That's why I asked Janet what the rash was, what was wrong with her legs, if a jellyfish had stung her. I did it because I knew she would be angry and because I knew she couldn't say anything back, because if she did, she would have to admit how she did it, how she didn't use enough soap because she was always so slap-dash, impetuous about everything, and even though she was becoming a woman, she was still messy and careless so now she had a rash. Her rash went even deeper red when she put on her Bain de Soleil suntan oil. Then she stretched her legs out into the sun and ignored my question.

"You can tell we just got here," Janet said. "Look how white we are compared to the English family. Judging by their tans they've been here at least a week."

"Jennifer said they have a whole month of vacation this year. We're only here ten days," I said.

"You shouldn't compare us to other people," Janet answered.

Now the sun was high in the sky, the water was really warm. I put on my mask and fitted the snorkel into the side strap, then took the mouthpiece in my mouth and plunged in. On the right-hand side of the bay at Paraggi, where the raw sewage from the pensione came out of a pipe, there were fewer fish than on the left-hand side where there was no sewage. I would snorkle by the big rocks that lined the left-hand shore.

When you put your head under the water, you could hear your heart beat in your ears. You could also hear distant outboard engines better than you could when your head was out of the water. I tried it many times. Head under water, I could hear a boat coming. Head out, nothing. Head under, it was closer now. Head out, still nothing. Then it rounded the point. Now I could hear it head out of the water since the point of the bay no longer blocked out the sound. Dad had told me to be careful of how sound was amplified underwater. He said if I was swimming underwater, and someone exploded something, my eardrums would pop because water magnified the sound, so I should watch out. I never figured out how to be careful of this. How could you tell if someone was about to drop a bomb in the water near you?

The boat had some people in it from a yacht. The Very Wealthy as Dad called them. The Very Wealthy were not merely rich people, let alone middle class; they were so rich that they could own yachts! Dad told us that if you had to even ask how much money you had to have to own a yacht, then you knew right there you didn't have enough.

Dad said, ''Maintaining a yacht is so expensive that it ends up costing more than the boat itself; only the Very Wealthy can bear those sort of expenses.''

Yachts would anchor in the next bay from ours. If you swam out far enough, you could look into the bay where they were moored, where the Very Wealthy kept their boats, in a harbor that was the most wonderful, glamorous, and interesting place in the world—Portofino.

The Banini hurried forward to help two girls in two-piece bathing suits, really small immodest ones, out of the boat from the yacht. An older man, my mom said ''clearly *not* their father,'' as she glanced meaningfully at Dad, waited to disembark until the Banini had pulled the launch far enough up on the beach so he could step out onto the dry sand. He had cream-colored white pants and white shoes on.

Why would the Very Wealthy leave their yacht to

come to our little beach? Dad explained that the riches of the Very Wealthy began to bore them. That sooner or later they ran out of things to do with their money and the things of this world, and started looking for other things to amuse them, like sitting on our beach during the day so that their yacht would not get boring. He also said that the Very Wealthy loved to parade their wealth like the Pharisees, and that there was no point being rich unless people could see you were rich since the satisfaction one could get out of worldly riches was fleeting and temporary, and that unlike spiritual wealth that was not corruptible, material wealth brings with it the terrible burden of always needing to have more.

They got out of their boat and paraded their wealth before us, then they sat down in deck chairs—of course they each had one—and the Banini brought them drinks, *alcoholic* drinks, from the snack bar. My parents exchanged more glances with each other. And Janet tried to exchange a glance with Mom too, but Mom wasn't looking at her, she was looking at the bathing suit of one of the wealthy girls.

"That's a very expensive bathing suit she's got on," Mom said.

"You look much more beautiful in yours," Dad answered. Dad was cranky but he was loyal.

3

THE BAZLINTON FAMILY had full pension. We had half pension. They had all three meals a day at the Pensione Biea. We had breakfast and dinner. But for once, the fact that we had less money to spend on our vacation than the English family paid off. We ate picnics on the beach every day while Jennifer was led back up to the Pensione Biea. She had to get dressed, sit at the table, eat a long four-course lunch, then take a nap after which she would return to the beach. By this time it was 3 P.M. Now *she* was the one who seemed odd. Now it was *her* parents who were out of step with the marching orders of the rest of the human race. We said grace, a long grace, but Jennifer had to take naps!

At about eleven in the morning Mom would hail one of the blue buses that ran between Portofino, Paraggi, Santa Margherita, and back. Armed with a giant wicker basket, she rode the bus to Portofino. There she walked in the back streets from shop to shop and purchased our picnic.

We gorged ourselves on the bounty of a Mediterranean August as we sat in the shade of our umbrella and scanned the horizon of the Gulf of Genoa. Figs bursting pink and milky, grapes that were in huge, odd-sized bunches still warm from the sun, vast sheets of wax paper on which micro-thin slices of prosciutto marched in solid ranks of pink and white tenderness, olives of every size and color, nimbus clouds of fresh buffalo milk mozzarella cheese floating in a bath of whey, tomatoes—long, thin, orange ones and huge, fat, misshapen red ones, *red* with a flame of yellow or green at one end, so fresh that they smelled like the bruised leaves of the plant when you pick them off the vine. All this our mother spread before us along with a loaf of fresh saltless bread and a square of focaccia, oozing olive oil, which I loved but my fastidious sisters would not touch. Calvin's ''grease bread,'' my sister Janet called it.

After Mom had eaten a little, she would sit back in her deck chair, a queen among her grateful subjects, and we, ranged on towels about her, would keep eating while she read aloud.

And so it was that my outer eye and inner eye, my nose, and my taste buds conspired together each lunchtime with my ears to offer me a surreal kaleidoscopic vision of an intensely bright world. A world of slow-moving Italian families, hot sun on blood warm water, peppery tastes, stories read aloud of Huck Finn or Ratty and Mole on their beloved river, all tangled with crusty bread and wafer-thin slices of salty pig flesh, which melted in my mouth.

The water lapped, and I awoke from the part in *The Wind in the Willows* where Ratty's boat had just tipped over and his beautiful picnic basket had gone to the bottom of the river.

"Were you asleep?" Rachael asked accusingly.

"No I was not!" I said.

"Then tell me what just happened."

"The basket has gone to the bottom of the river!"

"No, before that."

"I . . . I, well I *do* know!" I said.

"No you don't, you were asleep!" said Rachael.

Then Mom would rescue me. "Rachael, we're on *vacation*, we are all supposed to be resting. If he took a little nap that's fine."

Rachael looked darkly at me for a moment then said, "Well he doesn't sleep at night if he sleeps in the day, he'll keep *me* awake!"

The shadow cast by the mountain that loomed behind our bay began to fall on the other end of the beach. Gradually it crept toward our end. As it inexorably moved toward us, it cleared a path as surely as if it had been some deadly poison gas. Where the shadow fell the beach emptied. Mothers stood up and shook out the sand from crumpled damp towels, children took one last swim as fathers implored them to get out of the water and go to the beach cabins to shower off and dress. With a rhythmic "clack," "clack," the Banini began to slowly make his way up the beach folding deck chairs, closing umbrellas, and emptying the ashtrays, which stood on metal spike legs, into a garbage can he carried with him.

"We've got about ten more minutes of sun," said Dad. "Last chance for a swim."

"Why don't you come in with us, Dad?" we shouted.

"Not today, maybe tomorrow," he replied.

Mom added her stock reproof to my father's athletic indolence, "It's a *real* shame that your father won't go in anymore! He was always such a fine swimmer."

"Oh, come on, Dad!" we'd say.

"The water's too wet! It gets wetter each year." Then Dad would laugh, but we had heard this joke so many times that all we did was roll our eyes.

"All you do is work on vacations," said Janet.

"I have a lot of reading material to catch up on, Janet . . . anyway I enjoy reading," Dad answered.

"Who would want to sit on a beach all day reading the *Presbyterian Perspective* and never go swimming?" asked Rachael.

At this point Mom would intervene lest we go too far and put Dad in a bad mood.

"That's enough, dear, you mustn't talk to your father like that. Look the sun is almost gone, if you want a swim you better do it now."

Why exactly we needed to avoid swimming in the shade, after the sun had sunk behind the olive-clad hills, I never knew. But at the time I took it for granted that this was just one more unarguable truth.

After dinner that night we went for a walk, rather, *the* walk since it was always to the same destination: Portofino.

To walk to Portofino, you left the pensione, walked down the main road for about five hundred yards, a perilous journey in which you were all but hurled into the sea by every passing bus or car on this narrow coast-hugging ribbon of asphalt, to a small set of stairs cut into the rock face from which the path between Paraggi and Portofino is carved.

Climbing up these steps you came to the actual path, the kind of luxurious, tiled, beautiful footpath that only Italians bother to make but then forget to maintain. A path hung with every good-smelling green-bursting thing. Gardenia bushes among them.

"Oh, the smell of Italy!" Janet waxed lyrical. There was plenty to wax about. The walk from Paraggi to Portofino is an olfactory delight. A blind person could take equal pleasure in the walk as any sighted individual. Gardenia, fig, wild rose, arugula, thyme, wild basil, and goodness-knows-what-else wafted to our grateful noses, sometimes helped along by our hands as we would pluck a leaf here, a blossom there, and crush them between our fingers in order to smell them better as we strolled along in the twilight.

When you got to the high point of the path there was a wall to sit on. From this wall you could gaze into the harbor, bay, and town of Portofino. With a corn-colored moon hanging over the motionless velvet mantle of the sea to one side and the harbor to the other, it was, as my dad said, just like an opera stage set.

The yachts of the Very Wealthy were moored in a glistening row of white prows and shining glass. Behind them in a semicircle was a pastel line of buildings whose facades touched each other, a crescent-shaped backdrop of pinks, oranges, blues, whites, rusty Pompeii reds, and ochers. Portofino, a fishing village where the "catch of the day" was more likely to be movie stars and billionaires than any local seafood. Portofino, whose tiny grocery stores were tucked into back streets and whose boutiques nestled on the first floor of the buildings on the harbor square. Boutiques that sold belts, shoes, boots, and scarves for more money than ANYTHING you could imagine. Portofino, with its floating bar on a barge anchored in the harbor that had a solid bronze sculpture of a huge crab over the door to the bar's landward lounge. Portofino, where you could look into the cabin of a yacht and see, with your own eyes, Rex Harrison having an espresso with Peter Sellers! Where you could watch Jackie Kennedy stroll along the quayside in a tight white T-shirt with the words "St. Tropez" on it. Where you could watch Princess Grace duck into an art gallery to buy an original Salvador Dali drawing and come out with it wrapped in brown paper, just as if it were a bar of soap, as my dad said. Portofino, where there were no cars allowed into the town so that when you were ten years old you could have the run of the whole place as long as you remembered to meet everyone at 10 P.M. by the Hotel Nazionale for the walk back to our more modest lodgings in Paraggi. Yes, 10 P.M.! "We only go to Italy once a year," Dad said.

For the next three hours the town was mine. I knew *everyone*. We had been coming here for our annual summer vacation since I was three. Portofino was heaven. In heaven you are free, and in heaven all the angels are friendly to little boys.

One such angel was Gino, the resident painter who was almost famous. To better show me his paintings, Gino would have me sit on his lap at his easel in order to explain to me exactly what his erotic surrealistic paintings symbolized.

I did my rounds among the pagans, and was effusively greeted by each one to whom I appeared as a lost cousin from the wilds of the north who, having finally come to his senses, had returned to the warm south.

"Calvino! Where 'ave you been?!"

"And your mama and papa? They are here too? And your beautiful *sorellas*?"

"'Ow long you staying?"

"Only ten days! Madonna! Why you no takea longa time here?"

After I reintroduced myself to my beloved friends, I heard the church clock of Santa Christaforo, perched on the high rocky spit of land that separated the bay from the open sea, strike ten. I raced back to the square, over the uneven cobbles that smelled of fish, up to the row of potted palms that formed a discreet barrier between the late diners at the Hotel Nazionale and the open town square. There Mom would already be waiting with Dad as we children would converge from the four corners of the town. Rachael from the shoe store where, in a redolence of new leather, she had been sitting talking to the old lady who owned it, one of the many black-clad eternal widows who populated Italy. Janet from a café table where she had been sipping a San Pellegrino *aranciata* with the worldly American exchange students she had met who were drinking beer. And me from Gino's studio and the kitchen of the Ristorante Centrale where I had been allowed to watch as a rabbit for tomorrow's lunch was being skinned and gutted.

Dad had his arm around Mom's shoulders. She had a soft look in her eyes. Dad looked younger and kinder than he had on the beach. "C'mon, kids." We turned to walk back to the pensione accompanied by the sound of running water as a boy began to hose down the sidewalk in front of his establishment. "*Buona sera, signore*," he said.

"*Sera*," Dad replied.

4

IN THE MORNING I decided to snorkel all the way around the bay. Last year I had tried it but had been too little to finish my exploratory expedition so had given up halfway, climbed out on the rocks, and walked back to the beach.

Now I was sure I could do it.

"Be careful!"

"Sure, Mom. Anyway I'll be hugging the shore, anything happens I can climb out."

"Well, I hope you'll be all right!"

"Oh, leave him alone, he's a big boy now."

"Thanks, Dad."

When I looked down to the sandy sea floor, the water was clear, but if I dived down, then looked off to the side, into the sea's depths, the water fell away into a rich mysterious turquoise. A distant volume of water from which I could well imagine a sudden terrible looming shape appearing. A shark! Like the ones that assaulted Tintin in *The Adventure of Red Rackham's Treasure*. If I looked the other way toward the rock wall of the shore I would see fish, startled by my appearance, dart into crevices. The tentacles of an octopus hastily pulled deep under a rock. A little cloud of sand and pebbles hanging for one instant in the clear water, disturbed by the octopus's frantic escape from the looming of my body against the sun above—a threatening cloud blotting out the light. When I reached under the rock, the octopus jetted away, out the other side with a squirt of black oily ink left behind to confuse me. Not confused, I followed it, swimming above it as it hugged the sea bottom, its tentacles opening then shutting behind as it convulsed, surging forward, then stopping to surge once more. Finally it settled on the sandy floor, its color changing from the dark mottled gray of the rock wall to a drab speckled brown—a sandy shape on sand, but still not quite invisible if you knew where to look. I dived down to it and almost touched it. Then in a turbulence of panic, it shot off again, this time heading for the turquoise wall of deeper water. One last time I held my breath and dove down to it, now a distant shape twenty-five feet below me, a clear outline of brown against the near white sand of the bay. But the pain in my ears and the tightness in my chest told me that the octopus had won. I struggled to the surface and took a deep breath after blowing the water out of my snorkel. Unfortunately, I did not clear all the water from the tube. My next breath included a gurgling mouthful of saltwater, and my own spit caught in the curve of the snorkel pipe. Coughing, I poked my head above water, spat out the mouthpiece dripping with warm saliva, and sucked in a deep breath while treading water.

A moment later I readjusted the now-cold mouthpiece, tipped the quarter inch of water out of my almost airtight mask, took a slow breath to check if the tube was clear (it was), then ducked back into my quiet blue world. The octopus had vanished.

Heading back to the rock wall, I spotted a fish feeding in the undulating brown seaweed as it curled in the slight eddies of a quiet breaking surf. A surge of water so mild that the wake of any passing speedboat pulling a water skier caused twice the waves of the gentle summer swells.

The August Mediterranean was placid. A tideless and uniform giant paddle pool with only a little raw sewage seeping into it to mar its clear perfection. Around the sewer pipe grew knotted clusters of shiny black mussels. Some in shells the size of teardrop-shaped oranges. Others, babies, tiny as the tip of a ballpoint pen. I treaded water staring at the mussel bed, I would watch, fascinated, as the effluent from the pipe hung motionless in the otherwise crystal water below me. Brown-gray, the cloud of detergent, bathwater, human waste, and shards of toilet paper rocked with the fluorescent bright green seaweed that clung in ribbons to the mouth of the jagged pipe. Tiny fish would dart in from a circling school to snatch an unspeakable morsel here and there from the gray-brown cloud of waste.

When a long sanitary napkin lazily emerged from the pipe, magnified to mattress size by the water, the startled fish raced away. I, however, a boy with a healthy mother and two sisters, knew this was no predator but the constant, if discreet, companion of women. It was an item that had no name but was part of that second world of which we never spoke—at least not casually. A world in which being "Off the

Roof'' during ''That Time of Month'' was kept hidden, not out of shame, but because the inner workings of women's bodies were, like the exact nature of the Trinity, above casual discussion.

Here in the great leveler, the sea, where things were what they were, the pad began to float up to the surface, a few air bubbles preceding it. It had just enough buoyancy to propel it gradually upward toward the sun. A slight, very slight, out-of-focus trace of dissolving blood falling away behind it, as it rose in the dappled light, obscured the background momentarily as it undulated upward.

As I backed up, using my hands to propel me into an unsteady reverse so that I would not block the pad's ascent and spoil the fine effect, my left little toe grazed a half-open mussel shell. Its vivid yellow-orange interior disappeared as it snapped shut at my light touch but not before the edge of the shell had opened up a slight painless cut at the extremity of my toe.

A small wound I forgot until later, hot sand, now caking the opening, began to irritate.

''Go wash it off in the seawater,'' said Dad. ''The salt is a natural disinfectant.''

So spoke my father, a doctor of theology. After letting the sea do its natural best to cleanse my little toe, Mom put a Band-Aid on it, and I was pronounced well.

''Can I go back in after lunch?'' I asked.

''Sure, the water'll be good for it,'' said Dad.

When my temperature hit one hundred and five, Mom decided she should do something. Since it was four in the morning and all the *farmacias* were closed, she had to get the manager to call the local police station to ascertain the name of the *farmacia* in the area that had a twenty-four-hour emergency phone number to call for special nighttime service.

Two hours later Mom reappeared triumphant from her late night taxi ride. Sensible Italy had no silly rules about needing a doctor to prescribe medicine, so she was able to come to my room loaded with antibiotics, lotion, bandages, and aspirin.

By noon the next day, when my fever was at a stunning one hundred and six degrees, Mom decided that perhaps a doctor should be summoned despite her deep suspicion of the quality of the Roman Catholic Italian medical establishment.

Mistrust of Roman Catholic backward medicine notwithstanding, the pensione owner's family physician was duly summoned. He appeared unexpectedly next to my bedside. I tried to fly away. Somewhere between one hundred and four and one hundred and six degrees, I had been borne by my fever into quite another and not altogether unpleasant state of consciousness.

Hovering near the ceiling I was enjoying my newfound ability to fly, the only problem being a matter of motion control, hampered as I was by the fact that any sudden movement of my head would result in my losing my grip on the operation and doing slow loops and weightless somersaults against the powdery white-washed ceiling of my bedroom.

Like an errant helium balloon I could not come down. This disappointed me. If I had been able to hover a little lower, I could have navigated out of the window and then, hugging the hills, could have realized a lifelong dream to skim over the contours of the land. It was all I could do to remember to move my head v-e-r-y s-l-o-w-l-y.

With one dramatic flick of the wrist, my doctor-magician swept the sweat-drenched sheet off the other me, the one still on the bed. A detective of illness, he ran a cool manicured finger from the glands of my swollen scrotum (was I finally flowering like my sisters? My testicles were now man-sized enough), to the swollen glands behind my ears, then back, retracing his steps to my leg, past the knee and down to my red foot, and finally to my pus-gorged, sausage-sized toe.

"Ha! I 'av find the evil sick in you, boy! Madonna! I weel safe you, boy! Fear nussing, Mrs. Mama! I am 'ere! He 'as the *infezione*!"

Extracting an ancient glass syringe, a huge thick needle, and a long steel plunger, the doctor lovingly assembled his arsenal. Squaring his shoulders to the task at hand, he injected the first thick milky dose of penicillin directly into the hollow between my little toe and the next one. When my screaming subsided, he reloaded and did the honor to my rump.

The doctor then instructed Lucrezia, her father and mother, as well as their visiting cousin, who naturally had joined them in watching me, that I was to be packed in ice until my fever had dropped to nearer normal.

Lucrezia, armed with two champagne buckets, was sent up the road to La Busola, the night club that, with its "pounding music," annually came so close to spoiling our vacation because of Dad's sleeplessness. Once there, Lucrezia shoveled ice into her buckets from the large freezer in which steaks, fish, and bottles of vodka were stored and then brought them back to my sickbed.

As the ice progressively did its work, it was harder to float. Soon I exchanged my wings for mere blurred vision and finally sleep, a sleep punctuated by the low murmur of my mom's voice as she sat next to my bed and read aloud to me when I became restless.

In the morning she was asleep on Rachael's bed, her Bible open on her lap.

5

•••••

ONCE A YEAR, on our Italian vacation, we would leave the beach early to spend the afternoon strolling along the waterfront of Santa Margherita. We would unfavorably compare the lot of the English tour groups who inhabited the huge waterfront hotels and ours. They, poor misguided fools, had purchased "package" vacations in England. Probably, "they were just working class people who didn't know any better," said Mom.

We would walk along the palm trees and fountains that bordered the beachfront with the busy street and the wall of ornate hotel facades overlooking the traffic to our right and the sea to our left. On the beach thousands of migrant holiday makers sat in rows of deck chairs arranged in huge squares, as if the seating from some vast tightly packed auditorium had been transplanted onto the hard-pressed beach. Head to toe, they reclined with their radios, card games, cigarettes (the British working class apparently not knowing that ''Tobacco is a filthy weed and from the devil doth proceed''), and alcoholic drinks.

As we surveyed them, we pitied them. Little did they know that, as Dad said, they'd been sold a bill of goods. They might have spent *less money* and found a decent pensione in a less crowded spot, paid for half pension, and been free of the crowd, like us.

''But we wouldn't really want all these people on our beach, would we, dear?''

Mom was practical about such matters.

In a way the foolishness of the British working class was also part of God's great plan to take care of His faithful servants. We were grateful they were *not* on our beach. We were grateful that they liked the cheap pleasures of a worldly night life, the excitement of the flesh, that they sat in rows on the beach and were jammed into the tiny subdivided rooms in what had once been sumptuous Victorian hotels before they were renovated to accommodate factory workers from Leeds, Luton, and Liverpool. Dad explained that ''people like this actually enjoy their lemming-like existence.''

Mom said, ''When you're spiritually empty, you need to always fill up the empty hole only God can fill, and you fill it up with anything that will help you to forget your spiritual emptiness.''

''Like alcohol,'' Rachael chimed in.

''Like cigarettes,'' I added.

''Yes, dears, that's right.''

Janet said, ''Even noise. That's why they always have loud worldly music on so they won't be able to hear God's still small voice.''

''Why yes, darling, that is absolutely right! That is very perceptive of you,'' said Mom.

Rachael shot Janet a murderous glance. All she had thought of was alcohol, and Mom hadn't thought that "very perceptive." Janet was supposed to be on Rachael's side in the battle for control of the airwaves, this talk about loud worldly music in the same breath as empty holes only God can fill was not going to help Rachael in her campaign to be allowed to listen to jazz, with its "worldly savage beat," on the radio. That was probably why Rachael, who was meek but nevertheless less prudish than Janet, went for broke on this occasion and brought out the heavy artillery, partly to change the subject from the topic of "worldly music" and partly to be just plain ornery and embarrass us all. "But the thing they use most to fill up their lonely and empty spiritual holes is sex, isn't it, Mom?"

Janet and I glared at Rachael. Now we would get The Talk. Rachael refused to meet our eyes but looked pleased with herself nonetheless.

"Rachael!" bleated Janet.

"No, it's all right, dear," Mom said. "Rachael is quite right. The relationship between men and women is a beautiful gift from God to each person who is called to marriage. But misuse of this precious gift is a tragedy. It's not *fun*, it's just sad! Like a bad child sneaking down to the Christmas tree early on Christmas morning and ripping open all his presents before the rest of the family is awake. It spoils it for later. When God put Adam and Eve in the Garden of Eden, then they had a perfect relationship with each other. That's the way it's supposed to be. One man and one woman for a lifetime. And when they become one flesh, then this is the fulfillment of the *physical* side of marriage. But the *physical* side doesn't mean anything unless there is a *spiritual* side too. And the only people who can really know the fullness of how marriage is supposed to be are born-again Christians who are also the bride of Christ.''

Mom took a deep breath. Dad was looking straight ahead. He never contributed to The Talk. It was Mom's Talk. It was her job to put ''these things'' into perspective. Let her give The Talk, let her draw the neat little diagrams showing how the ovaries were connected to ''the wonderful womb.'' And how ''wonderful and beautiful'' it all was and how we weren't ashamed of the wonderful gift God had given each of us to ''use at the right time,'' in ''fulfillment of marriage.'' He, Dad, would pretend he was somewhere else. Mom was the head of the household in the department of sexual piety.

''Like you and Dad, Mom?''

''Oh, Rachael!''

''No, it's all right, Janet,'' said Mom. ''Like Dad and me? What do you mean, Rachael?''

''Like you, and Dad, I mean the beautiful fulfillment . . .''

''Oh I see.''

''Rachael!'' squealed Janet.

''No, Janet, it's good to ask these questions.''

Janet glared at Rachael, Dad stared stolidly ahead, I stared at the fountain we were passing with its rococo nymphs playfully helping a wide-hipped Venus out of her plaster shell to the greater glory of Italy and in remembrance of the war dead of 1914–18. Mom got her very sweet ''I'm-very-glad-you-asked-that-question'' expression on her face. Her voice went up an octave because she was so cheerful in answering Rachael's good question. It was all just ''*so normal*'' and ''*healthy*'' to talk about ''these things.''

''Yes, Rachael, your father and I *have* had the joy

of a faithful marriage in which we *have* sought the Lord's will *before* our own.''

''So you didn't unwrap the 'presents' before Christmas?''

''Rachael!!''

''No, Janet, it's all right,'' said Mom.

But Dad had had enough of this. ''Maybe you and Rachael want to talk about all this when you're *alone*.''

He gave Mom a Look. Not *The Look* but still a Look. So the whole thing petered out. For the time being that is, for with Mom, it was all-or-nothing in ''these matters.'' The slightest question, even a mild inquiry to clarify which came first on the reproductive map, say the ovary or the egg that God made that ''floats down the delicate little tube so all those little seeds from The Male can fertilize it,'' would result in The *whole* Talk. You could no more get a short answer than Congress could expect a president to step up to the podium in a State of the Union address and simply say, ''Things are fine, thanks, good night and God bless.'' Mom was a force of nature: once unleashed on the subject of the human reproductive system, The Talk ensued.

Janet suggested we split up. I could come with her, and Rachael could walk with Mom and Dad. We would meet next to the Gelateria Centrale at 4 P.M. for ice cream. That once per vacation treat we had to grudgingly admit was better in plebeian Santa Margherita than elite Portofino, the chocolate ice cream being of a particular, perfect toothsome darkness at the Centrale.

Janet and I set off. We left the seaside thoroughfare and plunged down a small alley lined with shops. Here the smells preceded the tiny crowded stores. The smell of fresh roasted coffee let you know that a moment later you would walk past a store with a huge jute sack in the window full of coffee beans. The coffee competed with a tangy smell of soap that wafted from the little dry goods, hardware, and postcard shop next door. The smell of blood and poultry innards was not quite so pleasant as it hit you from the doorway of a poultry butcher. Nor was the hard wall of odor coming from a fish stand. But the leather and glue smell of the shoe repair establishment was wonderful, and worth stopping for. The cobbler sat on his stool in the doorway of his tiny shop, his mouth jammed with steel nails, his glue pot caked with dark honey-colored glue, its brush thick with years of dried drippings. His stained blue apron hung over his knees, forming a generous lap in which a large white and orange cat slept while its master fit a shoe onto the shoe iron and, turning it deftly, hammered a perfect semicircle of nails into a new shoe heel to reinforce the freshly applied glue.

Looking up, the cobbler spotted me watching and beckoned me over. Handing me the glue brush he motioned that I should apply the glue to the next shoe heel. A small crowd of passersby gathered to watch me, one of the chosen people, in other words, a child, perform this important task. When I had successfully spread the glue the onlookers applauded. In Italy children were little kings and queens who could do no wrong and for whom even casual strangers felt obliged to take personal responsibility.

As Janet and I walked we picked up that inevitable escort any girl over twelve and below the age of thirty, especially a foreigner, especially an American foreigner, is given free of charge by the male populace of Italy. Three young men were now walking ten feet or so behind us, rather behind Janet. They seemed pleasant lads, one was even quite handsome. They were probably about sixteen years old.

"Just ignore them, and they'll go away," hissed Janet.

"Hello, baybee!"

"Hello, beuteeful girl."

"Hello, you America, me Italia!"

"*Bella*!"

"*Veni qui*."

"*Hi, Americano*."

"Keess me, beauteeful!"

Janet had me by the hand, pulling my arm into an involuntary straight-arm fascist salute as she hurried us along, retracing our steps in order to find Mom and Dad, who, as she said, "will *make* them go away!" This last directed to the three boys who laughed uproariously and redoubled their efforts.

"Hi, America!"

"I lovea you preetty!"

"Chicago, New York!"

"Hello, baybee. Hello!"

We rounded one corner and then another, passing three French girls in bathing suits walking in the opposite direction, who had five boys following them, calling out in heavily accented pseudo French.

"*Ciao! Ma jolie*."

"*Bonajoura, bella*."

The French girls seemed to be enjoying the attention. But Janet was made of sterner stuff. Indeed she was not about to let anyone look at *her* Christmas presents before it was time to share, "that most precious gift, our bodies, the temple of the Holy Spirit," with the person God chose for her, as He had chosen Rebekah for Isaac.

As we came to the next corner in the alley, Janet pick-uped her feet and ran, then in one fluid motion, she stopped, let go of my hand, turned, and magnificently swept off one of her heavy, wooden-soled clog sandals. Holding it lightly by the toe she raised this instrument of virtue over her head just as the three laughing boys rounded the corner.

"Hello, America!"

Thwack! Janet cracked one over the top of his head. Janet was *strong*, she was built more like Dad than like Mom. She could give you the worst Indian wrist burn ever. She had arm-wrestled our sixteen-year-old cousin Paul into red-faced ignominy. These poor boys thought they were following one more silly tourist who would giggle at their advances. Wrong number! And great was their fall. As the first boy's knees buckled, he had an expression of rapt and surprised attention on his pleasant olive-skinned face. When Janet turned the wooden clog on edge and clipped the second boy smartly on the bridge of his nose, he wordlessly slid down the wall of the small cheese store we were next to and carefully settled his face in his hands where he no doubt began to rethink all the received wisdom of Italian manhood. The third boy, the tall, handsome one, made the classic mistake of the French Army in World War II, he defended the wrong place at the wrong time, leaving his flank open. Janet, with a sweeping underarm softball pitching swing, gave his "Christmas presents" a resounding uppercut. This made him grip his testicles as he doubled over, and that was the very moment that he should have left his hands where they'd been, on top of his head, because Janet's next blow was an arching tennis serve that slammed down on the back of his head, now bowed in reverent pain.

As we ran back the way we had come, we passed the French girls. They were now walking arm in arm with their "attackers" and were giggling.

No such foolery for us! Rachael might have talked to the unfortunate boys, but not Janet! No one even got to peek at *her* presents let alone a tug at the ribbons.

6

IN OUR EVENING rambles about Portofino I would sooner or later wash up on the doorstep of my friend Gino. He would be in his "summer studio" in the evening. A vine-covered courtyard up some steps carved from the living rock behind a restaurant. Beyond the door at the stairhead lay a dim open space, which Gino shared with the restaurant, a storage area for their kegs of draft beer, vast wicker-clad bottles of table wine, crates of lettuce, spinach, and stacks of empty Coca-Cola bottles. Gino would sit on an empty keg and paint by the light of a row of dim decorative light bulbs that were hung from the trelliswork above. There, squinting through a constant curl of acrid cigarette smoke (he consumed some forty filterless French Gitane cigarettes per day), Gino would paint. He never permitted anyone to watch him work but a few select friends, of whom I was one, as was the old man who waited at the bus stop to carry luggage for guests going to the Hotel Nazionale or the Splendido. The old man sat in a drunken stupor in an old deck chair, the arms stained dark with his years of inert reclining, while I squatted on the floor or perched on a spinach box and watched Gino smoke, drink, and paint a little in between drags on his cigarette and sips from his glass. Gino imbibed his whiskey from a heavy chipped water glass, all opaque with unwashed age. We sat in silence broken only by the sounds of the milling crowd in the square below.

Gino would become a little bleary after drinking half a bottle of his Johnny Walker Red Label, but at the same time he became even more polite in a slow motion sort of way. Finally he would laboriously clean his brushes, then rise unsteadily to his sandaled feet. Taking the work in progress from his easel, he replaced it with a blank white canvas. Then, returning from a small cupboard he kept there for storing his art material, he would carry a tiny eight-millimeter film projector and a case or two of film back to where we waited.

Setting his keg next to the projector he would thread the film through the gate, loop the leader onto the take-up reel, then flip the motor and light switches.

The movies we watched had all been shot by Gino. ''Mia 'obby,'' as he explained before each screening. ''I takea them 'uste for mia!'' Gino struck his breast to indicate how close this hobby of amateur filmmaking was to his heart, then sat down to watch his cinematic excursion.

Gino, the old man, and I would sit for perhaps one or two hours watching the silent world of the exuberant life of Portofino as Gino had recorded it on film. The faces I saw were often recognizable to me.

The fishwife silently screaming, *"Pesce fresco!"*—I had no idea Gino ever rose before noon and I knew she only came into the square early in the morning. Gino was a man of many parts and hidden depths—tourists getting off the cruise boats that hugged the shore between Rapallo and Portofino stopping at jetties along the way to pick up fat, sweating German families with their Leica cameras in brown leather cases; English clans with a nanny leading the way, fat-cheeked, sailor-suited three-year-olds in tow; stoic Swiss who were doing their duty in taking an annual holiday but were silently wishing they were back in a nice clean park in the suburbs of Zurich or Kloten; and a handful of gangling Americans. The Americans were all a good head taller than the Germans and positively towered over what appeared to be the European pygmies surrounding them. They smiled a lot and it seems were forgiven for being perpetually lost and needful of direction to "The *Ristorante*" or "The *Toiletta*" at every turn. Sometimes Gino would follow a pretty Italian girl; an undiscovered Gina Lollobrigida, she would invariably have a scarf and perhaps sunglasses. Laughing in black and white, hand on hip, she would turn and shake a flirtatious finger at Gino and his unsteady camera. Not really because she wanted him to stop filming but as an excuse to face the camera at a better angle.

The next shots were all taken at a funeral. A sea of black suits and pasty white faces. Then, inexplicably, there were shots of Jerusalem taken from the back of a Jordanian camel whose head would swing into the frame from time to time. I did not know Gino ever left Portofino! This was a revelation indeed.

When the film ran out, it revolved heavily on the take-up reel, the bright light of the projector suddenly dazzling on the canvas ''screen'' as the last of the film went through the projector gate. Gino was asleep and so was the old man. It was a quarter to ten; the clock tower had just struck the quarter hour. Gino's cigarette was out between his lips, his saliva having soaked brown up to the hot ash. There was a sip of whiskey left in his glass. I pulled the plug of the projector, afraid to risk hitting the reverse button as Gino had done one night, sending what seemed like thousands of feet of shoelace-thin, tangled film spurting into a floor-sized plate of cinematic spaghetti. The hot white light slowly cooled to a glowing orange dot deep in the lens of the projector, and the ping, ping, ping of the lazily turning reel slowed, then stopped. The old man, remembering some past grievance, stirred and muttered angrily in his sleep.

I slipped out, ran down the steps, avoiding the thin cats clustered, unhealthy and persecuted, on the lower step. Then I raced back to the square, worried that because I was late I'd be in trouble. But no one had noticed.

7

DISPLEASED WITH MY family, I adopted another one. My new family was large and Italian. A vast clan of cousins, brothers, sisters, friends, two grandmothers and a mother and father. The oldest daughter had three tiny children, each dressed in adult clothes scaled down to fit the toddlers. Her children were about the same age as her mother's latest offspring. All of them played together on the beach under the watchful gaze of the younger grandmother, who was still ambulatory. The older one, confined to her deck chair, sat in the shade of the umbrella, wearing a heavy wool shawl, black, with tassels, over her head and shoulders. Her one concession to the sweltering beach was that by noon each day she would have laboriously removed her thick brown stockings, rolling them down one at a time exposing her ivory-colored legs, while one of her grandchildren stood guard in front of her, discreetly holding a towel to protect her grandmother's modesty.

During our vacation I blended in with this euphoric tribe as if I too were somehow related to them. When lunch was served or drinks handed out, when ice cream was purchased from the man who would walk up the beach shouting *''Gelati!''* and dispensing vanilla ice cream on sticks covered with a paper-thin layer of chocolate from his ice cream box, then I got my share along with the rest of the pack. I have no doubt I could have stayed with them forever, perhaps returning to Torino or Bologna with the grandmother on the train while Papa followed in the Fiat with a Mama or two and the bambinos.

At lunch even we children were given a little red wine with our *panino*. Faced with an alcoholic beverage I would have a brief crisis of conscience each day, remembering that I was a fundamentalist Protestant child of the light in a dark, corrupted ocean of Roman Catholic paganism and alcohol-consuming superstition. The superstition was evident everywhere, from the little cross the grandmother wore over her black blouse to the St. Christopher medals all the boys in the clan wore around their thin olive-brown necks.

When one of the babies would tumble off an overturned rowboat and begin to squall and bellow, thirty brothers, sisters, and cousins formed a phalanx and marched en masse back to Mama, who roundly scolded them all for their neglect then casually placed the tyke on her breast as she continued an animated discussion with the friend of a friend who had stopped by to pay her respects. One could feel the darkness of just how lost these Italians were. They were obviously not saved. None of them were born again or knew Jesus. If they had had Jesus in their hearts, they would never have done things like crossing themselves before eating lunch (we worship Jesus in our hearts not through outward pagan signs), drink alcohol (every real Christian knows Jesus made grape juice not wine out of the water at the wedding at Cana), or wear such immodest clothes (our bodies are the temple of the Holy Spirit). Some of the girls had really "terribly small provocative bathing suits on," as Mom said.

There was a constant sense of betrayal in my heart as I enjoyed the darkness of these sadly lost Roman Catholics. Like Judas, I was a secret betrayer of the truth; when they offered me a little wine in some water with a *panino,* I took a sip. Not, however, before I looked back to our side of the beach to check if anyone was watching me—I could see they weren't. Dad was lying on his stomach reading a back issue of *Christianity Today* about Billy Graham's Crusade in Wales. Mom was sitting in her deck chair reading her Bible, and Rachael and Janet were far out to sea swimming to the point and back.

The wine tasted like salad dressing. Later that night, wracked by guilt, I confessed to Rachael that I had had a sip of alcohol. I made her promise not to tell Mom, and she agreed not to on condition that I would ask God for forgiveness right then and there and promise never, ever to do something like that again. Because, as she reminded me, "You never know whether you're an alcoholic or not until that first taste. Then if you have alcoholic tendencies you just drink and drink. It ruins your life and takes you far from the Lord." I knew she was right. I felt far from the Lord already. That one sip had put a "spiritual wedge" between me and God. How could the Roman Catholic family ever come to be Christians if all they saw when they looked at me was an example of depraved alcoholic worldliness? A drunk. Someone who had given himself over to the pleasures of the flesh as they had. Now having had this sip of alcohol, I was living a lie. My parents had trusted me to go and be a light unto those Italian children living in darkness—after all, we were missionaries. Mom had even said she would pray that the Lord would ''open the door of opportunity'' so that I could share the Lord with those poor deluded children who thought they were saved by works and by wearing pagan saints' medallions, when they were actually lost because the True Church was the Early Church and that was what we belonged to, because in the Reformation all the dark side of paganism had been swept away by brave Reformers whom the Catholics burned at the stake, and now I was drinking wine just like the Spaniards did while they laughed and swore and tortured real Christians because they would no longer worship Mary, whom we know was an ordinary girl, not anything special, but they worshiped her because they were pagans who served the Pope not our Lord. Now I drank wine too! I was backslidden and needed to recommit my life to the Lord. And I would, too, as soon as the vacation was over.

Jennifer came over and joined the Italian family along with me. She was an only child. In England they were mainly Protestants, so they did not have such huge families like the unhappy Italians who were in slavery to Rome and superstition. Jennifer and I played with the Italian children, digging deep holes in the sand until they filled in with seawater. Then the more you dug the more the sides of the hole caved in until all you were doing was just maintaining the hole you had started, not getting it any deeper.

Jennifer giggled at night when she watched us say grace. Once I had asked her what she believed and she had said they were C. of E. Dad said that meant Church of England and that they were closer to the truth than Roman Catholics but that nevertheless they prayed for the dead and said "Eucharist" when they meant "Communion." He said there were some real Christians in the Church of England but not very many. Most of them were "only nominal believers. In fact so few attended church regularly, that 'C. of E.' has come to mean Christmas and Easter, because that's the only time most of them bother going to church!" So I should witness to Jennifer if the Lord provided an opportunity, Mom said. The Lord almost never provided the opportunity. No one ever came up to me and said, "Sir, what must I do to be saved?" so I could quote John 3:16 and get them to invite Jesus into their hearts.

When my mom would ask us if we had anything we wanted to share concerning our witnessing at family prayers, I never had much to say. My sisters did a lot better. Janet had actually brought a boy home she had met in Lausanne to ask Dad questions about God, and she got him to pray the sinner's prayer. Later he backslid and said he didn't believe anymore, but at least Janet had tried, and Mom said it wasn't her fault, that the cares of this life had raised up and choked his faith, and that if his "profession of faith" had been real the Lord would "bring him back to Himself by gentle chastisement in His own good time."

Instead of witnessing to Jennifer, I lied to her. She had asked me what my dad did. This was a perfect opening of the Lord. I could have told her how he had come to live in Switzerland after the war to be a missionary to Swiss Roman Catholic youth. And that he was a Reformed Presbyterian minister who traveled around Europe preaching the gospel to youth wherever local Christians needed encouragement in their outreach to lost Roman Catholics. And how the youth of Europe were either backslidden Protestants, who had forgotten their great Reformation heritage (some of them didn't even know who Calvin, who I was named for, was!), or worse, Roman Catholics who were in bondage to the Pope and Satan and were in the dark because they had never heard the real gospel or had been born again to a new life in Jesus as their personal Savior. Then I could have asked Jennifer if she had invited Jesus into her heart. Rachael would have.

But I lied because I was embarrassed. Whenever I tried to explain what my dad did, people, even children, would get a funny polite stare on their faces and say, ''Oh, how interesting,'' then avoid me as much as they could after that, the same way you see people kind of step aside when funny-looking Hasidic Jews in hats, long coats, and beards come walking down the street, as if they didn't want to catch something, as if they might wake up in a long coat with weird ringlets of hair hanging down the side of their heads and all kinds of stuff strapped to their foreheads, if they got too close.

Just like Peter denying Christ, I lied to Jennifer because I wanted her to like me. I said, ''He teaches.'' Which was almost true in a way, but it's what's in the heart that counts, and I knew Jennifer wasn't thinking that Dad taught the Bible, the Calvinist principles of the doctrine of Total Depravity, and Calvin's Institutes to lost Roman Catholics.

To say ''teaching'' was a good lie. Teaching

sounded boring, so I didn't get asked more detailed questions. No one cares where somebody teaches. Once I had told a boy I met that my dad was a doctor, and his mother overheard. She had asked me where he practiced. I said in a hospital in Philadelphia. She said she had a brother who was also a doctor in Philadelphia and maybe Dad knew him, which hospital was Dad at? That's when I decided that I would always say he was a teacher. And if they asked where, I'd say he taught at the American School in Geneva. But no one ever asked.

On vacation it was risky to lie to people about our family. My mother and sisters were so anxious to witness to people that there was a good chance they might start talking about The Things of the Lord to somebody who thought we were only a regular family of teachers. Then they would stand there staring angrily at me because I had betrayed them and said we were teachers, and now it turned out we were Calvinist missionaries. If they had been warned they would never have strolled over to my mom and said, "You must be the mother of that lovely little boy." Now they were trapped, and my mom was sharing The Way of Salvation with them and telling them that if they let Jesus into their hearts, they could be saved. And they had only expected her to say, "Why yes, I hope he's being good" or "How long are you in Paraggi for?" or "And are those *your* lovely children?" But because I had lied to them, they had innocently wandered over to talk to a born-again fundamentalist, and now they didn't know how to get away short of just turning their backs and running for the pensione, checking out, and taking the train to Rapallo or La Spezia to finish their vacation as far away from us as they could get.

I might have lost Jennifer as a friend when Mom told me to ask Jennifer if she would like to come to our church service on Sunday morning in Mom and Dad's room in the pensione. There we would sing hymns, pray, and listen to Dad preach an hour-long sermon to us, his congregation of Mom, Rachael, Janet, and me.

Once Rachael got Lucrezia to come, so she could experience real Christian worship along with us. She had been a little late in coming up to the room to join us for church because she had gone to Mass first, which made us all very sorry for her, and we prayed she would see the difference between dead liturgy and the living gospel preached by a minister who really Stood on the Word and who didn't follow tradition but who followed Calvin instead. She knew enough English to understand some of what Dad said. Rachael tried to teach her the choruses of our hymns. She sang with us, "I'm gonna let it shine! This little light of mine! I'm gonna let it shine, let it shine, let it shine, let it shine. . . . Won't let Satan blow it out, I'm gonna let it shine! Won't let Satan blow it out, I'm gonna let it shine . . ." Janet showed her how to hold her finger up to be the little "candle" of her light and make a blowing motion instead of actually singing "blow it out" during the second and third choruses of the song. Lucrezia seemed to enjoy this. Dad said maybe we had planted a seed that day and next year we could water it more.

I lied to Mom. I said that I *had* asked Jennifer but that she showed no interest in The Things of the Lord, so couldn't we just pray for her instead of my asking again. Mom said that would be fine, and even if she just heard us singing our hymns through the pensione window out on the beach, the Lord might "begin a work in her heart that would eventually bear fruit."

I made sure to not sing very loud so that if Jennifer did hear singing, she wouldn't hear my voice and maybe wouldn't know it was us. But if she did guess who it was, I had my story ready. I was going to tell her that we were members of the school choir where my dad taught and that we had to rehearse for graduation day.

Some kids I met told lies to be special. I told lies to be normal.

8

• • • • •

OUR FAMILY LIFE revolved around Dad's Moods. His emotions were extremely delicate, like orchids. If his Moods had been sent by parcel post, they would have been plastered with *"Handle with Care," "This Way Up,"* and *"Fragile"* labels. Anything could summon the storm clouds of a Bad Mood. Mom's perpetual lateness, a theological review of something Dad had written that was unfair, as all bad reviews of course were, any particularly long bout of giggling on the part of my giddy sisters, and worst of all his Dark Days, in which depression would settle on him and cling tightly wrapped about him in a smothering and stormy embrace.

Janet came up to our room and sat down on Rachael's bed.

"What's wrong, Janet?" Rachael asked.

"Oh, Dad's yelling at Mom in their room, I don't want to listen."

In this short exchange Rachael and I learned all we needed to know. Janet wanted to sleep in Rachael's bed that night instead of across the hall from Mom and Dad. Rachael moved over, and Janet crawled in. At home in Switzerland we often would go to each other's rooms and huddle together against the rise and fall of Dad's angry voice punctuated by the low murmur of Mom's rejoinders. Dad didn't care if we heard him yell, but Mom tried to keep her voice down so at least her part of a fight would be a secret.

We would strain to catch the drift of the argument in progress, yet at the same time not really want to hear what was being shouted lest it become a really bad fight. Then we would hear unspeakable things that left us no place to look for the shame of it all. It was agony to even glance at your sisters when Dad was being really bad because we were all so embarrassed that we had such a wicked father. What would people think? Also we avoided each other's eyes because we knew somehow this was our fault too. We had a hand in Dad's Mood.

"You should have talked to him, Rachael."

"That's not fair! I did talk to him, and he seemed in a good Mood then. Why weren't you nicer yesterday, that's when his Mood started! You should have taken a walk with him. Mom says when he gets a walk, it helps his Mood."

"Well why don't *you* go and knock on the door now. Ask something as if you don't know he's yelling, maybe it'll distract him, then Mom can get away."

"He knows we know he's shouting; he'll only get madder because he'll know I'm trying to break it up. Last time I went in in the middle of a fight, he screamed at me that he knew I was trying to 'handle' him. He said Mom was getting his own children to manipulate him. It only makes it worse!''

We would sit waiting for the screaming to stop. Waiting for the argument that Dad was having with himself and his demons to end, so Mom could escape and come and report to us on just how bad a Mood he was in, so we could all unite in our effort to plot a strategy to get him out of his Bad Mood.

I had seen a documentary movie on some men who had trapped a rhinoceros in a wooden pen; they were all working together in the movie to get the animal out of the pen without getting killed. It made me think of our family efforts to get Dad out of his Bad Moods.

On this occasion the big Vacation Fight ended when a few hours later the pensione owner knocked on Dad's door and said that the other guests were complaining because of all his shouting. Dad told him he would never come back to this pensione again if that's how he was to be treated. The manager said fine, but for tonight he'd have to be quiet. Dad told Mom to pack up right there and then. He told her if she didn't pack us all up right now, he'd just walk out and leave her. And when Mom said, ''But, Ralph, be reasonable,'' Dad screamed, ''I mean it, Elsa—forever!''

After Mom had packed her things and Dad's—he made her pack his clothes since this fight was her fault, because if she was a better wife, he would not get into his Moods and they'd still be on vacation and happy—he sent Mom to our room to pack our things and get us ready to leave.

She came in and turned on the light. As soon as it was on, huge moths began to come in the open window from the dark outside.

''Dad's in a really awful Mood. The worst he's

been in for a long time. He wants us all to leave tonight.''

We were shocked. He had never gone this far before. Last year he slammed the glass door between Mom and Dad's room and the balcony so hard it shattered and once he had thrown a potted ivy plant at Mom in front of Janet, which showed how mad he was even though he missed her and the pot shattered against the wall. But he'd never cut our vacation short before. He always swore he'd never come back at the end of every vacation, but we all knew that he had a whole year to cool down from his fury at the ''pounding music'' at La Busola, so it didn't worry us, and we always came back. But now we were all up in the middle of the night, so it looked like he meant it.

''Mom, is he really going to make us leave?'' Janet's voice shook. She was about to cry.

''Yes, dear, I'm afraid he's serious. The manager aggravated his Mood at the worst possible moment.''

Rachael suddenly screamed, ''I hate him! I hate him!''

Mom got angry. ''Don't you ever say that again about your father. He has his weaknesses. Satan attacks him at his weakest point, which is his temper. But he loves us all very much, and when he's not in one of his Moods, you know you all love him too!''

She looked around at us waiting for one of us to agree with her. But we just stared at the cracked slate gray tiles on the floor while the moths made big flapping shadows on the wall. We weren't going to say we loved Dad when he was spoiling our vacation worse than ever before.

''It's your fault, Mom!'' Janet said. ''If you just put your foot down, he wouldn't treat you this way.''

Mom always answered the same thing. ''I'm afraid

it's too late to do that now. You see, in my family my father never raised his voice in anger. When I found out about your dad's temper, I was so shocked I didn't know what to do. I had never been exposed to working-class behavior of this kind before. I let him get away with it. Now he's in the habit, and it's too late to change. I was totally unprepared. My father was an *educated* man."

Mom turned to me, and so did my sisters. They looked pretty accusingly at me, then my mom said, "You just make sure you learn from all this and *never* ever treat *your* wife this way!"

"He'd better not," Rachael chipped in.

"He won't dare to if I'm around!" said Janet.

I knew I never would, because now I wanted to kill Dad and I knew I never wanted to be like he was and have my children want to kill me.

I said, "I never will, Mom."

The girls and Mom all nodded their heads in satisfaction as if they had forgiven me, and they believed some good would come out of this yet if I had learned my lesson. Mom always said she was praying for God to be watching over the right little girl of "His choosing" for me to marry when He'd lead us together at "the time and place of His choice." That little girl would have been pleased to see how God was using even my father's sin to teach me a good lesson on how not to be.

Mom started taking my clothes out of the cupboard, she dragged the big blue suitcase out from under my bed and packed my T-shirts. When she put my mask and snorkel into the suitcase, I burst into tears. Rachael came over to comfort me and hugged me. We rocked back and forth together while she whispered in my ear, ''He's an awful man, an awful man,'' over and over again.

Janet went back to her room to pack and came back just a couple of minutes later with her bag. Before that year's vacation, she said that she was going to travel light since she was sure the Russians would attack during the summer and she wanted to have only what she could easily carry in case we had to walk back to Switzerland as refugees to get to the American embassy and catch the last boat or plane back to America—as the dark clouds of war rolled over Europe. If we didn't get the last boat or plane, then her bag might be small enough so the Communists would let her take it with her to the concentration camp in Siberia. That's why she had brought her thick ski sweater with her on our summer vacation to Italy along with the other stuff she really needed—two bathing suits, some underwear, one dress to wear at dinner, a pair of shorts, and a T-shirt with ''Summer Bible School—Camp Pocowa '57'' on it. Janet had also hidden a present from our grandfather, the educated one on Mom's side of the family, in the lining of the small plaid bag. It was the *Amazing Smallest Bible in the World.* The whole Bible was printed in tiny letters you could read only with a magnifying glass. It was the size of a big postage stamp and was about an inch thick. The paper was even thinner than regular Bible paper. Janet had made me hide a plastic magnifying glass that was part of my pencil set in my bag. That way, she said, ''If they search you and find the magnifying glass and rip the lining out of your suitcase to see if you have the *Amazing Smallest Bible in the World* and don't find it, then they might not search me and take away the Bible.'' If the Communists stopped us after they invaded Paraggi or caught us walking to Switzerland to our embassy, I should get in line first, Janet said, so she could keep the *Amazing Smallest Bible in the World,* and that way we could have God's Word with us in our concentration camp and would be able to "rejoice in all things" and witness to the other prisoners.

When Mom was done packing, she went down to tell Dad that we were ready and to ask him about what should we do now. She came back crying to say he was serious and we had to all go out and sit at the bus stop and wait for the first morning bus to take us to the Santa Margherita station, where we'd get the train to Genoa and then catch the train to Milano and on to Switzerland. "The vacation's over! That's final," Dad had said.

While we sat at the bus stop in the dark, Dad paced up and down the road. I prayed a car would come around the corner and kill him so we could finish our vacation.

Mom came out after the rest of us had been outside for about ten minutes. She had stayed behind to pay the bill. Dad said, "So that's it, see what you've made me do! There's no going back now!"

The first glimmer of the dawn began to appear around 4 A.M., but according to the schedule the first bus wasn't until 5:38.

When the Banini arrived on his bicycle at about a quarter to five to start to rake the sand and put out the deck chairs on the beach, he looked at us very curiously but said nothing at all even to me. Italians understand families, and he could see something was going on so he just nodded to us all, and we looked up at the hills behind the bay and wished the bus would come so we wouldn't have to explain anything to anyone.

"Elsa, come here." Dad was almost to the corner of the road, so he had to shout. Mom walked slowly up the dark road to Dad. Janet said, "He's going to kill her!" Rachael began to recite the Twenty-third Psalm. But when they got together, Dad only put his arm around Mom's waist, and they disappeared around the corner. They were gone for a long time. What would we do if they were still gone and the bus came? We got sick worrying about that because if we did the wrong thing, it would put Dad in an even worse Mood, and he was already as bad as we had ever seen, so who knew what came next? If we let the bus go, he might scream at us that we were undermining his authority, because he had said we were supposed to take it to the station. But if we stopped it and he wasn't there and he had to run to catch it, he might blame us for trying to give him a heart attack.

Before the bus arrived, Mom and Dad both came back around the corner just as the sun came up over the hill and lit up the tops of the cypress trees around the pensione. Mom was smiling, and Dad had his arm around her shoulders.

They walked right up to us, and Dad said, "Children, I have something I want to say. I want to apologize to you all. I've been very sinful and I ask your forgiveness."

We all turned red and wished that he wouldn't be so humble, which was as embarrassing as when he was really angry in front of people.

But we all said, "We forgive you, Dad."

At least Rachael and Janet did, and I mumbled "Uh-huh."

We all hugged, and Mom cried a little.

While Dad was kissing Mom, the bus came and stopped because we were standing there with all our luggage. Dad waved it on. The driver shook his head because Dad should have waved him on before he stopped the bus. Otherwise, how was the driver supposed to know we were standing there with all our luggage at 5:38 A.M. just for fun?

Dad said, "Well, everyone back to your rooms." I asked Mom how we would get our rooms back since she had gone and settled the bill and told the owner we were leaving and never coming back. Mom pulled me a little behind the others and whispered, "I didn't pay the bill. I told the manager we'd be back." Then I whispered, "Mom, how did you dare?" and she answered me, "I know your father, that's how." So I asked her what the manager had said, and Mom told me he had been very understanding and said that he and his wife had fights too and never mind, because he understood all about how complicated life was, especially *amore*.

9

THE NEXT MORNING we all slept in late, even me. Lucrezia left our table set for breakfast, though the other tables were already set for lunch for the guests who had full pension. Their tables had wine bottles sitting on them with their names written on the labels. If they didn't finish the bottle at dinner, the glass or two of wine left was still theirs to drink at lunch the next day. We usually had our mineral water bottle returned to us each night with some water left in it from the night before. If it was the fizzy kind of water, *gazzato,* by the next night it was always flat. I liked having our bottle with our name on it on the table just the same. It was bad enough that we were the only family on vacation at the pensione who didn't drink wine. So it was nice to have something to mark our table as normal, at least sort of.

Our huge white cloth napkins were also returned to us each night. We got clean napkins every Friday night. Until then your napkin was put in a little paper envelope you wrote your name on when you arrived. If you forgot to put your napkin in its envelope after supper or breakfast, Lucrezia put it in whatever napkin envelope she happened on first at your table. So you might get Janet's napkin at breakfast, all smelling of fish from the night before because she had used it to rub off her hands after eating mussels in garlic-tomato sauce with her fingers. It was one thing to wipe your lips on your own napkin's mess, but it kind of made me a little sick, especially at breakfast, when I realized that, because of the pattern of tomato sauce and lipstick or some really big, dried crusty excrescence, I was stuck with somebody else's napkin. If the girls found they had mine, they got really mad at me because mine was always the dirtiest, they said. They would go "Ugh!" and drop it in front of them on the table and say "*Whose* is this?" while they looked at me all disgusted. If I didn't admit it right away and speak up, then Dad would get mad and say "Get that thing off the table!" I'd have to reach for it, by which time Jennifer might look over from her table and she'd be looking at me all prissy and good like she was saying "ugh" too, then she'd giggle. Mom would see the napkin and say, "You really ought to remember to wash your hands before supper. Look, the napkin's filthy from you wiping your hands on it!"

The real reason why my napkin would get so used-looking was that at the pensione they served lots of food you ate with your fingers. Mussels, clams, dishes filled with olives, bread dipped in green peppery olive oil, plates of crunchy carrot sticks, celery, and big slices of red and yellow peppers. It was all delicious but a little messy. After you ate, Lucrezia brought out a little silver finger bowl with lukewarm water in it and a slice of lemon floating on the surface. The finger bowl had been sitting in the sunlight all afternoon since Lucrezia filled the finger bowls and sliced the lemons into them late each morning. Thousands of little bubbles always formed in them. They looked like pearls clinging to the bottom. When the bowl was put down, I tapped it to watch all the bubbles rise to the top.

We would rinse our fingers in these bowls, then wipe them off on our napkins. Mom always rubbed the floating lemon slice on her fingernails. She said it was good for her cuticles. When she wiped her hands on her napkin, they didn't leave any marks, but when I dried off my hands, the napkin seemed to get a lot more used up. On Friday her napkin always looked about like it had when she got it the Friday before. But mine looked like somebody had spilled something. A lot of dirt would come off my hands during the week and Janet said we would all die of cholera if we had to live with me much longer.

After our late breakfast Dad asked me if I would like to go on a hike. Our vacation hike was a tradition. We lived in the mountains in Switzerland and often went hiking there. Why Dad wanted to hike in the hills above Portofino when we were on our seaside vacation I never knew. I didn't dare to say no since I knew it was important for a father and son to be together. Mom said so.

Mom and the girls put on their bathing suits and went to the beach while I got dressed! My T-shirt was already sticky before we even crossed the road and started up the little trail with all the lizards on it behind the brick building that the Banini kept his tools in and that smelled of old paint and dead fish.

As we started up the path Dad walked in front to "set the pace." If he was in a good Mood, he would set a pace that I could keep up with easily. But if he had been fighting with Mom, the pace would be set so as to punish me for the fight. As we left Mom behind and the walk took on a life of its own, then Dad's Mood would improve and he would slow down for me, and after I caught up to him, we'd walk on together.

The trails we walked on in the hills above the Mediterranean were of all different kinds. Bits and pieces of old Roman roads, donkey paths up to hill farms and olive groves, even some roads that Mussolini had had his engineer corps build before the war to service hilltop military bunkers. When you passed the bunkers, you could imagine soldiers in them with machine guns waiting for the Allies to come up the very path you were on. As we rounded a corner Dad pointed to a bunker ahead.

"By this time they would have opened fire," he said.

I looked into the dark mouth of the overgrown gun port. "How could you get past them, Pop?"

"Well, some men would come up from the side and lob hand grenades into the gun port. That's how you'd take 'em out."

Now I was glad we had gone hiking while the girls sat on the beach. Dad only asked me once on every vacation to go with him. And I always forgot how much I really liked our hikes until we were back up in the hills again. Dad and I would finally get up to the top of the mountain range that ringed our bay and find the Roman road that followed the spine of the mountain. We could walk side by side because the Romans had made the road wide enough for a chariot, whereas the lower trails were just for donkeys with a man walking behind who hit the donkey when it slowed down or stopped to graze from some bush or the low branches of a fig tree.

Dad and I walked in silence for about the first hour. Then we came to a farmhouse with some chickens in the dusty yard in front. A big black dog ran to the end of its chain barking at us. The chain made it flip over backward when it played out and jerked the dog to a stop. The farmer came out and yelled at the dog, then it stopped barking and got all humble and sad so its head drooped down between its shoulders and its tail curled between its legs. When it turned around to slink away, I noticed that it had something wrong with its private parts. One of its testicles was about the size of a grapefruit. It was all pushed out behind its hind legs since there was no room for it to hang down where it was supposed to be.

"No wonder it's in a bad mood," said Dad. Then he winked at me. This was the sort of thing Dad and I could say when the girls stayed with Mom and we hiked alone. If they had been along, we all would have pretended we didn't see what was wrong with the dog. With me and Dad alone we could say exactly what we thought. If I needed to pee I'd just say right out, "Gotta take a leak, Pop," and he'd stand in the path or even say, "See if you can hit that rock down there."

If Mom had been along then I'd have said, "Excuse me, I have to go to the bathroom, Mom." Then she and the girls would have all looked at each other and smiled a little, and Mom would have said, "That's quite all right, dear, we'll just go on ahead and wait."

Then they'd all have walked on and stood on the

path with their backs turned, and I would have turned my back and tried to kind of spread my pee out so it wouldn't puddle and make a splashing sound and attract attention. Once I had let it puddle and splash, and when we all started off together afterward, Rachael whispered to me, "You sounded like a horse going to the bathroom!" Then she giggled and ran up the path before I could say anything back. I couldn't yell after her because Mom would have got mad if I'd shouted, "At least I don't have to squat down and try and hold my underpants out of the way so I don't soak myself like you!"

When Dad and I were alone, we peed and we never turned our backs and we even gave each other helpful advice like, "I would go on the other side of the path. Don't want to pee into the wind." Then we'd laugh and pretty soon after that we'd talk about the girls and Mom and other family stuff. Dad might tell me he was really ashamed of his temper. And now when he talked, I didn't get embarrassed because it was like Dad wasn't my dad, but just a friend.

So I told him how I got embarrassed at Mom's long prayers at the table in the pensione. And he asked me if I could keep a secret, and I said "Yes," then he said, "I do too." And I said, "You do?" Dad nodded his head. "Yup." Then he really surprised me. "Sometimes I envy those Roman Catholics, they just have to cross themselves before they eat." Then he laughed. That surprised me a lot because Dad usually talked about how dark and superstitious they were. But when we talked about the Roman Catholics when Mom wasn't there, Dad seemed to like them better. Maybe that was because Mom had been brought up in a missionary home and Dad had been converted pretty late in life from the working class. Like Mom said, Dad hadn't been raised in a godly atmosphere like she had. His mom was a foul-mouthed hardbitten un-believer even to this day, Mom said.

I got the idea that maybe I wasn't the only one in our family who got a little tired of always having to witness to everyone and all. So I asked Dad if he ever was embarrassed to stick up for Jesus like he should. And he said he used to be, but as the years had passed he had learned to get used to it and to being "called out from among them" and to always being different from everyone else and a Bible-believing Christian and all.

But he told me that if I wasn't comfortable sharing my faith, he understood and that I shouldn't worry about it right now. Then before I thought about it, it slipped out that I had lied to Mom about having invited Jennifer to church when I really hadn't. Dad got serious and said that he didn't mind me not witnessing as much as I should but that lies were bad and that if I lied again he'd punish me. I asked him if he was going to punish me for this lie, and he said, "No, because you told me about it of your own volition, so it wouldn't be fair." He said no more about it. He didn't say, like Mom would have, how hurt he was, and how I had not only grieved her but also how I had grieved Jesus who wept over Jerusalem and wanted to gather Jerusalem like a hen gathers her chicks. If it had been Mom instead of Dad, she would have hugged me and said she forgave me and then said, "Let's just pray about this, dear." She'd pray for a long time, so long that when I opened my eyes I would get a little dizzy and the room would spin around.

The farmer beckoned us to his house, and we went because Dad said that way up here the farmer never saw anyone, so we could not refuse his hospitality and should give him some company.

The farmer was very pleased to hear we were *Americanos* and he kept on saying "Peettsabourga." So Dad figured out that he must have family in Pittsburgh and said, "*Famiglia?*" "*Sì, sì,*" said the farmer. They both shouted at each other as if that would make what they were saying easier to understand, but it didn't since neither one really spoke the other's language. The farmer gestured for us to wait, then went into the farmhouse. He came out with three glasses and a bottle of white wine with no label on it. He poured out the wine into the glasses. I looked to see what Dad would do. Mom would have tried to make the "poor dear man" understand we did not drink alcohol. But Dad pretended to sip his wine. When the farmer went back inside to get some olives and figs, Dad quickly poured out the wine into a big terra-cotta pot that had a little miniature orange tree growing in it.

"Quick, pour yours out," he told me. So I did.

When the farmer came back, he smiled and pointed to our empty glasses.

"*Buono!*" he shouted.

"*Sì, sì, buono,*" Dad bellowed back.

The farmer wanted to pour us some more but Dad said, "No, *grazie,*" and motioned we had a long way to go. So the farmer laughed and imitated how we would walk, all staggering and swerving, if we had more, and he and Dad laughed as if they had been drinking wine together for years. Dad clapped him on the back and said thank you and "*Arrivederci!*" Then we walked out of the yard and when the dog growled at us again, the farmer kicked him as if he had just insulted his best friend. Before we turned the corner on the Roman road, we glanced back and waved to the farmer, and he waved back and called something we couldn't understand. It was all very friendly.

When we walked around the corner, the view suddenly opened up, and we could look down to the sea below. It was "at least one thousand vertical feet down," said Dad. He said we could go home to Paraggi by way of the bay of San Fruttuoso or by way of Santa Margherita. The hike by way of San Fruttuoso was two hours longer than the one to Santa Margherita. I could choose, he said. I decided we should go by way of San Fruttuoso. Dad said it was a good choice because that was the most "spectacular walk in these parts with a stunning view."

As the path wound along the hilltop between the pine and cypress trees, you could look down into one little inlet after another far below. Between them the rock cliffs fell sheer to the water. From the cliffs grew huge, misshapen, long-needled Scotch pines. They hung out over the water at odd angles and made you want to climb out on their long gnarled limbs and drop down into the blue-green water below.

One bay we looked into had a sailboat anchored in it. We could look almost straight down on the deck. We saw a man and woman lying there stark naked.

"I bet they don't think any one is up on the cliff watching them!" Dad said, and he laughed.

"Let's shout at them and see what they do," I said.

Dad said that would not be kind, but he let me do it anyway. At first the two people looked out to sea, thinking it was a voice from another boat. But when they realized it was from above them and there were people up there who could see them, they scrambled around as if the deck of their boat had suddenly gotten very hot. They snatched up towels and covered themselves. The man shouted things at us, but Dad didn't answer back.

He said to me, "Just because most people are too lazy to hike nowadays doesn't mean everyone is. They should have remembered that somebody might hike down the path above them *before* they took their clothes off."

"I bet they didn't know the path was up here." Dad said I was probably right about that.

When we got down to San Fruttuoso Dad said he had a surprise for me. Instead of walking back we could take the tour boat that he just happened to know stopped here on its last run of the day. So I got to ride back to Paraggi. The boat trip took forty-five minutes to cover the same distance it had taken us five and a half hours to walk.

When we got to Paraggi the sun had dropped behind the hills and the beach was in the shade. But Dad said I could have a quick swim anyway. I had been looking down at the sea below us all day and wishing I could fly down the cliffs to it and cool off. Now as I plunged in from the dock, the water felt even better than I thought it would.

10

WE WERE IN Paraggi for my eleventh birthday. On that day my relationship with my fellow creatures in the bay changed drastically. The day before I had been a mere observer of aquatic life. A fellow creature in the secret turquoise realm. Now all that changed.

At 12:30 Mom told me to get dressed. She said we were going to have lunch that day in the pensione. When we were all at the table, Dad came in carrying an armful of presents, which he put by my place at the table while Janet, Rachael, and Mom sang, "Happy birthday to you." The families sitting at the other tables joined in the song. Jennifer sang very loudly and deliberately off-key so her mother looked at her angrily to make her stop. But I smiled at Jennifer, and she made a funny face.

"Can I open them now?" I asked.

Mom said, "No, wait for dessert."

Of course I knew dessert was to be a birthday cake and it would probably be one of those weird Italian cakes, all soggy with liquor and heavy with thick marzipan "icing." Not a cake made from a Betty Crocker chocolate cake mix like the Ladies Aid Society always sent us from America for special occasions and Mom mixed up and baked. That was O.K. because I didn't have a sweet tooth anyway. The main thing was to blow out the candles and get the cake over with so I could open my presents. I knew I'd have candles because I had seen them in Mom's suitcase back at home. That's when I remembered it was going to be my birthday while we were on vacation. I had forgotten about it till then, but Mom hadn't.

When I opened my presents Jennifer knelt up on her chair in order to see what I was getting for my birthday until her mom told her to sit back down. I knew she wanted to see so I held up each thing toward her as I opened it. Some of the people in the restaurant clapped at each present. Others just kept eating and looked at their plates because they had sung to me and now didn't want to get any more involved with my party. It was the Italians who clapped and the German family who kept on eating. Jennifer's parents smiled and nodded, and Jennifer clapped for the first present, which was a pair of flippers—swim fins.

When I opened my big present, Jennifer didn't clap because she was jealous. I could see that. She just sat down and wouldn't look over anymore. That's because this was a real boy's present, and she knew that she would never be allowed to borrow it, maybe not even be allowed to touch it.

It was a spear gun. Not a little toy but one with a spring-loaded spear with three steel barbed prongs. It had a safety catch like a real weapon, a nylon string attaching the spear to the gun so the fish wouldn't swim away with your spear stuck in him, a heavy grip, and a brass trigger. The spring that shot out the spear was so powerful that to load the gun I had to lean all my weight on the barrel to push it down on the metal shaft of the spear until it clicked into place once the spring was compressed inside. Then I would snap on the safety. Dad showed me how and he told me not to unsnap it until I saw the fish I was going to shoot.

Mom said, "Oh, Ralph, it looks awfully dangerous."

"It is, Elsa, it's a real weapon."

My sisters looked afraid of it. Janet said, "Don't ever have that thing near me!"

"He won't be allowed to keep it except when he's going to go out and use it," said Dad.

Mom and Janet and Rachael all exchanged grown-up girl glances and looked at Dad and me as if we were both little boys and they knew things we didn't and were a lot more mature. But I didn't care, I had the gun.

I'd wanted a spear gun since I was about five or six. Dad always said that he'd get me one when I was old enough not to kill myself with it. Now I *was* old enough.

Dad and I left lunch early while Mom and the girls stayed at the table and had tea with lemon in it. We went out to the beach where Dad showed me how to keep the spear pointed away from myself at all times. He reminded me not to shoot myself in the foot by accident and showed me where I could spearfish with my new gun.

"No closer to the beach than the big pine tree on

the castle side of the bay and no closer than the end of the pier on this side. Got it?''

''Yes.''

I knew that these were those absolute kinds of rules that you couldn't even think about breaking.

''And another thing,'' said Dad. ''You are never to lend this weapon to anyone else or use it when anyone else is swimming with you. Never!''

''Yes, Dad.''

Unlike most rules, these were enjoyable rules because they showed me that, as Dad said, ''This is no toy, it's a real and dangerous object like a car or a rifle.''

I realized I was getting to manhood now and I told myself that even though it would be fun to point my spear gun at Rachael and make her scream, I wouldn't because when I had this thing in my hand I was a man, and Dad said men didn't put people at risk.

It took a little getting used to, swimming with the flippers while keeping your arms still so you could hold your spear gun, but by the time I had swum opposite the big pine tree on the hill above the far side of the bay, I was used to it enough that I decided I could look for something to kill.

I saw a tiny wrasse floating motionless on the face of one of the huge rocks that littered the cliff wall of the bay. It was quietly sucking in tiny particles of plankton I could not see but knew were there because Mom had read to me about them from our book *The Wonderful Secrets of the Deep*. I held my breath as I swam closer, then I slowly moved my arm forward so that the spear points of my gun were about six inches from the unsuspecting wrasse.

I pulled the trigger, and nothing happened because the safety was still on, so I reached over and unhooked it. It made a tiny click, and the startled fish darted away to another part of the rock. I could still see it and I gently kicked with my bright yellow flippers so as to make no noise while I followed it. As the wrasse settled down and started sucking in more plankton, I pulled the trigger again. This time the handle jolted, and the spear points made a crunching sound as they hit the rock. There was a cloud of smoky mud from where the spear had knocked the sediment in the crevices of the limestone rock off into the water. The spear points had hit on either side of the slender yellow-and-red-striped fish. It darted away unhurt with a flick of its black, translucent tail.

I looked down at my spear hanging from the white nylon cord in the water below me. I could see that one of the points was bent where it had hit the rock. As I swam toward the shore I jarred my mask with the butt of the spear gun and water got in. I couldn't see and the water got up my nose. I felt like I was dying. I dropped the spear gun, and it sank to the bottom. I could hear the "chink" of the metal tube as it hit the rocks on the sea floor even as I pulled off my mask to blow my nose into my hands.

I got the mask back on and looked to see how far down my new birthday present was. It lay only about fifteen feet below me. I could dive that far, so I was very relieved because I knew that if I lost the best present I had ever been given the first time I tried to use it, Janet would say she knew I wasn't old enough and how she never approved of this idea in the first place. And also that I'd never get another one.

When I dived down and got the gun, my ears hurt from the water pressure so I turned around quickly and kicked hard to get back up to the surface. I was surprised how easy it was with the flippers to dive down and how quickly I could propel myself back up.

I crawled out on the rocks of the shore and pulled the spear after me. One of the outside prongs of the trident was bent so that the space between it and the next prong was now too wide. I looked for a hole in the rock to stick the spear point in so I could bend it back. It took a while but I found one and slowly, so I wouldn't snap the metal, I bent it into shape. Soon I was back in the water again, having reloaded the gun before I got back in. Dad had said that in a couple of years I'd be strong enough to load the gun under water with my arms, but for now every time I fired it, I'd have to get out and push it down, so he had said, "Make each shot count."

This time I decided that I'd find something to shoot that was big enough so that the spear points could impale it. Also that I'd swim over to the sandy side of our bay so as to be able to shoot fish against the sand and not bend my spear point again on the rocks.

When I was right out in the middle where you never saw any fish at all, I looked down and my heart sort of froze. I stopped breathing and couldn't believe that right below me was the biggest octopus I had ever seen in all the years I had been snorkeling.

It was swimming slowly across the sandy bottom. After a couple of seconds of squirting itself forward, it settled down and started to change color. It just lay there, its huge bulbous head swaying in the water.

As soon as I saw it I felt afraid to shoot it and yet knew that if I didn't, I'd be sorry the rest of my life. I floated above it, making a plan. It was out in the open; how could I sneak up on it? The longer I waited the more nervous I got, thinking the octopus might take off and go deeper, where I couldn't reach it.

I couldn't think of any clever way to approach it, so I just dove straight toward it. It sat perfectly still but at the last minute as I held out my arm, sticking my spear out toward it, it darted away and left a cloud of sand and ink to mark the spot where it had been.

Now, deep underwater, I discovered how well my flippers really worked. I kicked with all my might. I did not want to lose this octopus. I was swimming right behind it as it jetted forward over the sand. I desperately wanted a breath of air and wished Dad had given me Aqua-lungs along with my spear gun so I could breathe underwater!

I knew I was going to have to go up for air very soon. My body would make me abandon the hunt in another second. My chest hurt, and I started getting that panicky smothering feeling that you get when you keep your head under the bathwater while your mom sees if you can beat your record for holding your breath. Now on top of running out of air, I was deeper than I had ever gone. My ears were ringing with pain, and I knew that if I waited to the last second, I would run out of breath and gasp in water before I made it back up. I already knew I would have to spit out the snorkel mouthpiece and just gasp for air when I resurfaced. There would be no time to blow the water out and then breathe in carefully.

I fired the spear gun because I wanted to at least try to get the octopus. Yet even as I fired I knew I had no chance of hitting it. I shot to the surface yelling all the way in my head because my ears and chest hurt so much. I managed to hold on to the spear gun, and as I swam up, ripped off my mask and snorkel and breathed out a lungful of carbon dioxide so I'd be ready to gasp in the oxygen as soon as my head was back in the air.

When I had taken two big breaths of air, I started to see in color again. Things had gone black and white the last couple of seconds underwater.

I checked to see if I had everything. I did. My mask and snorkel were in my left hand and my spear gun was in my right hand. I decided not to put my mask back on in case I dropped my gun. I didn't ever want to have to dive that deep again.

I began to swim back to the shore. About halfway to the beach something odd happened. All of a sudden I felt things crawling on my right arm.

I let out a yell because I was startled, but then realized it was probably just a piece of rope or something like that floating in the water. Because my mask was off all I could see in the water were the reflections of the little white clouds. I couldn't look below to see what was touching me without my mask.

Then I really screamed because this thing had me. It was winding around my arm, and it climbed up to my neck and started holding on to my chest. I even felt it touch my leg and stomach. So I screamed and screamed and called, "Dad! Dad!"

Dad had always said if I was in real trouble to call and he'd jump in and help me even though the water was "powerful wet," like he said. Now I *was* in real trouble, so I yelled for him. I was being grabbed by something that was going to kill me or at least bite me so deep the blood would spurt out everywhere, and I'd die of the loss of blood like the man did in the story Mom read about the Great White Sharks of the Australian Barrier Reef in our book *The Wonderful Secrets of the Deep*.

I could see people on the beach running toward me. There was Dad jumping off the end of the dock in his shorts and T-shirt. And there was Mom screaming,

"Ralph! Ralph! He's drowning!" And there was Janet screaming, "Please, Lord, save him!" and Rachael running up the beach to get the Banini to do something.

Now the thing was all over me. *Really* all over me! I looked at my arm and I saw a tentacle and suckers sticking to it. Then I realized all at once what it was and I understood the whole thing, but now I was even more scared than before because I had heard a story about what giant squid were capable of and now I knew it was a giant squid that was attacking me because I saw the tentacles and the suckers. I waited to feel the bite of its beak rend my flesh as it pulled me beneath the waves, a victim of the dreadful and mysterious deep where no man has gone.

So I screamed even louder and that was when Dad swam up and saw what was happening and said, "Why is that octopus on you?" and "Why are you screaming? I thought you were drowning!"

We swam in to shore together. Everyone on the beach was gathered in a big crowd just as the Banini ran out with a life ring, which if I had been drowning, would have done no good because I had been too far out. But like Mom says, the Italians aren't very practical.

I walked up the gentle slope of sandy beach with the giant octopus crawling all over me that I had shot at and missed. Only I hadn't missed because one of the prongs of my spear had stuck into the middle of one of its tentacles and caught it. Because it was underwater, it didn't weigh anything so I hadn't known I had it. It had wound itself around the nylon cord that held the spear and had slithered its way up to me and wound around me and hung on.

So I tried to act like I had not screamed for help

and instead had just been yelling triumphant things like "I got it!" Dad told me not to tell barefaced lies, but he said it in a low voice because Jennifer was there watching, and Dad was a compassionate man.

11

As I came up the beach Jennifer screamed and ran away from me. The octopus was a writhing mass of legs firmly attached to my arm and shoulder. I tried to act as if I were enjoying the situation and had in fact done this on purpose, that this was how I always caught octopus. The octopus began to crawl up on my face and head. I threw down the spear gun, tripped over my flippers, and yelled, "Help me, Dad!" But Dad looked as horrified as everyone else.

The Banini squatted down next to me, then did something that made my sisters scream and turn away and start running up the beach, saying things like "I can't believe he did that" and "I'm going to be sick." Some mothers pulled their children away though a couple of men kept watching to prove they were braver than the women, but you could tell they were getting sort of queasy themselves.

What the Banini did that made them all sick was

to lean over and bite the bump between the octopus's eyes right off and spit it out. When he did this the octopus convulsed, then went slimy and limp on me—all flaccid, heavy, and spent. It was paralyzed, dead, lifeless. Its color changed from a florid red brown to a light, blotchy pale sandy color. The Banini picked it up from where it had flopped off me. He unscrewed the head off my spear gun, the trident part, and worked the barb out of the tentacle it was stuck in. After that he held the octopus in his hands and, with one quick motion, turned it inside out. It made a squashing sound when he did this, a sucking gurgle. Its insides hung out all yellow and blue, sort of like a sheep's stomach I had seen that spring when the farmer on our road killed and gutted a lamb that had had its hind leg chewed almost all the way through by a dog.

The Banini took out his big Opinel clasp knife and made a few deft cuts after which all the guts fell out into the shallow water by the beach. They floated there all afternoon. Little girls would dare each other to see who would go up to them and touch them, then they'd scream and run away while their mothers yelled at them and said if they did it again they'd slap them.

No one went swimming near the octopus guts for the rest of the afternoon. By the next day they were gone; I checked. Two days later I saw them lying at the bottom on the sand by the end of the pier and little fish were pulling them around as they swarmed over them and took tiny bites. But they never touched the big yellow sack sort of thing.

When the Banini had finished cleaning the octopus, he turned it right side in again and dropped it in a bucket and handed it back to me. I looked at him, and he understood my look to be a question and pointed to his mouth and said, "*Mangiare*!" Then he smiled and patted my cheek and pinched it to show he was proud that I had killed something I could eat. So I nodded and smiled and patted my stomach and said, "*Sì buono*!" to show I had eaten dozens of octopuses and loved them. Then I couldn't get out of it, so I marched up to the pensione kitchen and handed the bucket to Lucrezia and her mother, who pulled the octopus out and said, "*Che bello pulpo*!" Which meant, what a beautiful octopus! And I said, "*Sì*," and they said "*Bravo*!" but I was thinking I should have left it alone.

That night, while the rest of the family had charcoal-grilled veal chops, which were my favorite Italian food and which were only served once each year when we were staying at the Pensione Biea and which Mom never made for us at home because we were missionaries and the Lord provided for our needs but not that well, I got a huge serving platter full of deep-fried octopus pieces.

Rachael said, "You must be kidding!" when I asked her if she'd like a few, hoping she'd say yes, and would I like some of her veal chop.

Janet said, "It makes me sick just to see it again."

Mom said, "No thank you, dear."

Dad never ate deep-fat-fried food since he got his ulcer and since God had not healed him because these trials of the flesh are to test our love of the Lord, like the Apostle Paul with his thorn in the flesh.

So between Dad's spiritual warfare and my sisters being cowards I got stuck trying to eat this huge pile of octopus. And I tried not to remember what it looked like when the Banini had its guts hanging in one hand while he cut it with his knife and still had a little juicy mark on his chin from where he had pressed his face against its head when he bit off its nerve bump and killed it.

I found that, with octopus, bigger is not better. I had had little rings of fried squid before and they hadn't been so chewy. But *my* octopus was so chewy that I swallowed most of the pieces whole after I'd chewed them for a long time and as I chewed them, the crisp fried batter came off and left rubbery octopus that started to taste fishier and fishier and reminded me more and more of how slimy the octopus had looked in the bucket when it was dead and how the water bubbled up around it in the sun by the kitchen door before Lucrezia's mother had thrown it into the kitchen sink. Then I started to feel the little suckers with my tongue and I looked down at my arm where I still had faint round marks from its sucking on me, and I wondered if the ones in my mouth were the same suckers that had made the marks.

"How are you enjoying the catch of the day?" Dad asked.

I said it was great and that it was "the best fish I've ever tasted."

"You can't beat really fresh seafood," Mom added.

"Nope, I guess you can't," I agreed.

I kept eating and eating. It turned into an endless nightmare. Chewing and chewing, I got fuller and fuller and Dad said it sure smelled good and that if it wasn't for his thorn in the flesh, "I'd have some, it smells so good."

When I remembered how that yellow sack had smelled when the Banini cut it with his knife and how it oozed stuff that looked like spit, when your mouth is really full of spit because you've saved it to spit over the balcony and see if you can hit the line of ants going to the dead mouse on the flagstones by the house, that's when I threw up. Not a little bit but a lot and not neatly the way I saw Mom get sick once, just sort of coughing a little up, but hard, what Mom said later was "projectile vomiting."

Rachael pitched over backward in her chair as she tried to get away from me, and Janet threw herself sideways and hid under the table.

Dad stood up and said, "Damn that octopus!" And since he never swore, except at Mom when he was fighting with her, I knew he was very upset.

Mom jumped up as if she had sat on a very sharp fork and said, "Oh dear!" Then she looked at Dad and said in a shrieky sort of voice, "Ralph, he's vomiting all over!" And Dad shouted, "I can see that! Do you think I'm a moron?"

I noticed a lot of things even while the octopus was squirting out of my nose into the breadbasket and filling it up and covering the bread sticks, which were made in Milano and had instructions on their packages about how good they were written in six languages, even Japanese. I noticed Jennifer point at me so her parents both looked, and I noticed how they left the dining terrace and didn't eat their *cassata* ice cream dessert, which is a pretty good dessert once you pick all the pieces of candied fruit out of it.

Rachael said, "Stop it, *stop* it!" over and over, then burst into tears.

So Janet slapped her and said afterward it had been to prevent hysterics, and she had learned this, about slapping preventing hysterics, at her first aid class at Summer Bible School. But Rachael said she was just being mean and taking out her feelings on her.

When it was all over I was led from the dining

terrace back to my room, and everyone I passed stared at me to see what somebody looked like who could do such a thing to a perfectly nice pensione.

But Lucrezia's mother came up to me and patted my cheek and said, "*Poverino*!" which meant she was sorry for me and wouldn't make us leave the pensione.

Dad started to take it out on Mom, and I heard the beginning of a fight. His tight voice got very polite in a way that meant as soon as he was alone with Mom, he would be very rude. The polite part I heard Dad saying was, "That was a very interesting little episode, Elsa. What exactly did you have in mind by letting him gorge himself on that fool thing?"

Mom said that she was sorry, and Dad said *he* was too. But the way he said it meant, "You bet you'll *be* sorry for ruining my whole vacation just when my ulcer was starting to heal."

Then they went to their room after Mom cleaned me up and tucked me into bed and prayed with me and kissed me good night and said, "It could happen to anyone, dear." But I knew it could only happen to me and that I'd stay in my room for the rest of the vacation so I wouldn't have to see anyone ever again, especially Jennifer.

When Rachael came in she was really nice to me and not just in a "Christian charity" sort of way. She sat on the end of my bed and told me about how embarrassed she had been when she found out at summer Bible camp last year that she had gone around for a whole day with a split in the back of her Bermuda shorts. And how she knew that everybody had seen her underpants and hadn't said anything out of politeness but how she never wanted to ever see them again. So she understood how I felt and if I did decide to stay in the room, she would bring me my food on a tray at mealtimes, but not octopus, though, and we both laughed.

Then she asked me if I wanted to pray about it, and for once I was so sad about something, I said, "Yes, let's take it to the Lord in prayer."

So Rachael prayed, "Dear Heavenly Father, we just thank Thee that Thou knowest us in our inmost parts and that we have no secrets from Thee. And we just claim Thy promise that 'When two or three are gathered together there will I be in the midst of them,' and so we just ask that You will reach down and touch Your servant, Lord, so that he may be able to enjoy the rest of his vacation. And also that You will touch our dear father's heart so that he will be in a good Mood tomorrow and not be too mean to Mother. In Jesus' precious name we pray. Amen."

Then Rachael asked me if I felt better and I said, "A little."

She said, "The Lord will do a work in your life."

I said, "I hope so."

Rachael told me to "cast my burdens onto the Lord."

"I'm trying to."

Just then there was a knock at the door, and if I could have commanded my bed to swallow me up, let alone a mountain to move, I would have, because it was Jennifer. Then a sort of miracle happened, and the Lord did touch me in His mercy after all because Jennifer said, "I just wanted to pop round see how our patient is doing." She said it like her mother would have. Then she said, "Mum says you must have food poisoning and that the health inspectors in Italy are notoriously lax. She hopes you're feeling better and wants to ask you if you'll join us tomorrow for a row, presuming you are fully recovered. Daddy is going to let a boat in the morning and we plan to be out a half day. Mummy will bring a lovely picnic.''

Then she walked over to my bed and felt my head and said I had no fever, so she believed I could indeed join them for a ``bit of a row.''

I looked at Rachael, since she was the next one up in the chain of command, and she nodded.

So I said, ``Thanks, that will be great.''

Jennifer said, ``We start at 9 A.M., punctually.''

As she went out the door she turned around and blew me a kiss. That made me kind of funny feeling but not in a bad way.

When Jennifer was gone, Rachael said, ``Now *that's* an answer to prayer! You see, you don't have to be embarrassed!''

I agreed because now I had been invited back into the society of polite humans who had forgiven me for throwing up at dinner and were even sorry for me and had not said that my octopus had made me sick but had provided me with a scapegoat, food poisoning, just as Isaac had been spared when God provided Abraham with the ram caught by its horns in the thicket.

12

• • • • • •

THE ROWBOAT THE Bazlintons had rented was not really a boat at all but was actually two, ten-foot-long, cigar-shaped pontoons fastened together by benches bolted across them at right angles. One bench faced forward and had a nice rounded back to it so the passengers could comfortably sit, three abreast, and look at the scenery. The other bench had no back. The person rowing sat on it to row.

Between the benches it was open. You could look down and see the water sliding green-blue between the pontoons.

These "rowboats" were just for people on vacation. No fishermen ever used them. They had numbers painted on the sides so the Banini could keep track of who had what and how long they had it and if their time was up, or if they had forgotten that their hour's rent was due at four-thirty and came back at five instead and had to be charged for the extra half an hour.

If the people being charged extra were Germans, they would compare the time on their watch to the Banini's and argue that his watch was wrong or that he had put their departure time on his blackboard wrong, or that he had all the boats' numbers on it incorrectly. The Banini would wait for them to stop explaining his mistakes to him, then just ask for the extra fifty or one hundred lire all over again, very politely but firmly, until he got his money.

If the people argued longer than normal, other vacationers would come over and start to gather in a little circle to see how it would all come out. If the people who didn't want to pay the extra money were Italian, they never pretended the Banini had got the time wrong but just started to argue about how the rent for the boat was too high anyway and how the Banini was a Fascista Capitalista and how when the PCI (the Italian Communist party) won the next election, all the boats would be free for everyone, and the Banini and the people whom he worked for, who thought they owned the beaches, would be put in jail. Then the Banini would say that, if everything was going to be for free, maybe it would be a good idea for them to lend him their new Fiat parked up by the pizza and espresso bar so he could go visit his mama that afternoon. The other man would shout that the Banini was a *porco-cane* (a pig-dog) and then other Italians nearby on the beach would all come over, and the Christian Democrats would take the side of the Capitalista Banini, while the PCI families, who had little pictures of Communist partisans shot by the fascists in the war in their cars instead of saints' medallions, would take the side against the Banini and all the Capitalistas who were ruining Italy. The Socialistas would try to be reasonable and take the middle ground, but because you can't argue very effectively in Italian without taking a strong position, the Socialistas would have to join in with the "people"—PCI rowboat-renters—against the "lickspittlers of the Vatican oppressors and the Capitalist Swine who served neo-colonial American interests."

The Banini would finish what he had to say and turn his back and walk away but only for a couple of paces; then he'd turn around and say a lot more about how subversive the boat-renter was and also maybe something about *his* war record and how *he* knew who the *real* collaborators had been.

Then the boat-renter's family would all scream things and hold back their PCI papa who was being so insulted that soon he would have to fight the Banini. They all screamed at the Banini asking if he was trying to get someone killed with his inflammatory loose talk about people's war records.

Other men would step forward to get between the two men who were soon going to kill each other, but then they'd start arguing among themselves about who had really started this, so you couldn't tell who was who anymore or which ones were Capitalist Running Dogs and which were Stalinist Butchers.

Then the PCI man who would not pay the extra fifty lire on principal, because you had to take a stand against the CIA and America somewhere and this was it, picked up the boat washrag and with a sweeping motion wiped all the boat times off the Banini's blackboard so as to bring *true equality* to Italy and to show he wouldn't sit still while the partisans were called collaborators and Wall Street brokers bought and sold the world.

The Banini turned to the crowd and asked them if they had seen what the PCI man had done. He shook his fist at the sky and asked the saints and Mary the Mother of God if *she* had seen what the PCI man had done.

Then he took a step over to where the man's wife had put down their beach ball, towels, and picnic basket and he picked up the PCI man's towel and threw it into the water to show the PCI that if they called in the Soviet tanks, like in Hungary to crush freedom, and wiped off blackboards with the time people had left in their rowboats, then, then, Then (!) saints above (!) they would have a fight on their hands, and he could count on *that*!

The PCI's friends and his wife had to beg him not to fight the Banini and the Capitalists and the Papal Stooges, and the PCI wife had to show the PCI baby to her husband and beg him in the name of the PCI's saints and the Communist Mother of God not to fight for the baby's sake because did he want his children to be fatherless in this Capitalist wilderness?

Then the PCI father picked up his baby, who had started to cry because of all the shouting, and he held his baby up to heaven to show God, who, if not actually a member of the PCI, was nevertheless his witness, that the *Banini* had made his baby cry and to show that if he had done this to a sweet innocent bambino, he would stop at *nothing*!

The PCI grandmother who was on vacation with the PCI family ran up the beach, screaming that the PCI father was going to kill the baby in his rage. The pensione manager, hearing somebody screaming about murdering an *innocente*, came out of the kitchen wiping his hands on his apron, which was all bloody from the chickens he was gutting for our supper. He came down to the beach to ask what was going on, and then the Banini told him what the Communists were trying to do, and the Communists said their towel was ruined, and the manager said it was only wet and would dry.

The Communist man then said the Banini could have his filthy fifty lire and grind the faces of the poor for all he cared, because soon justice would be done. And he laughed very loudly to show how he would not be sorry when the justice happened to the Banini and to show how he would laugh even if the Banini begged for mercy.

Then he threw a fifty-lire coin out into the water and took his children by the hand, and the mother and the grandmother all walked up to where their deck chairs were and they all sat down and if the children said anything, they got slapped and told to sit still because couldn't they see Papa was upset enough?

The Banini got the net on the long pole he used to fish up things tourists dropped, like earrings or sunglasses, and he found the fifty-lire coin and put it in his leather boat money pouch.

When the next boat came back, he didn't charge them any extra since the times were gone from the board. But they were an English family, and the father said he remembered when they had left and that he knew he owed the Banini an extra hundred lire, and he paid him and said they had had a "splendid time."

Then the Banini walked over to the Communists, who were now having a glass of wine and some bread and grapes with amaretto cookies. And he showed the hundred lire to the PCI father and said how the English man had remembered he owed more and paid it without having been asked, even though he didn't have to because the times were wiped off the blackboard.

The PCI man and the Banini both laughed at how

the *Inglese* were imbeciles because who would ever pay when he didn't have to and how the *Inglese* had something missing upstairs. The Banini then sat down and accepted a glass of wine. He and the Communist told stories to each other about how crazy the English were in the war when they had both been captured by them in North Africa. And how they had even heard how the English would pay their taxes without lying and how that proved they were *stupido* even if they were polite.

The Bazlintons had rented their boat for a half day, so we didn't have to keep an eye on the time as much as you do when you rent by the hour. Mr. Bazlinton, Jennifer's hearty father, and Eunice, her tired-looking mother, had decided we would row out of the bay toward Santa Margherita, then pull up on the little pebble beach halfway between our bay and the Santa Margherita beach. There was no way down to this beach from the road above, so the only people on it were those who arrived by boat. And since it was a pebble beach, not sand, no one went to it except the English. When we pulled the pontoon boat up onto the beach, it was empty. Mr. Bazlinton unloaded a picnic hamper the size of a suitcase. And Eunice unpacked a little Primus stove, a bottle of fresh water, and a little saucepan that fit into the ring over the burner. She boiled water and made a thermos full of tea. She and Jennifer and Mr. Bazlinton all drank a lot of tea before they did anything else. I wished we had something cold to drink. Mr. Bazlinton said that there was "nothing like good hot tea." And I agreed, there wasn't. In my head I was thinking that you could take what he said two ways. Then Eunice told Jennifer and me to go play until lunch and she would call us when it was all laid out.

We walked to the end of the beach, about one hundred yards from Jennifer's parents, and started to climb on the rocks. There we found a lot of stuff stuck in the crevices where it had washed up from the waves in some winter storm. Jennifer found a rubber thing like a balloon that wasn't blown up. The part where you blow was too wide around and its color was like a rubber band, sort of milky brown, not red or green like a regular balloon.

Jennifer held it up between her thumb and forefinger like she didn't really want to touch it. Then she giggled and asked me if it was mine. I just stared at her because I didn't get the joke, so she giggled some more and said that if I didn't know what it was, *she* wouldn't tell me.

I said I didn't care what it was, and I grabbed it away from her and said I'd take it to her mother and ask her. Then Jennifer said, "Go on, I dare you." Which I thought was stupid because dares are for scary or dangerous things, and this was probably just something from a kitchen appliance or a part of some machine or maybe a hospital sort of thing.

I walked up the beach swinging it in my hand; Jennifer walked next to me giggling. When we got closer to her mother and dad, she suddenly snatched the thing away and threw it into the water and said, "You really mustn't." And because it all seemed so dumb and because I didn't know why she was being so giggly about it all and because I was a little nervous about her parents who were "such nice English people, so refined" like my mom had said, I didn't bother going in after it.

For the rest of that vacation Jennifer would look at me and giggle and say, "He doesn't *know*, poor dear!" I never did figure out what I had done. It was one of those things that was a real mystery and sort of drives you crazy like when you know a word but can't remember it and just as you are about to say it, Rachael shouts out the wrong word trying to help you remember the word you've forgotten that was on the tip of your tongue, and then you know you'll never remember it. By the end of the vacation all Jennifer had to do was look at me and roll her eyes and I would get mad and walk away from her. It happened so often Mom asked me why I didn't want to play with Jennifer anymore. What had happened, she wanted to know.

The way she asked it it sounded like she was suspicious I had done something bad and was ashamed, and that's why I wouldn't talk about it. But because I didn't even understand what Jennifer had meant or what the thing was, I just said that girls bored me. Mom kept asking though, and so in the end I lied to her, saying Jennifer "took the Lord's name in vain." Then Mom was pleased with me that I did not want to hear profanity, and she told Dad, and he said that he was glad I was developing "spiritual sensitivity."

Mom said that I did not have to play with Jennifer anymore if I didn't want to and that we would pray for her instead. Janet said that upper-class British had "dreadful language" for educated people, as bad as Dad's Unregenerate working-class mother.

When we rowed back to our beach, I sat up on the front of one of the pontoons, and when the water got shallow enough to see to the bottom of the bay, I put on my mask and lay on the pontoon with my head in the water and watched the sandy bottom slide by underneath us. I saw a few fish way down where the water was turquoise green. They looked so far away I couldn't tell how big they were. As we got closer to the shore, we went over a vivid patch of green seaweed, and I wondered if some sewer pipe came out there that I didn't know about because we were still a lot further out than I usually snorkeled.

Jennifer hung on behind the boat and got pulled along in our gentle wake. Eunice sat with her head thrown back "to get a little more sun under my pale Surrey chin," she said.

Mr. Bazlinton rowed very well since at Cambridge University he had been on the rowing team. Though, as he said, he had not rowed "tubs like this but the real thing."

When we got to the beach the Banini waded in and pulled us up to where Eunice could step off the boat onto dry sand and not get her toes with their bright red polish wet. I thanked the Bazlintons for a great time, and Mr. Bazlinton said, "Jolly good, old chap, glad you enjoyed it."

Then I took my mask and my towel and ran up the beach. Just as I got back to Mom at our deck chair, Jennifer called out "balloon," and I could hear her laugh.

13

IN THE MORNING it was raining hard. Not a summer storm where huge warm raindrops made craters in the sand and the sun came back out, but a pelting steady autumn rain. It was cold, and the sky was a solid battleship gray. The Banini didn't even bother to come to work, and no one was on the beach except the German family who were dressed in rain slickers and were walking briskly from one end of the beach to the other and back again while their dad timed them with a stopwatch.

Lucrezia stared out the dining room window. She was polishing wineglasses. She did it without even needing to look at her hands and would just glance at each one against the light before she put it upside down on a tray.

I was eating breakfast alone at our table, hot chocolate and rolls to dip in it. I would butter the roll and when I dipped it in the hot chocolate, the butter would melt off so by the time the cup was half empty, the chocolate had a pool of melted butter floating on it.

Lucrezia saw me watching the Germans, and she tapped the side of her head to show how crazy she thought they were.

The service bell rang. Lucrezia looked up at the wooden box on the wall in which there were rows of painted numbers. Under each number was a hole and when someone rang the bell in his room for service, a little red metal tag would drop down into the hole under the number of the room where the person had pressed the *servizio* buzzer.

I saw it was Number Seventeen. That was my parents' room. They were ordering breakfast. Lucrezia reached up to the *servizio* number box, pulled a handle on the side that made the red tag for Room Seventeen go back up. Then Lucrezia sighed and reached into the cupboard to get out the things she needed to set up their breakfast tray.

The first morning you were at the Pensione Biea Lucrezia would take note of what you had for breakfast. After that, when you came in and sat down or if you pushed the *servizio* button, she automatically brought you what you had ordered the first day. It could be coffee, tea, or hot chocolate. You could also ask for a glass of milk, and unless you told her not to, she would serve it to you warm so a skin would be on it, and you could really taste how different Italian milk was from Swiss milk.

Lucrezia put two plates, two huge silver-plated knives with ''Hotel Splendido'' stamped on them (even though this was the Pensione Biea), two cups, saucers, the little pots of Yugoslavian apricot jam, sugar cubes, individually wrapped in white paper with a picture of Pope John XXIII on them, and last the coffee and hot milk for Dad and the tea with lemon for Mom.

When Lucrezia was ready I decided to follow her to Mom and Dad's bedroom so I could ask them what I could do that day since it was raining.

When we got to their room, it was pitch dark. Dad always closed the shutters and pulled the curtains because he liked a really dark room to sleep in. If we ever stayed anywhere that did not have heavy curtains or shutters, Mom would look around the room and say, "I'm afraid Ralph will not sleep very well. He'll wake up early and be in a terrible mood." We would all work hard to prevent this by doing whatever we could to help Mom find a way to get the room properly dark. If we could, we'd hang blankets up or even bath towels. Once we stood a whole couch on one end and pushed it against the window to help Mom get the room dark enough to keep Dad in a good mood.

Because of the night club, La Busola, at the corner of the beach Dad also kept all the windows tight shut at night so he couldn't hear the music as much. Even though it was a cool morning with the rain and all, it was still as hot as it had been the day before in Mom and Dad's room.

The air smelled like Mom and Dad. I could smell Mom's face cream and Dad's morning smell, sort of like the smell of burned toast at a distance with a little bathroom smell mixed in. Not really bad, but different enough so you noticed it.

One side of Dad's face looked crumpled up because he always slept on that side. And his hair was all pushed over, so he looked a lot more bald than in the day when it was brushed straight back.

Lucrezia said, "*Buon giorno*," put the tray down,

then went over and opened the curtains, the windows, and the shutters. When she had snapped the shutters back into place against the wall of the pensione, she asked Dad if he wanted the windows left open a little. This embarrassed me because I knew Lucrezia thought the room smelled ''close'' as the English would say. But Dad said no, so she just shut the window up again, and I knew how she would tell her mom about how it was like a cave in there and how these Americans were not like the Germans and English who kept their windows open and liked fresh air.

When she was gone Dad got out of bed, went over to the sink, and peed in it. He always did this in rooms with no toilet in them. The toilet was down the hall, and all he had was the bidet or the sink to go in unless he wanted to stand in the shower and spatter his feet or walk down the hall in his pajamas and meet people who would look at him and his crumpled face and pushed-up hair.

Mom sat up and started brushing her hair and tied it back. Later she'd put it up in the bun she always wore, but for now she just tied it back with a black ribbon. Then she rubbed a little face cream on and put on her lipstick. All the while sitting in her bed. Mom said that a wife should always try to be beautiful for her husband all the time if she expected to have a romantic marriage. She said marriage was a picture of Christ and His Church, and we all were the bride of Christ. While Dad ran a little water in the sink to flush his pee down it, Mom was smoothing down her nightgown and blotting her fresh lipstick with a Kleenex so it wouldn't be too red like women wore who were more worldly than Mom and wanted to use makeup to attract attention to themselves in a way that was *not* pleasing to the Lord. She blotted her lips even in her room where the only man was Dad, who was after all allowed to be attracted to Mom as much as he wanted to be, because Mom said that within a godly marriage a man and a woman should enjoy the gift of love that God had created.

When Dad turned around he didn't even look at Mom but just said, "Don't touch my plate with all that stuff on your hands." And he turned to me and said, "Elsa rubs all that junk on, then touches my food with it so it tastes like I'm eating something that got dropped on a bathroom floor."

Then Mom said, "Oh, Ralph!" and laughed to show Dad we all were enjoying his humor. I laughed a little to help her out because we all did what we could. But Dad didn't say anything or even smile. He got back into bed and said, "Hand me that tray." So Mom did.

Mom took her tea things off the tray and balanced them on her lap and was careful not to touch anything of Dad's on the tray so he would not taste her face cream. Then she poured out Dad's coffee and fixed it the way he liked it with two lumps of sugar and a little milk. She felt the side of the dented silver-plate coffeepot and said, "Oh dear, I'm afraid the coffee's not very hot again." I waited to see if this would put Dad in a bad mood or not and whether he'd press the *servizio* button and make Lucrezia come back again, get his coffee, take it away to warm it up, and bring it back.

But he only said, "Let's say grace." And before Mom could start to pray, and make his coffee really cold, Dad hurriedly said, "Dear Heavenly Father, we come before Thee to thank Thee for this food, and I pray that Thou wilt lead us in Thy will. In Jesus' name, Amen.''

He looked up and took a bite of his roll almost before he finished saying amen. But Mom kept her head bowed a minute longer and her eyes closed to show she was more spiritual than Dad. Dad didn't even glance at her because he knew exactly what she was doing but wouldn't give her the satisfaction of catching *him* looking at her when she opened her eyes and said, ''Amen,'' very softly, as if she was ''praying in secret'' but really knew all along that she was actually getting even with Dad for having been so surly about her face cream first thing in the morning and not even noticing how she was being like the bride of Christ and all.

She poured out her tea and the pot steamed up and Dad glanced at her and said, ''It seems *your* tea is hot enough.''

''Would you like my tea? Here, let me take your coffee. I don't mind, dear.'' She said it all in a sorry, meek and mournful voice to show how sacrificial, unselfish, and humble she was. And how good she was, compared to Dad, who put such a lot of store by ''the cares of this life.''

''Aren't we so sweet?'' he said. The way he said it meant the opposite. It meant he knew Mom thought she was a lot more Christ-like than he was, and what's more he knew she was too, but that it didn't make him like her any better.

At home when we all had to stop what we were doing to have a special Day of Prayer and Mom made up a Prayer Chart—our direct phone line to God, she said—and put all the times of the day down in a column of boxes in half-hour slots from 6 A.M. to 6 P.M., Dad would only put his name down for a half an hour of prayer. Mom would put a red line through six boxes and take three whole hours from 6 A.M. till 9 P.M. and another two boxes at the end of the day. She said it was just so wonderful to talk to the Lord she needed all that time to just begin. Rachael always took at least six boxes of prayer and Janet once took six like Mom, but next time was back down to two boxes of prayer. I took one box like Dad, which was plenty for me, because to tell the truth, after about half a box, I'd start thinking about something else. And once my mind wandered so badly from The Things of the Lord that I found myself thinking about whether my Little Thing was ever going to get as big as my dad's, and then I started to think about the time Jacky Keegan stuck his in a Coke bottle and it went hard and he couldn't pull it out again and he had to *show his mom what had happened*! She had called my mom up and said that I had played a dirty game and that I could not play with Jacky unless I promised not to get him into trouble anymore. Which wasn't very nice of her since I didn't get Jacky to stick his Little Thing in the bottle in the first place. If he had listened to me and just let me smash the bottle by hitting it with a rock, his mom would never have known. His mom, who was also a missionary, had been sent out by the mission board to help my parents in the vineyard of the Lord to bring in the sheaves of wheat from the field and to catch men for Jesus like in the hymn, "I will make you fishers of men, fishers of men, fishers of men—I will make you fishers of men if you f-o-l-l-o-w me." She would not believe me, and said I was a truly bad boy, and had a perverse unregenerate mind.

Then I remembered that I was supposed to be praying that the Lord would meet our needs and that the mission board would still support us even though my dad's denomination, the PCUSA (Presbyterian Church United States of America), had just split into two parts. The other part had a much weaker view of Scripture, and Dad did not know if he could be faithful to The Things of the Lord and work under the authority of men who, at their last conference on the inerrancy of Scripture, had allowed a paper to be read by a theological professor from Dallas Seminary who said that he did not believe that Christ would reign as king during the millennium, and who believed that after the rapture the end would come *without* the millennium!

So we had to have a Day of Prayer to ask God to lead us through this fiery wilderness of apostacy. But after I prayed that God would lead Dad to make the right decision about whether to stay in the PCUSA or look for support from the new mission board of the split-away PCCCUSA (Presbyterian Church of Christ and Covenant United States of America), a denomination that would not allow people to read papers questioning the essentials of the faith like the millennium and the rapture, I let my mind wander and get overgrown with worldly weeds, like Mom would say. And while I tried to pray, all I could think of was Jacky's Little Thing stuck in the bottle, and I wondered if Dad had ever gotten his stuck in a bottle and whether the bottle would break if his went big, because his was a lot bigger than Jacky's to start with.

Once I had come into Dad's room at home without knocking, and he turned around, then turned away real fast because his was big. I couldn't see very well because he only had his bedside light on, but it looked bigger than the zucchini Mom grew in our garden and stuffed with hamburger and cheese to make ''Mennonite Meatloaf'' every Wednesday night before Bible study.

I waited for Dad to eat enough breakfast so I figured it would be all right to ask him something without the answer being ''no'' before he even thought about it. I said, ''Since it's raining, can I walk over to Portofino by myself and spend the day there?''

Dad was about to say ''no'' when Mom said, ''That seems a little risky.'' Dad looked at her and said, ''I don't think it's a bad idea. Just be back by six so you can change for supper. And do *not* go out to the lighthouse and climb on the rocks, the waves are too high today!'' I said, ''Thanks, Pop.'' And got out in a hurry before he could change his mind and add other things to the list I wasn't supposed to do.

I went to my room to get the hundred and fifty lire of spending money I had saved up by not buying anything at all yet on this vacation. Rachael woke up and asked where I was going, but I pretended I hadn't heard her question and slipped out the door.

14

IN THE COLD rain I could not smell the walk as well as at night when the path was warm. But it was just as exciting in the day to come to the high point on the walk halfway between Portofino and Paraggi and to look into the bay with all the yachts at their moorings. During the night when the rain had begun to fall there had been a storm at sea. The swells that were rolling in from the horizon were much bigger than usual, and the boats in the harbor were bobbing up and down so hard you could see the violent movement as they bucked against their anchor chains.

Portofino was empty. The rain had driven the little old ladies, who sat in their doorways making lace, indoors. Half the boutiques had their blue or green shutters up. The tourists who walked around taking pictures of famous people coming to and from the yachts were back at their hotels in Santa Margherita and Rapallo. The red and white excursion tour boats were bobbing at anchor, all tours canceled, a large "*Chiuso*" sign hanging over the clock that showed the time of the next boat's departure.

The waves were crashing so hard on the high rocky narrow peninsula of land protecting the port to the southward seaside that fumes and jets of spray were coming right over the top of the peninsula on which the church of Santa Christaforo sat and were splattering in big puddles on the granite docks and jettys of the town below.

People who had to walk around that side of the port would time their movements in order to stay dry. They dashed from a doorway to a boat or from a storage shed back to the main square, to avoid the spray from the pounding surf on the rocks below the church.

Sometimes they miscalculated and would get a good half a ton of water dropped on them as it arched up in the air, at least one hundred feet, then fell with a loud, machine-gun splatter, on the flagstones of the port.

Then they would stand there and look all around to see if anyone had watched them get soaked. And if no one had they just went on to wherever they had been going. But if they caught somebody's eye, then they would make a big show of shaking off the water and looking down at their ruined clothes, cursing and shaking their head as if they could not understand how such a thing could be allowed to happen to them.

If the person was a woman, she would squeal and run and show how it was not her fault because it was an accident, and if a man was with her she'd step back and look down at her clothes and show the man how terrible they looked. And he would take off his coat and hold it over their heads even though it was too late. Then he'd have to hold the woman even closer so as to be able to hold the coat over them both. She'd laugh and put her arm around his waist, and if he saw a friend he'd call out something, and the friend would laugh and shake his hand at the man, which was to say he knew all about things like this. If the woman had on high heels she'd take them off, and they'd scamper soaked into the bar by the jetty that was always open no matter what because it was a real bar, and not just one for tourists.

I saw one couple come dashing into the bar where I was standing drinking a *limone* soda in just that way. The pretty girl took off her soaked sweater and the men in the bar all gathered around to see if she was all right or if she had been hurt or something. And she told all about how the water came down while she pulled on the front of her white blouse so it wouldn't stick to her and be immodest because you could see her lacy bra under it through the wet cotton.

Then the bar man handed her a dish towel and apologized for the fact that it was all he had for her to dry herself with. The men in the bar suggested different drinks she should have to warm her and make sure she didn't take a chill.

But the bartender knew best. He fixed her an espresso and put a dollop of brandy in it even though her boyfriend said he thought a shot of Branca Fernett would be better for her.

She stood at the bar with her shoes up on the rail in front of her and the bartender and other men passed her shoes around and discussed whether they were ruined or not.

Then the woman noticed that one of her silk stockings had run and she wailed and said oh no and that it was "*Cattivo*!" All the men crowded around to see the run and they shook their heads and groaned right along with her that this could happen to her and at how she was right to be worried about what she could wear now because all her clothes were at home in Genoa and she was here to visit her grandmother this afternoon and her grandmother was very particular and already thought her skirts were too short and by the way did the men think her skirt was too short? And they said no it was perfect, but the run went pretty high up so maybe she should take her stockings off. It would be fine because her legs were so nice and brown.

So she started to take off one stocking by lifting her skirt to unfasten the garter and all the men were looking very helpful. But the man she came into the bar with took her by the arm and led her toward the door marked "*Gabinetto*" and pushed her inside and told her to take off her stockings in there. When he turned around, the other men all groaned and swore at the man because now they couldn't see the pretty girl. He didn't smile back at them and went back to the bar and picked up her shoes and paid for the drink, and when she came out of the toilet with her stockings in her hand and smiling all around at everyone, he snatched them away from her and stuffed them in his jacket pocket and pulled her by the wrist out of the bar onto the dock.

The men at one end of the bar went back to playing cards, and the other men at the table finished their drinks, stubbed out their Gauloise cigarettes, put on their yellow slickers, and went back to work fixing a broken boat winch now that the wind had died down.

I heard the bell tolling on the other side of the square from the other church in Portofino. Not the one getting soaked above the harbor but the one up by the road that the tourists never visited. I stepped out of the bar and waited until the next spray hit the flagstones, then I ran out to the square until I got past the big puddles that showed where the spray could get to. I walked to the church as the bell tolled for a noonday mass.

When I got to the church door, I stopped and dipped my fingers in holy water and crossed myself. Just like the woman in black with the gray crocheted shawl over her head had done ahead of me. This was one of my favorite things to do on our vacations in Italy. I knew that Roman Catholics were not saved and not Christians, and I knew it was wrong to concentrate on the ''mere external signs of piety,'' but still I liked to pretend I was a Catholic when the rest of the family was not there to see me.

When we had communion twice a year at home in our church, which we held in our living room, all it was was Dad passing some little glass cups around. They were the same size as Mom's thimble, only cheaper-looking and made out of glass. They had grape juice in them. We ate a piece of bread cut into little squares and Dad would read about the Last Supper and ask if we were each coming to The Table of the Lord worthily and were all saved. And since it was just us and Jacky Keegan's parents and Jacky in our church, and Dad knew we had all accepted Jesus into our hearts, I never knew why he asked. We'd sing a hymn, and Dad would pray, and we'd go outside from our church, which was really our living room with all the chairs turned to face the fireplace where Dad stood to preach. Then Mom would pick up the leftover communion bread to bake in the oven and make croutons for lunch for our soup, and I'd drink up our leftover grape juice out of the leftover full little cups, then go outside to play, unless Mom let me build a tower out of the cups first.

But in the Roman Catholic Church, even though they didn't believe in Jesus, or the Inerrancy of Scripture, and worshiped Mary and prayed to dead people and were probably the Whore of Babylon, they did things I liked to watch. It wasn't as if I was making fun of God or telling bad jokes about the Bible or anything sacred because we knew that none of their empty rituals were pleasing to God. So I didn't think it was wrong to play Catholic, but I knew that Dad and especially Mom would be really mad if they saw me taking the wafer and crossing myself and kneeling next to old ladies and even once lighting a candle in front of Mary and saying, "Hail Mary, full of Grace" just like the little South American boys did before the missionaries got to their village in our nighttime devotional storybook *Pete and Penny Play and Pray*, which had stories about how Christian missionaries had gone to explain about Jesus to the Roman Catholic pagan children living in darkness and superstition and trusting in men rather than in God and the Bible.

In our church we sang a hymn about the Bible. The chorus was "The B-I-B-L-E, yes that's the book for me!" And we got to scream it out and wave our Bibles over our heads because there was nothing wrong with praising the Lord joyfully and without ritual, superstition, and liturgy.

Then we'd play Sword Drill. We'd hold our Bibles by our sides and when Mom called out a verse, we'd draw our Bibles like swords, and whoever could look up the verse first got a sticker with a Bible verse on it to stick on his Sunday school attendance chart. I never won since I could hardly read because my mom was teaching me at home when she had time because she didn't want me in the Roman Catholic Swiss schools being taught by nuns. So she taught me, and I sometimes did some schoolwork with Janet, when she came home from the Protestant girls boarding school she and Rachael attended in Lausanne.

Janet taught me by giving me Indian burns on my wrist if I wouldn't concentrate. Mom let me take a lot of recesses out in the yard. So I had a lot of trouble finding the Bible verses or reading them. Rachael would sometimes help me look one up, and then I'd try to read it while she whispered the words to me. She had been at a real school in St. Louis before we had moved. Mom would say, "That's very good, Calvin," even though she knew I'd been helped. She and Rachael and Janet would all exchange sweet smiles just like the pictures of all the women in long dresses on the book cover of *Little Women*, which Mom had already read to me twice.

When I played Roman Catholic I never had to read anything and since the Catholics did not "Stand on the Word of God but on pitiful human tradition," like Dad said, they never did Sword Drill or stood up and screamed the chorus to "The B-I-B-L-E" but instead knelt down quietly in their churches with the air all hazy and blue from incense. They didn't know about the Five Points of Calvinism, the New Covenant and the Reformers like Zwingli, so they still used incense even though Jesus had said He "desired mercy not sacrifice," so they were really sinning and not getting saved because they had not done what Zwingli, who Dad said was even more reformed than Calvin, had told them to. But this was not surprising because "They are Vessels of Wrath, not the Elect predestined to be saved."

But the incense smelled good and the voice of the

priest was all quiet and comfortable, and echoed.

When Dad preached, he'd shout and wave his arms as he expounded The Word to us. And his sermons were very moving. Mom said so. We'd all follow along in our Bibles and read the verses to ourselves as he read them out loud. At least Rachael and Janet and Mom would, but I had to pretend to since I couldn't read. I'd turn the pages to the right place because I could read numbers, and I was able to see where Mom had her Bible open to. I always followed along because I wanted my Bible to be as worn out as my mom's, or at least as Janet's, because I knew that if I was going to grow as a Christian, I had to Live in The Word, and you couldn't prove you were Living in The Word unless your Bible was getting worn out. It was no use just crumpling up the pages or rubbing a little mud on them. Rachael could tell what you had done, and she told Dad, and he strapped me, not because I had soiled The Word since, as he said, "we're not Catholics or Eastern Orthodox, we do not venerate the physical book but only the One who inspired it." So he didn't mind me getting my Bible muddy, but he minded because it was a kind of lie to try and wear out your Bible and pretend you had done it the right way, which was to meditate night and day on it and bind it to your heart by prayerfully reading it. He asked me before he bent me over if I understood why I was being strapped and if I thought the punishment fair. And I said yes, but after he hit me three times, with my pants up since I had lied by "omission" not "commission," which would have been much worse and would have made him hit me with my pants down, I thought that really it wasn't fair because I hadn't volunteered to be a Presbyterian Reformed missionary to the Roman Catholics of

Switzerland, and so it wasn't my fault I couldn't read. If I couldn't read and Janet and Rachael could, because they went to a boarding school for missionary girls and had been to a real school in America that we left when I was two, of course their Bibles got worn out and they grew in the Lord more than me!

15

AT THE BEGINNING of each year's vacation in Italy I knew that the days would pass by horribly quickly. I knew that thinking about how we had ten whole days would only make them start to go even faster. By the fifth day we were there I would try not to think about the vacation being half over. And in the last three days I tried not to admit to myself that soon Mom would say, ''The day after tomorrow we'll be leaving.'' At home, ten days was a long time, but not here.

I was as sad as I always was, which was very sad, when Mom said that Rachael and I should pack that night, and just leave out our clothes and our toothbrushes for the train ride home. What made it worse was that on our last full day it had been raining. I had enjoyed myself in Portofino but I would rather have had a last day snorkeling and helping the Banini around the beach.

At dinner Janet held up her arm and said, ''My tan's already fading!''

Rachael said, ''I wanted to swim all the way out to the point alone once this year and now I can't.''

Mom told them, ''Give thanks in all things.''

''I don't see why,'' said Janet.

''Because God is sovereign, that's why,'' Dad answered.

''You mean He had a purpose in making it rain so I couldn't get more sun?'' Janet said.

Then Mom said, ''Janet, we don't say sarcastic things, especially about the sovereignty of God.''

''Janet might have said that in a mocking spirit but as a matter of fact she brings up a good point,'' Dad said. ''Yes, Janet, you did. All things *do* work together for the good of those who love Him, the Elect. You never will know what might have happened to you today if the sun had been out.''

''You mean if I had gone out to the point, I might have had a cramp or something and drowned, and God knew it so He made it rain to save me?'' Rachael asked.

Mom smiled at Rachael, and Dad gave her head a pat and said that Rachael was beginning to show discernment for the Things of the Lord.

But Janet muttered under her breath, ''Or might have been raped.''

Mom turned to her and seemed to grow six inches taller right where she was sitting, eating a plate of pasta with fresh tomato and basil sauce. ''What did you say, young lady?''

Janet wouldn't repeat it even though we all had heard it. I wondered why when we said something once that Mom said should never have passed our lips, since our mouth was the guardian of our body, which was the Temple of the Lord, she would make us repeat it again even louder.

Dad said, "If I were you, I'd obey your mother."

Then Janet said, "I said, 'or raped'?"

"That's an awful thing to say!" Mom said.

I knew that Janet was in trouble and that I could say a lot of things right now and Janet would get the blame for starting it all because she should know better and I was only a child. So I said real quiet and in a voice like little children use, "Mommy, what's 'rape'?"

Mom gave Janet a really long look and exchanged glances with Dad, who said to Janet, "Now are you proud of yourself?"

Then Rachael looked at her plate and wouldn't look up at anyone, even though I kicked her a little under the table to see if I could get her to look at me and start to giggle. Janet looked like Dad looks when he's discussing who authored the book of Matthew when someone says two people did. And I could see that if we hadn't been in the pensione dining room and the Bazlintons hadn't been watching us, Dad would have probably slapped Janet even though she was a teenager now.

Janet said, "I only meant that even worse things might have happened to Rachael than cramps and because it rained they didn't, because God is sovereign and kept her inside all day playing chess with me."

But Mom was angry and wouldn't let her get out of it, especially since I said again, "But, Mom, what *is* 'rape'?"

Mom said to Janet, "Really, darling!" Then she turned to me with a sweet smile and said, "It's not your fault, no one is blaming you."

Then Janet made a big mistake, or rather God did

because He's sovereign. Dad had said many times how the great Reformation hero, Calvin, showed us we are in a state of Total Depravity and so is our free will so we really can't even think with our fallen minds or choose to do good things because we are so depraved. So God made her say, "I only asked!"

Then God made Dad throw down his napkin and say, "That's it!" and Janet stood up with her face all red and the pimple on her forehead even redder than before and she walked away even before Mom said, "Go to your room, young lady, we'll talk about this later."

With no one having any way to choose anything because God is sovereign and all, and with all things working together for the good of the Elect, I wondered if something might fall on where Janet had been sitting that would have split her head open or cut her arms off since all things work together for good for those who love Him, and then we'd know why this had all needed to happen to spare her or something. I knew Janet loved God because her Bible was getting almost as worn out as Mom's, so she was one of the Elect all right. I knew something good would happen now. But it wasn't her avoiding anything falling down on her place because nothing did.

In the silence that followed Janet's departure, we ate and I started doing experiments with the salt shaker, which had rice in it to absorb the moisture from the sea air so it would still pour. My experiment was to see if I could do something halfway, then stop or change it so fast that I could get ahead of, or even beat the sovereignty of God. I started to pour out a little salt onto the table but just as more was about to come out, I suddenly stopped and started to shake the rice around in the cellar so God would lose count of the grains of salt. Then I started to put it down but instead yanked it up above my head. And I did it so fast that salt came out all over me. In a way that was good since God is sovereign; He knows your thoughts all the time, so how could I do something He hadn't planned for since the beginning of time? I was glad when the salt came out all over my head because it was a surprise to me and so it might have been a surprise to God too. But then I figured He knew I was going to do this thing with the salt from before I was born. So He was probably still sovereign and Calvin was right and had God figured. While I was thinking this, Dad said, "What on earth did you do that for?"

And before I thought, I just blurted out, "God made me do it."

Then Dad turned to Mom and said, "What's got into them all tonight?" He said to me, "Blasphemy is not something we tolerate, young man, go to your room!"

I knew by the way he said it that when he came to "talk it over" afterward, he'd spank me because blasphemy is taking the Lord's name in vain. So I walked to my room with that squirmy feeling you get when you are waiting for a spanking while your dad finishes his dessert.

On the way I ran up the front stairs and went down the back stairs, then went up to my room instead of just straight down the hall past the place where the little Madonna is in the wall with the plastic flowers in front of her and the red glass thing with a candle in it.

But I was too slow and I was sure God knew I'd go this unusual way even from before the creation of the world. It was no use, the whole thing was part of His plan, even the things we did to get out of His plan, like the thing with the salt shaker I did, were really part of His plan so you had to do it, and I couldn't have left the salt shaker alone even if I had wanted to.

I started to wonder why Dad would spank me for saying God made me do it when he always said Calvin was right and the people who didn't accept the sovereignty of God were not really Christians and that "free will" simply meant we were free to recognize God's plan, even though we could never change it or understand it because of our Total Depravity.

When the door opened and Dad came in, I had that watery feeling in my legs and I could not get my mouth to stop turning down at the corners all quivery. Then Dad said, "I've been talking it over with Mother, and we think that because this is the last night of the vacation, you're probably a little upset. So I've decided not to spank you this time but don't let me ever hear you say anything like that again." Then he gave me a hug and a kiss, and I hugged him back. When he left my room I was very glad and sat down and thought about how much I loved my pop. Then I wondered if God had known he would change his mind and not spank me and if this was part of the plan.

16

THE THREE SPEAR points and barbs on my spear gun each had a wine bottle cork stuck firmly on them for safety, and the nylon cord was wrapped around the handle so it wouldn't catch on anything.

Dad was in a bad mood because Mom hadn't been ready to catch the 7:33 A.M. bus from Paraggi to Santa Margherita. We had all stood at the bus stop while Rachael ran inside to tell Mom that the bus had arrived, and the Italian driver was shouting at Dad because he was keeping one foot on the bus stair so the driver couldn't close the bus door and leave without Mom.

Rachael had come running back out and called to Dad, "She hasn't paid the bill yet and still has to pack one more bag." Dad pulled his foot off the stair of the bus, and Janet, who had already gotten on and was sitting down in the back row, rushed to get off the bus before the driver pulled away. When he left he shook his head and then tapped the side of it to show he thought we were all nuts.

When Dad saw him to do this, he ran a little way down the road next to the bus and shook his fist at the driver and gave the bus a big thumping slap with his hand on the side as it pulled into traffic. The people riding on the inside all looked out and started talking to each other about Dad.

Dad walked back to where we were and he was fuming mad. We all sat still. Even Janet didn't say anything at all.

Dad said, "If we miss our train we'll miss all the connections, and if we do that we'll just have to sit on our suitcases in Milano until tomorrow's train to Switzerland."

Nobody asked any questions. We knew Dad was telling the truth because we'd spent all our vacation money on the pensione so we wouldn't have any left for a hotel in Milano.

When Mom came out Dad shouted, "Now you've done it!"

"What's wrong, Ralph?" she asked.

Dad yelled "Wrong!? Wrong!? I'll tell you what's wrong! You've made us miss the bus to the station! That's what's wrong, Elsa!"

"We'll take the next one, dear."

Dad yelled out at the top of his lungs, "The next one's at a quarter to and if, *if* it's on time, *exactly* on time, we'll have one and a half minutes to get across the street, up the stairs, across to the platform, and catch our train to Genoa!"

"The Genoa train's always late, so I'm sure we'll be fine dear," Mom said.

Dad said nothing else for a while, but we knew that if they got alone someplace, then Dad would have plenty more to say. When Mom sat down next to Janet on the bus stop bench, Dad turned his back and started to walk up the road toward Portofino as if he was looking for the next bus.

Janet said to Mom in a low voice so Dad wouldn't hear, "He ran next to the bus and shook his fist at the driver and hit the side."

Mom shook her head in sorrow and sighed, "Oh dear. Poor Ralph. . . . It's his working-class background in him coming out. You know he's only a generation away from a manual laboring family." Janet nodded and moved closer to Mom on the bench.

Dad, whose father ran away to sea at twelve and who fought in the Spanish-American War and worked on a coal breaker when he was eight where, Dad told me, you got hit with a stick by the foreman if you didn't sort coal fast enough, came running back because he had heard the echo of the bus horn as the bus pulled out of the parking lot at Portofino.

"It's coming!" he shouted.

The pensione door opened and Lucrezia came out carrying Mom's little travel bag and calling out to Mom. Mom ran over to meet her and thanked her and told her we'd see her next year and to remember what she had learned about Jesus in church in our room. Lucrezia kissed Mom on both cheeks and waved to us all. Dad didn't wave back because he was still mad at Mom.

The bus came and it was almost full with people going into Santa Margherita to work. We didn't get any seats except Mom and Rachael who sat down up near the driver.

The train in Santa Margherita was eighteen minutes late, so Mom had been right about that. But Dad was right too in a way, because the train was so late we still might have missed our connection from Genoa to Milano. Even though this was nothing to do with Mom, Dad blamed her for it and said, ''What else did you forget?'' every time Mom talked about whether we'd make the express from Milano to Switzerland or just have to sit on the platform all night.

In Genoa the train we had wanted to get was gone already, so we were even later now. Dad said that we would miss the train to Switzerland for sure, that even in Italy the express trains were never a whole hour late.

Mom said, ''Let's pray about this.''

We all looked at Dad to see if he was so mad he'd dare to not join us in prayer, even though this would not be pleasing to the Lord. We found out he was seriously in a bad mood because he said, ''You go ahead and pray, Elsa, I'm going to the newsstand to get a *Newsweek*.''

Mom and Rachael and Janet all looked shocked, and at the same time Mom looked happy because now we all knew whose fault it would be if we did miss the next train. Mom gathered us around to pray, and I made sure I was standing so I could open my eyes a little and see what Dad was doing in his rebellion against the Lord, because you never could tell how swiftly the Lord's anger might spill over on Dad like the Midianites smiting the Jews when *they* turned away from God. Maybe Dad would be eaten by worms like Herod as soon as he opened the *Newsweek* and read about worldly things while Mom did what she was supposed to and took the train to the Lord in prayer.

Mom prayed, ''Dear Heavenly Father, we just come before Thy throne to first thank Thee for being Thyself. And to ask that we might find favor in Thy precious sight. We also ask Thee to touch Ralph's hardened heart this day and Lord to encourage him in Thee that he might become closer to Thee and trust Thee more. For Thou art the Lord who didst part the waters and Thou art the Lord who didst say, Whatsoever you ask in faith so it shall be done unto thee. So we just come in faith, Lord, and claim Thy promises this day and ask Thee, Lord, not that a mountain might move or be cast into the sea, Lord, but that Thou wilt increase Ralph's faith so that he too wilt trust in Thy holy name. So Lord I pray, as did Thine servant Elijah, that Thou wilt send a sign to Thy people, Lord, and that the train in Milano wilt be late so that Thine servant Ralph wilt, like Jonah when *he* strayed from Thee, believe again in Thy mighty loving hand, Lord, who knowest every hair on our heads. So open Ralph's eyes as Thou opened the eyes of the prophets of Baal who doubted Thee, Lord. And may Ralph praise Thy name because Thou art mighty, and may he have the sign he needeth to have the faith, Lord, that he shouldst have faith even as I do, Lord, without a sign. And, Lord, we pray Thou wilt forgive Ralph for loving the things of this world more than Thee and for having refused to come to the foot of the Cross in this our hour of need. Touch his heart, Lord, we pray in Thy Son's dear name. Amen."

Mom turned to us and started to sing, and the girls joined in, and I tried to move a little way down the platform and look like I was with an Italian family who were slicing up a Motta Panettone cake and drinking cups of espresso from the station snack bar. But Mom beckoned me back into the circle of faith where she and Rachael and Janet were all singing "*This Little Light of Mine*," and so I was stuck, and that was probably good because Jesus said that if we deny Him before the world, He will deny us before His Father in heaven and bound we will be cast into outer darkness. We were not denying Him; in fact, all the people on the opposite platform turned around, and Mom smiled at them while we sang. Dad just glanced up and then kept on reading his *Newsweek* like Peter in the high priest's courtyard when he denied Christ and the cock crowed three times and he wept bitterly.

But Mom was looking so happy she almost looked fierce, and the girls were singing really loud so we were getting to witness to everyone on both platforms at once, which was probably why God made Mom be late in the first place because all things work together for good for the Elect.

All these people could see the light of Jesus shining in Mom's and Janet's and Rachael's faces because they had learned how to sing and smile at the same time. I tried it in front of a mirror once after Mom told me to let my joy show. But I couldn't do it. If I smiled I'd forget the chorus or sing it out of tune. Or my smile would look funny because my mouth was wide open shouting "Hallelu, . . . , Hallelujah, Praise ye the Lord!" and the smile would disappear. That's why when I sang I tried to keep my face turned away from Mom's so she wouldn't be able to check for joy because I couldn't make it shine on my face the way Steven's countenance shone with joy when he was stoned by the multitude. But he was only praying to himself, not trying to sing "*This Little Light of Mine*," so it was easier for him.

When we finally got to Milano we looked across at the platform where the express to Switzerland was supposed to be, and it was gone. Dad looked at Mom, and he looked pleased, and Mom just shook her head like Jesus weeping over Jerusalem because of her sorrow at his lack of faith.

Dad put down his suitcase and said, "Well, this is where we spend the night!" He turned to Mom and said, "I hope *you're* satisfied."

Mom looked at the girls, and I knew they all thought it was really Dad's fault.

We all sat down on our suitcases, and Dad said in a cheerful voice that really meant he was even madder now, "Isn't *this* fun! It's so exciting living with Elsa, isn't it, girls?"

Janet and Rachael kept quiet because the worst thing that could happen was if you answered Dad when he was in a Mood because then he'd start to fight through you at Mom, saying things to you loudly that really meant something else like he just had because when he said, "Isn't *this* fun!" he really meant, "*Now* do you see how hard it is being married to your mother?"

We sat looking at the men in the long blue coats with metal numbers pinned to their chests who were porters pushing carts piled up with people's luggage. Janet and I started trying to guess where people came from by how they were dressed. Then a porter asked Mom if we wanted our luggage moved someplace, and Dad said, "No, *grazie*, we are staying here!" The porter asked when the train we were taking was coming, and Mom said in a small voice, to show it wasn't her idea, "Tomorrow—*domani*."

"*Domani*?!" said the porter. "Why tomorrow?"

Dad said with a lot of meaning in his voice, "Some of us missed today's train to Switzerland."

Then the porter smiled and said, "But no, *signore*, you no miss the traino, it leave in a half the hours."

We all looked over at the platform where it was

supposed to be but it was as empty as ever.

The porter laughed and pointed behind us and said, "They changea to the other sidea because of the engines troubles. The traino is one and a half hours later! Not like in America, you never later. I 'af a brosser in Chincinattis!"

No one was listening to him, we were looking at Mom, and Mom stood up and her eyes were shining and she just said, "Well!"

Dad picked up his suitcase without saying anything and walked over to the train car that had Domodossola-Brig-Montreux-Genève marked on the side and he got in without looking around.

1965

17

I HAD SHOT a cat with my spear gun a few weeks before we went to Italy. Now we were on the train on the way to our vacation. The barbs had stuck in the loose skin on its back. I had been standing at the back door of our chalet in Switzerland, and no one saw me because they were all at a Monday morning prayer meeting being led by my mother, who was sharing all the things the Lord had done for her that week.

When I shot the cat it was sitting with its back to me. When the spear stuck into it, it jumped in the air and took off so fast it pulled the spear gun right out of my hand. Then it dragged the spear, cord, and gun behind it, until it came to the hedge that separated our chalet from the one next door. When it ran through the hedge the spear gun caught on the trunks of the hedge bushes and yanked the barbs out of the cat's back.

I was glad it had pulled loose because it was easier to shoot a cat than to think what to do with it when you hit it, and it was jumping around spitting and growling and all.

The prayer meeting had ended soon after, and by that time the cat had climbed the big apple tree and was sitting up in my old tree house Dad had built for me when I was little. Now it was growling in that low angry way cats do when they're upset. I could see its tail all bushed out swishing back and forth and I felt sorry for it. But I also felt pleased that my aim was good since I planned to spear-gun fish all vacation. Not just a little but really concentrate on it and try to eat fish every night at the Pensione Biea. Maybe even have enough for the whole family to eat. If I saw anything I did not know was good to eat or that might be good to eat, like the octopus was, but not good enough, in the sense that it was not enjoyable or made you feel sick, then I wouldn't even shoot it. I was going to swim out beyond the point of our bay to shoot the big fish that were out there. This was farther than I had ever been before. I had asked Dad about it, and he said that now I was almost fourteen he would move the swimming limits farther out for me since I was much older and more responsible.

He said that before I shot the cat, and I didn't tell him about doing it so he didn't change his mind about the responsible part.

I left a little blood, just a smear, and a couple of black cat hairs stuck to the barbs of my spear gun. This was because Mom had been reading a book to me by Jack London about men in the Yukon living rough, and it seemed like a good idea to leave the first blood of the hunting season on my spear like the Indians did when they marked their foreheads with a smear of blood from their first elk kill. As the blood dried I had to wet it a little and rub it around because otherwise it would have come off my spear like most of the cat hairs did.

When I bleed my blood sticks pretty well to whatever it gets on, but this cat's blood dried up then started to peel off the metal, like paint does off wood that hasn't been primed.

Maybe the cat was anemic or something. Janet was and she had to have shots of iron. I would see when I got home if I could find where she kept the bottle of iron medicine in her room which the visiting nurse injected her with when she came by on Wednesdays and gave her her weekly shot. I could treat the cat for anemia and then do a test to see if its blood got stronger and would stick to things the way it should. I knew where Mom kept the glass syringe and needles in the kitchen because I would see her take them down and boil them for thirty minutes so that they would be ready for the nurse when she came by to give my grandmother, who had moved in with us the year before, or Janet shots. I always asked Janet if I could watch her get the shot; she said no because we were older now so it wasn't proper for me to see her bottom anymore. So I hadn't seen it yet, the shot I mean. I had seen Janet's bottom fairly recently. When we had been on a hike Janet had told Mom she needed to go to the bathroom; Mom told us all to "go on a little and turn around." We did but I had looked back just in time to see Janet squat down and pull up her skirt. So I had seen her bottom very well, and it didn't look much different from how I remembered it from when I was allowed to see it when I was younger.

I said to Mom, "I'm going for a walk in the train, can I?"

"Are you asking me or telling me?"

"I mean, may I go for a walk?"

Dad said, "That's better, young man."

Mom said, "Yes, you may, dear, but not for long."

"You better be back here before the train gets to Stresa because a lot of people get on there and these are not reserved seats," Dad said.

I had plenty of time because we were just pulling out of Brig into the Simplon tunnel and wouldn't be in Stresa for an hour. I knew this because we had taken this trip every year since I could remember. I could even tell by the sound of the train if I shut my eyes where we were on the trip. In fact, I had done that last year on the ride home. I had kept my eyes shut from Milano to Brig. For four whole hours I kept track of where we were by counting the stations we stopped at and by the sound of things like the Simplon tunnel and the arcades the train goes through before it gets to it. Dad said it was remarkable. And Mom looked pleased with me and said, "We have a very bright child in this one."

No one asked me why I wanted to walk in the train and if they had I would have lied. I wanted to go for a walk to see if Jennifer happened to be on our train.

Once years ago she had been on the same train as us because she and her parents had taken the boat train from England, via Paris, to Lausanne, Switzerland, changed trains, and then boarded ours by coincidence. Mom had seen them and waved out the window to them on the platform and said, "Look, there are the Bazlintons!" They had boarded the first-class car and Mom didn't say any more because we were in second class and not even with reserved seats because that cost more. We had all been a little embarrassed when Mrs. Bazlinton had come to our car after Domodossola to say hello because we knew she was thinking to herself how crowded our part of the train was with Italians who worked in Switzerland as manual laborers who were now going home for their summer holiday. And how it smelled more of people in our part of the train than in first class. And how we were not all sitting together because there were only a couple of seats still unoccupied when we had got on the train in Lausanne so we were all spread out through the car.

I didn't mind if Jennifer knew we rode in second class. If she was on the train I wanted to see her anyway. On the last day of our vacation last summer Jennifer had given me a picture of herself in her English school uniform standing with two friends of hers from her girls school. They held field hockey sticks and had short plaid skirts on with high gray knee socks and what Jennifer called "cardigans," she meant sweaters, on top. I didn't care about the other two girls in the picture, but Jennifer looked very pretty. I kept her picture in my Bible in Exodus. I looked at it a lot when I was alone.

I walked through the train and kept saying "*Scusi*" to all the Italian people standing in the hallways. At one end of the car there was a family sitting in front of where the toilet is in the space by the door. They had put out some picnic things on a suitcase and were cutting up a salami. The mother was breastfeeding her baby. When she looked up and saw me staring at her and the baby, she didn't look shy or annoyed but smiled and said something in Italian to her husband, who then held out a piece of salami to me. I said,

"No, *grazie*," because I wanted to keep looking for Jennifer.

When I got to the first-class compartments, they were nearly empty. I looked into one empty seat after another as I walked down the hall.

In one compartment an elderly Swiss woman and man were sitting, and when they saw me look in at them, the woman reached over and pulled the blind down on the window facing into the hall. She looked angry that I was watching them and she said something in Swiss German to her husband that sounded scolding, though of course I couldn't understand what it was because no one except Swiss Germans speak Swiss German.

When I got to the end of the car there was no place left to look. So I walked back down the length of the train to our compartment.

While I had been away a man who had been asleep in the corner had woken up and was smoking a cigarette. Mom kept staring at him and then at all of us. But he just lit another cigarette while he kept his eyes on the copy of *Paris Match* he was reading.

Mom, seeing his magazine, guessed where he was from and said to Janet, very low so he wouldn't hear, "French." They both nodded because they understood each other perfectly. The way Mom had said "French" meant she was pretty disgusted with France and how dirty it was and how it was full of Roman Catholic atheists who smoked and drank and how they had murdered the Huguenot Protestants in the seventeenth century and were one of the darkest and most pagan countries in Europe where the men "urinated in public." When she and Dad went to Paris once to give a talk on Calvin's Doctrine of the Lord's Supper at an Action Biblique conference on evangelism, she had come home with a very bad impression of the French.

When the Frenchman glanced at Mom, who was staring at him, he looked up, pulled a blue packet of Gauloise cigarettes out of his pocket, and offered Mom one, thinking that she was staring at him because she wanted to smoke. She said very loud and firm, "*Non merci, je ne fume pas*!" She shuddered in disgust to think that he could have mistaken her for *that* kind of person.

Dad sat in the opposite corner reading our denominational newsletter from the world headquarters of the PCCCCUSA, our new denomination, because we had split again and our part of the split was now called the Presbyterian Church of the Calvinist Confirmed Confession United States of America. This split had been over the issue of whether Hodge or Warfield had a better idea of how to interpret Calvin's position on Total Depravity and Regeneration. I think we went with Hodge but I'm not sure. The main thing was we knew we were right, and the only real believers in Reformed doctrine left, so Dad and the other leaders made a new church.

Dad was reading about Pastor Bob White of Gabon. There was a picture of him on the back of the newsletter. He was in a white short-sleeved shirt and had on a thin black tie. In one hand he held a big Bible. His other arm was draped over the skinny shoulders of a black native man who only came up to his waist and was smiling a big smile full of happy teeth between thick lips. Under the photograph was a caption that read: "The Good News comes to the village of Wangogo—Pastor Bob shares the love of Jesus with a native."

Maybe it was this picture that reminded Mom that

Jesus had died for everyone, even the French, even ones who smoked. So she stopped glaring at the Gauloise man and instead started smiling at him as if she were Pastor Bob and he was the headman of the village of Wangogo.

The Frenchman looked a question at her because Mom was smiling and smiling so hard. She cleared her throat in a meaningful way and said, ''*Excusez-moi, est-ce que vous parlez anglais*?'' And the man said, ''*Oui*, I speeks the Eengleesh a leetle.'' Then Mom asked him if he would like to see something interesting. When she did this I suddenly got a feeling of panic like I was drowning because I realized what Mom was about to do. And she did it too. She reached into her handbag and pulled out a large walnut.

The man looked at it and said, ''*Non, merci*.'' He thought Mom wanted him to eat it, and like she didn't want to smoke, he didn't want to eat a large walnut just then. Then Mom did something with the nut that made him jump a little. She began to pull a tiny ribbon out of the nut. The man saw this was no ordinary nut, the walnut that is. Mom first pulled out a little piece of black ribbon about three inches long and a quarter of an inch wide. She said to the man that the black ribbon represented his sin. She asked him if he agreed or not. He nodded his head, fascinated, and Mom took this as a yes, so she pulled the ribbon out a little more, and the next part that came after the black was a section of red ribbon.

Mom said to the man, ''The red ribbon represents our Savior's blood.'' The man started to lick his lips. And Mom took this to mean he didn't understand, so she said, ''*Jésus! Jésus*!'' pretty loud. The man forgot to smoke his Gauloise anymore, and it went out because Gauloise cigarettes are all natural and don't have saltpeter in them to keep them burning if you didn't suck on them.

"Jesus died to wash your sins clean, so the ribbon in your heart is washed red and the black is washed away and replaced by white." Mom said this part as she tugged on the red section of ribbon and pulled out the white section. At least it was supposed to be "white as snow," but it was really a little yellow because the American Missionary Alliance, which sent out the Gospel Walnut Witnessing Kit, had used cheap satin ribbon in this batch of nuts. If you were going to be literal about it, you'd have to say that your heart would get "white as not-so-fresh egg yolk." But the Frenchman was not a fundamentalist, so he let it pass and accepted Mom's word for it that the yellow ribbon was really white and his heart would be the same color when he had agreed to believe what Mom was telling him with the assistance of "the miraculous little nut that helps you plant the seed of life in desperate human hearts," like the instruction booklet said that came with each Gospel Walnut.

Mom pulled out the last piece of ribbon. It was gold for streets of gold in heaven where the Frenchman could go if he stopped smoking and listened to the nut. Mom then turned the tiny wire handle on the side of the nut that was like a little crank. By turning it you made all the gospel message, "told with attractive ribbons sure to get the unbeliever's attention," go back into the nut. Once I had taken my Gospel Walnut and pried it open to see what was inside and where the ribbons that "told the story of the precious Savior's love" went when they were not out witnessing.

All it was that made it work was some ribbon glued

to a piece of wire in the middle of the hollowed-out nut that wound up when you turned the handle. It had once been a real nut and had been carefully cracked and scooped out, loaded with the Good News, and glued back together with a little bit of the lip of the nut shell cut out in front so "the ribbon of eternal life" could do its stuff.

Mom asked the Frenchman if he would like to accept Jesus into his heart right then before it was too late because the train might crash. The man wiped some sweat off his forehead with his sleeve and said, "I *suis* a Catholic." I could tell he thought that this would settle it since it would let Mom know he was already a Christian. But this only made Mom start to roll out the ribbon again, since if he was a Roman Catholic this was as bad as being an atheist, maybe worse, since you thought you were saved but weren't, and then your darkness was complete.

"You cannot be saved by trusting in good works. You must personally accept Jesus into your heart," Mom said.

Then the man said, "*Oui, oui.*"

Mom took this for another yes so she put her hand on the man's shoulder and said, "Pray after me—'Lord Jesus.' " Then she waited, but he didn't pray after her so she had to open her eyes and sort of leave the prayer just hanging out there.

"*Non*?" said Mom. "*Vous ne*, you don't understand. Repeat after me. *Répétez, répétez*!" Then she started again. "Lord Jesus."

And the man got the idea and said "*Jésus*." I couldn't tell if he was praying the Sinner's Prayer after Mom or swearing in French or calling on Jesus to help him or all three.

Janet and Rachael were looking all tender and Janet

had tears in her eyes because last year at Summer Bible School she had rededicated her life to the Lord so now she had a more Tender Heart for the Lost. And Rachael, who had never rebelled and always had had a tender heart, was looking sweet and happy because she was witnessing the rebirth of a lost soul and was rejoicing along with the angels.

But Dad just kept reading in the corner even though Mom had looked over a couple of times and said, "Isn't that so, Ralph?" in a way that meant she wanted Dad to enter into the witnessing and help midwife this lost lamb into the kingdom. Dad just kept reading; he had turned the page now, and I could see a chart on the back of the newsletter outlining the proper Presbyterian eschatological position of the End Times. The point on the chart where the Elect were taken up in the rapture was marked with a red arrow pointing up and a picture of a family dressed in their Sunday best all floating up to meet Jesus in the air. The mother's legs were already in the clouds so you couldn't look up her skirt.

Mom kept going with the Sinner's Prayer and said, "I come to you a repentant sinner."

The Frenchman sat straight in his seat and wouldn't pray because the conductor had just opened the door to our compartment and was saying, "*Billets, s'il vous plaît.*"

Dad stood up and reached into his jacket for the tickets, then remembered Mom had them. So she had to interrupt her revival meeting and get them out of her handbag and in the process handed me the Gospel Walnut to hold while she rummaged for the tickets. The conductor saw the nut in my hand and said not to crack open nuts on the little table that was attached to the wall because it would make marks on it. I started to explain that this was not an ordinary nut you could eat. But I stopped because I looked over at Mom, and she was watching me all happy and expectant. I realized she thought I was about to follow the booklet's instructions on how the nut was "a natural conversation piece that will lead from conversation to conversion!" I knew Mom always prayed for me that my heart would grow more tender for the Things of the Lord since I had refused to carry my Gospel Walnut at all times like the booklet said I should, and almost never witnessed with or without nuts anyway.

I looked at her and said, "Forget it," and stuffed the nut into my pocket. That was a mistake because the Missionary Alliance volunteer who had made Mom's nut had not sanded off the sharp wire handle after he or she was done getting the Good News into her nut. The razor-sharp wire poked through my pocket and stuck deep into my thigh in the tender white flat part where you can see the veins next to your groin. Nothing had hurt so much since I had broken my leg skiing the year before. I jumped and yelled out in pain, and everyone looked surprised. I reached into my pocket and pulled the nut out. The conductor shook his head as if he was saying now he'd seen everything, punched the tickets, and said, "*Changez à Milan.*"

Dad said, "What are you doing?"

"The Gospel Walnut got me," I said.

Mom looked sorrowful and sweet and smiled but said nothing. I could figure it out myself that the truth could not be hidden, and so it had poked me. It was a sign.

The Frenchman used this distraction to get back behind his *Paris Match*. He made sure to hold it close enough to his face so that there was no chance of Mom catching his eye or trying to make him finish repeating the Sinner's Prayer after her. But at least he didn't smoke anymore because he couldn't light his cigarette and hide at the same time.

18

AS WE PULLED into Genoa we were all shocked because the place where you catch your first glimpse of the sea was filled up with a new gray apartment building. Even Dad stood up and put down his reading material to look as we approached the place where we always had our first glimpse. We were all ready and waiting as the train came out of one of the tunnels you go through in the hills behind the city. If you didn't see the Mediterranean at that point, you didn't see it again until after you changed trains in Genoa and were well on your way to Santa Margherita. Then you saw the sea some of the way next to you because the track had been laid hugging the coast. But that wasn't the first glimpse—it was still exciting but not the same.

"I can't believe they'd do that," Rachael said.

Janet answered, "Don't be stupid. People need a place to live."

"Oh well, dear," Mom said, "the sea is still where it's supposed to be," and she sat down.

Dad said, "Overdevelopment."

We all sat down, and Dad started to read a paper on the Scottish revival of the Presbyterian churches. The rest of us sat sort of glumly.

Mom said, "Well. I was going to wait until we got to Santa Margherita to tell you."

Rachael said, "What?"

Then Mom got her "I've got a wonderful surprise" look on her face and said, "This year we're not going to stay in the Pensione Biea at all. I made reservations at the Hotel Nazionale in Portofino itself!"

This stunned us. We had been going to the Pensione Biea for ten years. We remembered the first summer Lucrezia was old enough to help serve in the dining room at night. I knew everyone on the beach. Not just the Banini but everyone. All the families who came on vacation when we did. Suddenly it hit me. Jennifer! Because of the pain in my groin from the Gospel Walnut I had forgotten about her for a little while. Now I remembered and as I remembered I reached up and touched the hard patch in my shirt pocket where I had put the snapshot of her.

"How are we supposed to get to the beach?" I asked.

Mom said, "Why, dear, don't be silly, you'll just walk on the path in the morning. We'll spend the whole day at the beach like we always do. It's all arranged."

"You mean I'm supposed to carry my spear gun and all my diving equipment all the way from Portofino to Paraggi every day? There and back?"

Janet said, "Talk about ingratitude!"

"I'll help you carry it," Rachael said.

Mom said, "Why don't you all listen to my plan before you ask so many questions?!" So we waited and she said, "I've rented a beach cabin, you know, one of those little changing rooms. We'll all keep our things in there. All you have to do is walk over, change, and there you are."

"Well, what about . . ." I began. But Janet pulled me by the arm and so I said, "What? what?"

Janet just pulled me into the train hall. Then she pushed me in front of her up the hall to the place where the toilet door was. We could hear the toilet flushing, and a man came out pulling up his zipper. Janet waited until he was gone and then shook me by the shoulders and said, "You ungrateful boy!"

I was mystified because I might have argued a little with Mom but not much and Mom hadn't seemed upset and it wasn't putting Dad in a bad mood because he was just reading and didn't seem to care where we stayed one way or another. He didn't know anyone on the beach, so what did he care?

Janet said, "Do you want to go live with relatives?" She pulled my hair like she was really mad and we had been fighting. This mystified me even more and hurt a lot because when Janet pulled your hair it stayed pulled for a good long time because Janet had the strength of ten. The bad warning sign was when she bit her lower lip in an unconscious sort of automatic way, then you knew she was about to do something. If you were smart, you'd try to get near to Mom, who would stop her before she slapped you so hard the marks were still there a week later or pulled your hair or whatever.

So I said as politely as I could, while Janet brushed a clump of my hair off her hands, "What relatives?"

Then Janet said, "I'll tell you what relatives," and

she bit her lower lip so I ducked but it was no use because she wasn't hitting but kicking and since I left my legs where they were she got me on the shin before I could think to call out for help or run back to Mom and tell her that Janet had finally gone out of her mind because she was being really mean for no reason at all.

I took a step back and sneaked a look at my shin, which I could see because I had shorts on, and sure enough it was red and would go blue. Jennifer would ask what I had done, and I'd tell her my horse had kicked me, not that my big sister had done it for no reason. I didn't have a horse and had never even been riding in my life but it seemed like a good lie anyway.

Janet said, "Because they're saving their marriage! That's why! Because Portofino's more romantic! That's why! Because the night club in Paraggi kept Dad awake all last vacation, and he said he'd rather leave Mom than put up with that again! That's why!" I took another step back in case she tried another kick or something.

"What do you mean?"

"Haven't you noticed how they've been fighting?" Janet asked.

"No more than usual since Grandmother came to live with us."

"You're a stupid little boy!" Janet said. And because she still had some of my hair stuck to her sweater where the static electricity made it cling and because my shin was hurting so much I had trouble putting my weight on it, I didn't say anything back seeing as there was still plenty of me left to hurt. Then Janet looked at me and said, "I suppose you deserve an explanation. But if you tell any one, *any one*, I'll kill you!" Because this was Janet saying it I didn't take this as a figure of speech but as a solemn promise. I nodded and she continued. ''This spring Mom told me that Dad and her were having marital problems. And that she was going to visit the wife of Pastor Oates at the mission headquarters in Brussels to get godly counseling. She said that Dad and her were fighting every day and had even had more serious problems than that.'' Now I began to see why Janet was so upset.

I said, ''Is this true?'' but not in a way that meant I was questioning Janet's story but just like you say, ''Oh really!'' in a way that lets someone know you're interested.

''Yes,'' said Janet, ''I'm afraid so.'' She paused for a very long time because Janet always has been dramatic, then she said in a whisper, ''There is another man.''

At first I didn't get it. I must have looked blank and stupid in a way that got her mad all over again because she said, ''Wipe that dumb expression off your face before I do!'' So I tried to look smarter and must have succeeded because she kept on talking and didn't hit me. ''Mom has a sinful attraction for Jonathan Edwards!'' Janet said.

Jonathan Edwards was a man who was staying with us. The mission board had sent him out to us as a trainee, an apprenticeship sort of thing. He was finished with his seminary studies at Westminster Seminary and was now Waiting on the Lord and the mission board of the PCCCCUSA to see what he would be led to do next. While this was happening and he was Waiting for God's Call, he was staying with us to help Dad in his ministry. Dad would joke with him about his name being Jonathan Edwards because there had been a famous Christian preacher by that name and Dad said things like "It's an honor to have you under my roof." And they'd laugh, then get back to their work stapling together hymnbooks they had translated into French for this summer's Bible School they were going to hold as a retreat for the children of Reformed Presbyterian PCCCCUSA missionaries from all over Europe.

"You mean . . ."

Then Janet said, "Of course not! Only that Mom has confided in me that the reason for her sinful thoughts is that Dad and her are very estranged and have not been, been, cohabiting."

I didn't say anything because even though I didn't know exactly what the word "cohabiting" meant, I could tell pretty much what it must be about by how red Janet's face went when she said it. "You're old enough to know about this. And I hope you love your mother and father enough to do all you can to be good and to stay out of their way on this vacation and let them have a second honeymoon! That's why we're going to stay at Portofino! So they can have a room that looks out on the harbor because it's romantic! It will be a perfect setting in which to have a second honeymoon! Mom said so!"

When Janet was finished talking I noticed she was clasping her hands in front of her and her eyes were all bright and her face was flushed, and I suddenly realized she was enjoying all this and I wondered if she was just making it up. Then I decided she probably wasn't because even Janet wouldn't dare to tell lies this serious about Mom and Dad.

She said, "Will you?"

"What?"

"Do everything you can to stay out of the way and let them be alone to restore the beautiful gift of God's love. To rekindle the flames of passion?''

''Yes.''

Then Janet said, ''Just say I took you to show you something.'' And we started back to the cabin, and I tried not to limp on the leg Janet had kicked, which was unfortunately the same leg I had broken, so it hurt a lot.

When we got back Dad was pulling down the suitcases because we were arriving at our station.

Mom said, ''Oh, Ralph, be careful, you'll break the light.''

Dad said to her, ''Like this?'' and he hit the light bulb on our train cabin ceiling on purpose with the suitcase and it broke and blue glass fell all over him and Mom.

Mom shrieked out all shocked, ''Oh, Ralph!'' and pulled us all out of the way. I looked at Janet and she looked very meaningfully at me and nodded slightly as if to say, ''See, I told you.'' I nodded back and wondered which relatives I'd be sent to live with when they got divorced and what we'd do with Dad's mom—our bad Grandmother. Then I got to thinking about why Mom would ever tell Janet something so private. As usual I couldn't figure Mom out, so I quit wondering about it and started thinking about the vacation instead.

We got off the train in Genoa and walked across to the local that would take us to Santa Margherita. I looked at Rachael to see if she knew we were supposed to help save our family, but she didn't seem to understand the look.

I looked at Dad and he was still fuming and had glass in his hair, and I looked at Mom and she had her sweetest expression on her face to show how *she* was not the family lunatic. We all knew who was. I got to thinking about how this was going to be an interesting vacation even though I'd have to walk to Paraggi every day.

19

THE HOTEL NAZIONALE in Portofino sits in the middle of the town facing across the main square to the yacht harbor. The view from the window of Room Thirty-six is spectacular. Mom had booked this front room specially for herself and Dad. The view from the window *was* romantic. When I looked out I thought to myself that this ought to do the job since standing there you felt like a king or a millionaire or something what with the yachts and all right there in front of you.

Mom told me to run along to my room and wait. She'd come help me unpack in a minute, she said. Since I wasn't having a second honeymoon, my room, Number Thirty-seven, was across the narrow hall. My window was up near the ceiling, and when I stood on the bed to see out, I found I was looking into a gray air shaft that only a little daylight came down from high up someplace. People's toilet windows were vented into it. The first and last thing I heard every day were sounds of toilets flushing and the creak of the wooden toilet paper holders as people in the hotel used them. I could hear voices too. One night I heard a woman scream and then slapping sounds followed by a man shouting. Mom and Dad were not the only people in our hotel who needed a special view or a second honeymoon, by the sounds of it.

Mom came into my room and looked around and said, "Bet you're glad to get your own room for once."

I said, "Yes."

But really I kind of missed Rachael because she'd read to me sometimes at night when we shared the room in the Pensione Biea.

"You're older now," said Mom. "Do you have any questions you'd like to ask?"

I knew what she meant, and it made me a little nervous. Mom had started doing something in the last year or so that I knew was really strange.

I had asked Jacky Keegan if his mom did it, and he said, "Are you kidding? No one's mom ever talks about stuff like that! Your mom's *really* weird."

Once Rachael had said that it bothered her too. She said, "I don't want to know all about that stuff. Especially not her private life. She's supposed to be our mother, for goodness' sake!"

We all knew about the "questions" Mom wanted us to ask. Mom had always talked a lot about how precious a gift God had given us in our bodies and how beautiful marriage was and all about the Christmas morning thing, how we were to save our bodies like presents, to share them only with the person of the Lord's choosing for us. How we were going to spend our lives with this special person God had ordained us to marry before the foundation of the world.

Mom had explained years ago how babies got to be born, how the male sperm swims by marvelous instinct up a little passage into the womb and meets the woman's seed and fertilizes it and how it grows and becomes a precious baby with its own fingerprints. She had drawn the diagram of the ovaries, like two balloons on strings, and had explained to me how in God's great plan once a month a precious little egg came down to be flushed out, and that was why Janet was in a bad mood and had almost broken my arm twisting it when I had only been teasing her, holding her bag of monthly pads over her head and shouting, "Tell me where you put these!"

Mom's talks had gotten a lot longer lately. I knew all I wanted to know a long time ago. When Mom started asking if I had any questions, it meant she wanted to discuss These Things some more and even tell me about how it felt and how I would feel when I put my seeds into my wife. Even stuff about her and Dad! Which is what got Rachael so mad she even told me about how she thought Mom was going nuts. Not nuts like you say, "He's nuts," but *nuts* as in really unhinged—the way Uncle Oswald got when he tried to kill Aunt Penelope because he said she was a vulture pecking up all his birdseed.

So I said, "No, Mom, I don't have any questions."

She sat down on the edge of the bed and as she did, her hair brushed the single light bulb that lit my room, and it began to swing back and forth a little, making Mom's shadow loom up behind her and her face look like she was smiling then frowning not because she was, but just because of how the light bulb moved over her swinging on its long cord hanging from the ceiling.

Mom said, "There are things a big boy like you needs to know." I wanted to say, no there aren't, but I just stood still. Mom went on. "You are at that special age now where you are going to go through some dramatic physical changes in your body. Changes that we need to talk about and you don't need to ever feel embarrassed of."

"I know, Mom, you already told me. Can I get unpacked and go and see if Gino's in his studio?"

Mom acted as if she hadn't heard me and kept right on talking. "Sex is a marvelous gift," she said, "we don't have to be ashamed of it."

I wished we didn't have to discuss it either, so I started moving toward the door, but Mom said, "Let's finish our little talk, then you can go." I waited, hoping she wouldn't use too many personal examples in our discussion she was having. "When your father and I were first married, he had so little knowledge about the physical aspect of marriage, I had to show him practically everything. You know how Grandmother is! But when *you* get married, because we've had our frank talks together over the years, and I've been a better mother to you than his mother was to him, you'll know a lot more about the precious gift of the physical side of marriage than he did on our wedding night."

"Please, Mom!" I said. "*Can* I go see Gino now?"

"There will be an enlargement of your testes," Mom said. "That's because they will start to produce the millions of wonderful little seeds that are for fertilizing the precious egg your wife produces." Mom didn't seem to notice I wasn't married yet.

"God has already chosen the precious egg to be

your child.'' Why was she talking about my wife and child? I was going to turn fourteen next week. Was Mom really going loopy? If so, what could Rachael and me do? Would Janet react to Mom's lunacy by kicking me to death?

''You have noticed that you have begun to develop a little bodily hair, what we call 'pubic hair,' around your Little Thing.'' I wondered who ''we'' were who had noticed the hair I had growing around my nuts. Did Mom have friends who came over to watch me take baths through the keyhole? Did they compare notes on how much bodily hair I had compared to their kids?

''You will have also begun to notice your feelings changing. You will have begun to feel differently toward girls and women. When you look at a girl now you will have certain desires that might frighten you, but we will discuss them and that way you can ask me all your questions.''

''Yes, Mom, thanks, I understand now.''

''No, you don't. You're not asking questions, and I know you must have lots of them.'' This was the part I hated most in our talks. If I didn't ask any questions, Mom would keep explaining for hours until I did. If I did ask questions, I felt I was being as weird as her and got embarrassed.

Today I wanted to get out to visit Gino and maybe even get over to Paraggi and see if Jennifer was at the pensione, so I hurriedly said, ''I don't understand about the 'wet dream' part.''

Mom's face lit up. ''I'm *glad* you asked that and aren't embarrassed to be frank and open about all this! What happens is that the little seeds, the sperm, build up in your testes and, for new ones to be made, some have to leave their little warm home to make room for the fresh supply. That way all your precious seeds are healthy and new all the time, so you can give your wife a good fresh seed for her perfect little precious egg.'' Mom still was talking like I was already married, but I let it go because I was in a hurry.

``Oh, I see.''

Mom smiled. ``So God has provided young healthy boys a natural means to get rid of, or as we say, 'ejaculate,' the unwanted seeds from time to time. What happens is that while you're asleep, you have a lovely dream about something that makes your Little Thing get hard as if you were about to put the seed into your wife. But since you are only letting a little extra seed out, what happens is that you get those wonderful feelings in your Little Thing we discussed last time you had questions, and some seeds shoot out. When this happens let me know. You're not to be embarrassed by this wonderful natural thing even if your sheets get a little wet. Just tell me and I'll change the sheets and it'll be our little secret.''

``Can I go, Mom?''

``Have you been touching yourself?''

``No.''

``Good, because masturbation is an expression of lust. Not natural like a wet dream. Wait for a wet dream. Don't touch yourself.''

``Can I go, Mom?''

``Yes, but remember any time you have more questions, make sure you ask me right away. If you want to touch yourself, come to me and tell me so we can pray about it and ask the Lord to send you a wet dream, which is the natural healthy way He has provided.''

When I got out into the hall I ran down the back stairs and out the side door of the Hotel Nazionale into the street. Then I realized I had forgotten to change out of my traveling clothes. But I ran on around the square to Gino's studio anyway because I knew if I went back, Mom was still unpacking my stuff and would think I had questions and would want to talk more. Or maybe she would want to pray for a wet dream right then and there.

On the way to Gino's I made sure everything was still where it was supposed to be. It was. Nothing ever changes in Portofino. No one puts up a new apartment building or anything like that. In the church the same old ladies looked up as I took holy water and crossed myself and knelt to pray. In the Boutique Brazilia, the lady remembered me and gave me a Baci chocolate from the big bowl on the counter. In the bar on the dock the same men were there who always played cards at the corner table.

When I got to Gino's studio he motioned me to a chair to wait till he was done painting the part he was working on of a large picture of a naked woman sitting on a motorcycle with her head on fire while a dog bit her foot. When he was done adding some details to the dog's tail, he got up, wiped off his brush, and said, "'Ow are you?" and offered me a drink. We sat sipping whiskey and water, and he explained about the problems he was having with a new gallery owner in Milano and how the new owner said that he was going to take a 50-percent commission like they did in New York. And what was Gino supposed to do about this greed since even a third had been a lot, and he could barely live on what was left as it was.

Then Gino poured me out a little more whiskey, and I told him my mother had gone out of her mind, and he said he wasn't surprised. He had heard that that was happening a lot recently because of the effects of the radiation from the testing of nuclear weapons in the atmosphere.

20

IN THE MORNING I left the Nazionale before they started serving breakfast at seven-thirty. The day was going to be hot. The sun was barely up and already the air was getting hazy. The early morning breeze was replaced by a thick summer stillness that seemed to make everything go a lot slower. In the square the fish woman was pushing her cart, full of tiny silver fish that the Italians deep fry and eat whole. She was bellowing up the echoing stairways of the buildings she passed, "*Pesce, pesce, pesce*!" As she walked she was eating a piece of focaccia. I hurried on so I could get to the beach at Paraggi in time to get some focaccia myself from the Banini before he went out to the rowboats.

By the wall on the way to Paraggi, I stopped to breathe in the verdant green smell. I closed my eyes and inhaled deeply through my nose. Fig, gardenia, wild thyme, oregano, arugula, and other mysterious green smells. I was back!

These ten days every year were the best of my life. And this year, because Mom and Dad had sent me to a boarding school in England last autumn, I was especially grateful for Italy, the path to Paraggi, and the smells, smells the English and Swiss never even dream of. The English boarding school was worse than Janet teaching me. I was finally learning to read, but I was so far behind the other boys in the school I had become a sort of joke, almost a kind of byword, a standard by which failure was measured. Teachers would say things to other boys like, "If you aren't careful, my lad, you'll wake up one fine day and find you've become thick as Becker here."

The good side of going to English boarding school was that when I met Jennifer this year I could tell her I was at a boys' school in England just like her school for girls. At last I would have something to tell her about myself that was true. This would make things easier because when you have to tell lies all the time because you don't want people to know about your family, it gets confusing. Especially if you have to lie each year to the same person and have to remember what your story was the year before in case the person was really listening and remembered that you said you were in the American School in Montreux and that your dad taught there and now you've forgotten and said that you are studying in the English school in Villars. When really of course you were just playing around the yard of your house as Mom kept an eye on you while she typed up prayer letters to send to our Reformed Presbyterian supporters of our ministry to Roman Catholic youth.

But now I could say, "I'm at school in England."

And if Jennifer said, "Where?" I could say, "Haywards Heath Sussex in Great Dunstable Preparatory School." It was like I had joined the regular human race! Of course I wouldn't say how, because I couldn't read very well yet, I had been put into a class of nine-year-olds when I first got there. Or how I had to do special work on Saturdays since the headmaster said I was the most "unfit boy" he had ever had the duty to "bring to the light of knowledge." I would say I loved the games and field day even though since I had never played cricket before I only got to do "sports" by getting up every morning and pushing the roller around on the cricket pitch to help keep it flat for the boys who got to play.

When I got to the bottom of the path from Portofino to Paraggi, I looked along the road to the beach and could see the Banini sitting at one of the tables up by the snack bar. He was alone and had a brown paper bag spread out in front of him. I couldn't see what was on it yet but I knew he always had focaccia and probably some sardines too. I yelled out so he'd see me and leave some food for me.

When I got nearer he stood up and called out, "Calvino! youa back!" I ran up and dropped my snorkel and spear gun and sat down. The Banini pushed over a big hunk of focaccia. I licked off the pieces of rock salt stuck to it and the green olive oil ran down my chin when I bit into a piece just like I had dreamed of doing hundreds of times when I closed my eyes in the Great Dunstable school dining room and tried to imagine Italy instead of England.

The Banini picked up my spear gun and pretended to be shooting with it.

"*Pulpi?*"

I said, "No," because I was not going to shoot any more octopus. "*Pesce*," I said.

He pointed to a place on the side of the bay where the big rocks were and he gestured how I should go over there because that's where the fish were this year.

When we finished eating we swam out to the row-boats and I helped the Banini bring the boats in to the beach the way we always did. On the way back, he rowed over to the rocks on purpose to show me where he had seen some really big fish a few days before.

We had all the boats tied together as usual. The Banini was rowing the front boat. I was climbing around from boat to boat and planning how I'd walk along the rocks to the place he had showed me, then get in the water and spear-fish from there. I remembered I had forgotten to bring a plastic bag for all the fish I was going to spear. I wondered if the Banini had one he would lend me.

I heard someone call my name from the beach. I looked up. It was Jennifer standing there. She waved at me and I waved back and wished there was a mirror in the rowboat so I could see if the cowlick on the top of my head was standing up or not. To make sure it wasn't I spit on my hands and smoothed my hair a couple of times. When we pulled up to the beach Jennifer waded out to help the Banini by pulling the nose of his boat up to the sandy shore. I jumped into the water like the Marines in newsreels I had seen jumping off their landing craft on Korean beaches. I miscalculated. I had jumped too soon so I went in up to my armpits instead of just to my knees. My head went under the water. When I came up I wondered what shape my plastered hair was in now. Did it look funny or good? Then I swam back out to behind the last boat and started to push it to show Jennifer I had jumped in the deep water on purpose like it was part of my job.

Suddenly I heard a voice right above me and looked up into Jennifer's face. She had climbed into the first boat of our boat train whose nose she had pulled to shore and had hopped from one boat to the next till she got to the last one that I was behind pretending to push.

"What do you think you're doing, silly?" Jennifer said.

"Oh hi, Jennifer."

"Why did you jump in? You can't do any good pushing."

"I always do this, I have for years. Someone has to do it," I said.

Jennifer shook her hair in my face and lay down on her stomach and hung out over the water with her pale blond hair falling all around me as I tried to push the boat.

Then she said, "Batty. You're batty. You've always been batty."

I just kept pushing and wishing I could think of some way to make it like I had finished the job but I couldn't so I pushed the boat up toward the beach while Jennifer's hair was in my face and she peered down at me and laughed. After watching me she reached over and pushed my head under the water.

When I came up I said, "Don't do that."

So she did it again and when I came up she said, "I love the hol's, because I'm able to see how batty you've become each year. You're getting worse you know. Worse and worse and worse. I expect in another year or two you'll be simply raving mad. Bonkers! Really stark staring."

I just kept pushing and wished again that the Banini would hurry up and pull the boats out of the water so it would look like I had finished my work but he didn't so I said, "There I think that'll do it."

I swam in to the shore while Jennifer clambered over the boats and was standing on the beach waiting when I walked up the sandy bank from the water. While I took off my wet T-shirt and shorts (but of course kept on my swimming trunks, which were underneath my shorts), Jennifer stood there tapping the side of her head and saying, "Poor dear, are the bells ringing very loudly in our wee little head today?" Then she laughed and what was worse she got the Banini to laugh at me too because my clothes were wet, which was dumb because his shirt and cut-off dungarees were soaked too. So why was he laughing at me? Jennifer picked up my wet clothes and wrung them out and said, "Let Mummy look after the poor lost child." She hung them over an oar to dry out in the sun.

I said, "Do you want to go snorkeling?"

"Not if you bring that beastly thing with you."

She meant my spear gun. So I said I'd leave it with the Banini and we would just go look at the fish not kill them. And Jennifer said, "I should hope not, you bloodthirsty boy!" By this time I had had enough of her banter so I dove at her legs and tackled her. She fell back on the sand and I made her eat a little of it. While I had her down and was wrestling to keep her under me so she couldn't get away, by accident I put my hand on her chest and suddenly I realized it wasn't Jennifer's old chest anymore, but that she had "developed" the way Rachael had. I pulled my hand away because it had been on her new breast. It was soft where her chest had always been hard before.

I pretended I hadn't felt anything and I wrestled even harder with her to prove it. I was careful where I put my hands after that. I decided that as soon as I was done making her eat a little more sand I'd get off her as quick as I could and never tackle her again because her body was like a mine field now.

Then Jennifer did a really terrible thing. Suddenly, just as I was about to get off her, she reached up and put her arms around my neck and pretended to be all serious and pulled my face close to hers so that I was practically lying on top of her and she said, "Now you have me what do you want to do, big boy?" The way she said it was serious but it was really an even worse kind of teasing than calling me batty because I had no idea what to do.

I pulled away and stood up very fast. Jennifer sat up on the sand and laughed at me and said, "You should have seen the expression on his poor little face, my dear," as if she was talking to someone else about me at tea in the pensione later that day. I felt my face get red because I thought that was exactly what she would say later to someone. Suddenly I felt that Jennifer wasn't my friend anymore and at the same time I wanted to be with her every minute of the day and hoped she'd go snorkeling with me.

21

MOM AND DAD'S second honeymoon didn't seem to be working out that well. Mom, Janet, Rachael, and I were all at our dining table on the terrace in front of the Hotel Nazionale waiting to be served our dinner but Dad had not come down from his room. Mom asked Rachael to go and ask him if we should wait for him or not.

When Rachael came back she said, "He says go on and eat. He's not coming down to dinner."

Mom asked her what he was doing. "He's sitting in the room staring out the window," Rachael answered.

So then Mom asked Janet to go up and see if Dad wanted dinner sent up.

Janet came back and said, "He says no, please don't send anything up. And if you do send up any dinner he says he'll throw it out the window into the square."

Mom looked at us and said, "We should stop a minute and bring this to the Lord."

And before I could ask her not to, she bowed her head and prayed for so long that the soup that was served to us while she prayed was completely cold by the time she was done.

When she said, "So we just lay our burdens at your feet. Amen," all the *pastini en brodo* in our bowls was stone cold and the manager had came over and asked what was wrong with our soup since no one had touched it. He asked if we'd rather have the prosciutto *con melone* to start with. Mom said no, we loved his soup and she smiled at us so we'd know what to do. We started to eat the cold soup and we all said how good it was. The manager stood looking at us as if he were in a lot of pain because Italians hate it when you don't eat your food right and he could not understand why we had all sat staring down at our soup plates for twenty minutes before we took one mouthful. Finally he wrung his hands one last time then went back to the other side of the terrace in despair.

When the roast chicken was served Dad finally came down because he was hungry after all, even though he was depressed. He had probably just wanted to miss enough of dinner to make a point to Mother as part of this vacation's fight. I wasn't sure what the point he was wanting to make was but I think it was to get back at Mom for getting up at 4 A.M. and going out to read her Bible and pray sitting on the rocks by the lighthouse. She had done that to show Dad how the Lord was her refuge in times of trouble and how Dad was that trouble and how instead of getting angry because he had thrown all her clothes out of the hotel window and screamed, "If you say another word, Elsa, I'll throw you out too!" which I had heard through my hotel room door the day before, he'd yelled it so loud, she had gone to the Lord in prayer like he should have done. So he was getting even for her goodness in the face of adversity.

Mom stood up and said, "Oh, Ralph, how nice you've come down to join us. We were just praying for you."

Dad said, "I bet you were," and sat down, which was pretty rude.

Dad shouted, "Garçon!"

And the waiter came over and said, "*Sì*?"

"Give me some chicken, can't you see I haven't been served?"

While the waiter hurried off to get Dad his food, Mom said very sweetly, "Here, Ralph, have mine," and pushed her plate of chicken and roast potatoes with rosemary over to him.

Then Dad said, "What a saint *you* are!" and he picked up her plate and held it out over the edge of the table and dropped it on the floor where it hit the big red tiles and sort of exploded. "I don't want *your* chicken, thank you anyway," Dad said.

The waiter came in with Dad's chicken, which he served Dad while he called for the boy from the kitchen to come out and clean up the broken plate and food off the floor. He never asked how Mom's plate got there, but a lot of people at other tables, who had started to watch us when Mom was praying the long prayer so our soup got cold, now stopped eating altogether and turned their chairs around so they could make sure they would not miss whatever we did next. I sat very still hoping they would not notice that I was part of this family. Janet didn't seem to mind the attention. She jumped up and threw her napkin down on her plate and started to cry and sob and her face got red and she yelled out between sobs, "I have feelings too!" Then she knocked over her chair and stomped off the terrace, pushing right between the potted palm trees that separated the terrace from the public square. Mom looked at Dad and said, "Oh, Ralph!" very accusingly, and Dad just ate bigger and bigger pieces of chicken until his mouth was so full food fell out of it every time he tried to shove more chicken in. Rachael started to cry too because Dad seemed to have really gone off his rocker. Not like Janet but all silent with her shoulders shaking quietly. You couldn't even hear her sniff, she cried so discreetly.

Mom put her arm around Rachael's shoulders and said, "It's all right, dear, Mommy and Daddy are just having a little fight."

Dad looked up at Rachael and said with his mouth full of chicken and rosemary potatoes, "Yeth, we're thine! Canth youth thee everythinth ith thine?" But he said it sarcastically and chicken fell out of his mouth when he said, "thine."

Mom said, "Oh, Ralph, can't you see she's really upset."

"Ith thee?"

He spit out his huge mouthful of chicken and rosemary and yelled, "Well, maybe this'll make her feel better!" And he swept all the dishes crashing onto the tiled floor with his arm and stood up. Then we all got up too, since our food was all gone now and a lot of the other guests jumped up as well so they could move faster if we started coming toward them or in case Dad made any sudden moves.

The manager ran over and asked if we didn't like

the food and he wrung his hands together so much his knuckles cracked.

Mom said to him, "No the food is wonderful. It's really delicious!"

Dad pushed through the palm trees and headed out into the square. Mom took Rachael, who was still crying silently, by the hand, and they walked into the hotel and went up to Mom's room. I walked away as slowly as I could so as not to attract the attention of the other guests who had started to talk again and compare notes on our family. Some saying one thing, others another, but all of them agreeing that there was plenty here to discuss.

I crept around the edge of the square so I wouldn't meet Dad or Janet, who had both gone the other way. I went up to Gino's outdoor studio behind the restaurant. I was very thankful he was there. When I walked in he was sitting watching his movies. I could see he had been doing this for a while because when he tried to stand up to motion me to a crate of parsley to sit down on, he weaved around because he had had a lot to drink already. We sat and watched his movies of tourists getting on and off the tour boat with a lot of close-ups of young handsome men, who were of great interest to him for "aesthetic reasons," like he said.

When one movie finished, I threaded up the next reel he handed me because he was now too drunk to be able to do it himself.

"Is your mosser still crazy?"

"Yes, and my dad too. They're getting worse."

"Tella me, what they 'avea beena doing?"

So I did. "Nexta timea youa eat you calla me so I canna come to the 'otel anda makea movie. O.K.?"

I said I would but Dad didn't smash the plates

every night so if nothing much happened not to be too disappointed.

We sat and watched while Gino sipped his whiskey and I sipped my whiskey and water. Gino turned to me after a while and said, ''Did you learna to read the book yet?''

''Yes, I am learning at the school in England.''

''Doa the teacher 'eet you weeth a steeck?''

''You mean caning?''

''Yes, wees the cane steeck.''

''Yes, but I have only been caned once so far. It wasn't about my reading but because I lied about not doing my prep.''

''What ees prep?''

So I explained it was after-school work, homework, like we said in America or at least like we Americans said in Switzerland.

''Eet eesa good youa read now. Why you go school een Eengland?''

I explained how a board member from the mission board of the PCCCCUSA had been visiting us and had found out I wasn't in school anywhere and that I couldn't read and how he had complained to the mission board of the PCCCCUSA back in America and how they had sent a letter telling Dad that the Lord had laid it on their hearts that his son should know how to read. And how since we weren't Swiss Roman Catholics and Mom wanted me to speak English, and grow up Reformed, and the only Reformed boarding school in Switzerland was for girls only, she and Dad had decided to send me to a boarding school for the sons of missionaries in England and how it was all paid for by the Missionary Alliance Family Help Fund for the Servants of the Lord.

"I don't understanda youa fasser, 'ees a priest, no?"

"No, we're Protestant missionaries to the Roman Catholics; Dad's a minister."

"But ef 'ees a priest, whya 'eesa married?"

I explained again he wasn't a priest, but a Reformed Presbyterian.

"Youa mosser, she'sa 'ees meestress?"

I explained again how Protestant missionaries got married and that way their whole family could witness for the Lord along with them.

Gino drank awhile, then said very loudly, "Jesus coulda read!"

I couldn't exactly see how that had anything to do with Dad and Mom, so I just explained again about how Dad had been called by God to be a light unto nations.

Gino paid no attention but stood up holding on to my shoulder so he wouldn't fall over; he lifted up his glass like he was toasting someone and said very loudly, "Jesus Coulda Read!"

I decided I'd better agree with him since he got notions about you if he thought you were disagreeing with him when he had drunk almost a whole bottle of Johnny Walker Red Label, so I lifted up my glass too and said, "Yes, Jesus could read!"

Then Gino maneuvered around and clinked my glass and said, "To Jesus' books!"

I didn't know what he was talking about but I sipped my whiskey all the same and said, "Yes, to His books!"

Then I hoped I would not be struck by lightning because I knew that if this wasn't taking the Lord's name in vain, nothing was.

Gino drained his glass all the way and then sat back

down in his chair very heavily, sort of fell back into it. I threaded up a new movie, new for that night that is, because I had seen it many times before. We watched the movie of the tourists arriving on the bus in the communal parking lot. I knew each black and white face getting off the bus. I had them memorized and I knew that as soon as the fat Belgian lady with the canes was helped down the stairs the next person to come off would be Jennifer. In this movie she was about eight years old and was with her mother, who lifted her down from the bus steps. She always stared straight at the camera and waved and smiled. I had seen it a hundred times but all of a sudden I got a hollow feeling in my stomach as she smiled at me for the umpteenth time from Gino's movie.

Gino put his hand on my arm and said, "That'sa you girl?"

"You know Jennifer, Gino, you know she's my friend."

"Yes a special leetle friend, no?"

He tried to wink at me but only managed to shut one eye and seemed to forget to open it again. Then he shut the other eye. I sat for a moment watching his cigarette go out. I took the glass out of his hand and put it on his palette on the stool next to him. Then I removed the cigarette stub from between his lips as he fell into a deeper sleep.

22

THE NEXT DAY we were sitting on the beach together eating our picnic when some sand landed on my sandwich as it lay on the towel in front of me. I looked around to see Jennifer standing behind me smiling and with one hand on her hip.

"You've eaten enough, you greedy swine," she said. "I want to climb out on the rocks. Come along, boyso."

Mom didn't look very happy to see Jennifer. "Jennifer, we're having our lunch right now. Calvin will be along to play when he's done eating."

"I'm done now, Mom," I said, as I jumped up.

"You haven't finished your sandwich yet," said Mom.

"Sit down and finish it," said Janet.

"It's got sand on it," I said. Jennifer giggled, because she had thrown the sand in the first place.

Janet looked at her in a way that meant she thought

Jennifer was intruding on our lunch and I knew if Janet had been related to Jennifer, Jennifer would have had to look out when Janet got her alone someplace.

Jennifer turned and began to run up the beach toward the rocks. I started after her.

My mom said, "Come back here this minute."

At about the same time Jennifer called over her shoulder, "Hurry up, you greedy boy."

I didn't know exactly what to do. Rachael said, "Oh, let him alone, we're on vacation for goodness' sake!"

So Mom said, "Well, I'll wrap it up for a snack later."

As I ran off toward Jennifer I heard Janet say loudly, "You're spoiling that child. When I was his age you'd never let *me* run off with some strange *boy*!"

Then I heard Mom say, "It's only Jennifer and anyway . . ." but then I was too far away to hear more. Jennifer was already at the rocks starting to climb.

When you climbed out on the rocks you first went under a high wooden deck that had been built up on pilings driven into the sand under the water. People sat on the deck to sunbathe. Under the deck the lap and gurgle of the little waves echoed. Since it was always in the shade under there, the rocks had a lot of green slime growing on them; you had to be careful how you put your feet down. There were also a lot of cigarette butts all over the rocks from years and years of sunbathers dropping their cigarettes through the cracks between the boards that formed the deck above. So the place had a strange smell of cigarette butts and seaweed and fish. A few dead ones were always stuck between the rocks.

You could sit under the deck in the dark and look out at the bright sea framed by the rocks below and the deck above. And you could also listen to people sitting right above you talking and hear what they said as if you were right next to them. Of course they had no idea anyone was listening.

Jennifer said, "Let's tickle their feet."

"I thought we were going to go snorkeling," I said as I lifted my mask and flippers to show I had brought them, but not the spear gun, because Jennifer wouldn't let me use it around her. Jennifer wasn't listening to me. She was hunting around on the rocks on her hands and knees. Soon she found what she wanted, which was a plastic straw that had fallen through the cracks above. Then she went back toward the rock wall where the deck was low enough so you could reach up and touch it and she began to walk along while carefully looking up at the deck. Then she stopped and pushed the straw through one of the cracks between the deck boards. There was a scream and the sound of thumping from someone jumping up out of his deck chair. This was because Jennifer had found a foot and stuck her straw through the boards into that foot and the person whom the foot belonged to screamed because it felt like a bee or something was starting to sting him. He leaped up and spilled his drink, which came trickling down through the cracks.

Jennifer doubled up in silent laughter and I laughed too. She said, "Isn't it marvelous," and went to look for the next foot.

Then I looked around for a straw and found one and we started to really go to work. I found a stomach lying on a crack and poked it really hard and it must have been a fat person because there was a lot of lumbering around and shouting and the boards creaked and bent. Then Jennifer got one that was a real squealer and it shrieked for a good long while after Jennifer poked it. And she whispered to me, "Right in the bum!" She laughed until tears came down her cheeks.

It became a competition. We raced around to see who could poke more people and who got the loudest screams. Soon the murmur of conversations turned into more like a roar above us as people began to leave the deck picking up their towels and radios and drinks as they scampered away. A lot of cigarette butts rained down because people were leaving the deck. And from what they shouted we could hear that they thought ants or something were all over the place biting them.

When we had the whole place in an uproar Jennifer came over and sat down on a rock and I sat next to her and she hugged me and said, "We met the enemy and triumphed!" Then she gave me a kiss on the cheek and I sat sort of stunned because I had wished she's do something like that since last vacation.

Suddenly a voice called out, "Calvino!"

I looked up to see who was yelling my name as Jennifer jumped up and took a step away from me. It was the Banini. He was crawling along the rocks toward us. He said, "I know eet wasa youa when I see people running. They say they bite the bugs in feets. But I know eet ees you!" Then he shook his hand at us to show what he would do when he caught us. Jennifer and I started to run the other way and the Banini called out, "Noa run on the wet rock! You falla and keel your head!" He stopped chasing us so we wouldn't get hurt, which showed he wasn't really too mad. We heard him swear in Italian and laugh. Then he turned around and left but not before saying, "I tella youa mosser!"

Jennifer laughed and called back, "Mya mosser noa carea!" Then she laughed some more and shook her finger at the Banini and he laughed because she was a pretty girl and so she could be as rude as she wanted and he didn't care.

We got out to the rocks beyond the deck and put on our masks and snorkels. I threw my fins into the water and put them on after I jumped in. Jennifer didn't have fins, which meant I could swim a lot faster and dive deeper. I dove as deep as I could until my ears hurt so I couldn't stand it and until things started going dark because my brain was deprived of oxygen. It was worth it because when I came up Jennifer said to me, "I've never seen anyone go as deep before, you dive like a seal." I said, "It was easy. I've been diving for years."

We followed a school of fish that were feeding on the bottom until they went so deep we couldn't see them anymore. That took us almost to the middle of the bay where a friend of Jennifer's family was rowing on one of the pontoon boats with his two little girls, who were about three years old and were pulling a big inflatable rubber Mickey Mouse behind the boat on a string.

The little girls' father invited us on board. We climbed up between the pontoons and sat with our feet dangling in the water as he rowed back toward the shore.

When we got closer to the beach, I saw Janet walk over to the place where you brought the boats back to the Banini and wait for us. She had Dad's binoculars in her hand and so I understood how she had known it was me on the boat because she had been watching us and waiting for me to get back. I got a sort of sinking feeling because when Janet got interested in what you were doing it was a bad sign.

When we got off the boat I pulled off my flippers as Janet walked over to me and said, "Are *you* in trouble!" Then I smiled at Jennifer to show Janet was just kidding around but Janet grabbed me by the ear and marched me back up the beach to where Mom and Dad were. I knew Jennifer was watching us the whole way. I wanted to die and to kill Janet too.

When we got to our family Dad stood up and said, "Let him go, Janet, you're not his father." Janet gave my ear a last twist so hard I heard it crack, but I refused to touch it or say anything because I didn't want to let Jennifer see it hurt a lot if she was still watching us.

"The Banini told us what you did," said Dad.

"We were just . . ."

"And I can't say we're very proud of you right now."

"It was not much of a witness to Jennifer for you to get her into trouble," said Mom.

"But it was her . . ."

"He needs a really good strapping," Janet chipped in.

Then Rachael tried to help me by saying, "Maybe he thought it was just a joke."

But Janet straightened her out. "Rachael, some things aren't funny! One lady said she was poked in the eye!"

Dad said, "If we were staying at the Biea as usual instead of the Nazionale I'd send you to your room." And he looked accusingly at Mom as if this proved even more how her ideas never worked.

"We can punish him another way," said Mom.

Janet said, "Pull down his swimming trunks and paddle him right in front of everyone!"

"Janet!" said Mom.

"Keep out of this," said Dad.

Then Janet said, "Well *I* would."

"One more word out of you," Dad said, "and you will be the one in trouble."

I looked at Janet and wished I hadn't because she looked back at me and mouthed the words, "You wait."

Dad said, "Your punishment will be that you cannot play with Jennifer for the rest of this vacation." And he sat down and picked up his copy of *Christianity Today* magazine and began to read an article about the growing divisions within the Lutheran Church.

I walked up the beach toward the snack bar to get away from my family and to plan how to kill Janet when the opportunity arose and also how I could see Jennifer without Dad knowing about it.

23

• • • • •

I LEFT THE beach early and walked back to Portofino alone. As soon as I got into town I climbed the steps to the church and went in. It was lit by the last rays of the late afternoon sun. The clusters of candles burning before the Virgin were glowing brightly in the failing light. No one else was there.

After I used the holy water and crossed myself I went over to kneel in front of Mary to pray. I lit a candle, and even put twenty lire into the box the way you were supposed to instead of just stealing the candle the way I did when I was little and came to play Roman Catholic.

In *Pete and Penny Play and Pray* they had a chapter on the false religions of the world and since the Roman Catholics were the worst, being the Whore of Babylon and all, the longest part was about a little Catholic boy they called Antonio and how sad it was that he believed he was praying to God when he was really worshiping an idol of Mary and praying, "Hail Mary, full of Grace."

I had learned how to pray to Mary from Antonio's story. Like Antonio before the Christian missionaries came to his village and taught him never to pray written prayers but just say anything he wanted to God, I prayed "Hail Mary, full of Grace." I didn't actually ask anything because in *Pete and Penny Play and Pray* they hadn't told you how Roman Catholics asked for things, just how they prayed false prayers that were written down by the Pope so he could make money from his poor deluded followers. So I said it again, "Hail Mary, full of Grace," and this time I crossed myself too.

It was then I got the idea on how to see Jennifer. Because the idea was really clever, I knew it wasn't mine but a miracle. I looked up at Mary and said, "Hail Mary, full of Grace, I thank thee." That sounded about right. Anyway it was respectful. I wished that there had been more false prayers in *Pete and Penny Play and Pray* so I could have known how to thank Mary properly, but I did my best.

I left the church and went down to the hotel to look for Rachael to ask her to help me to write a letter to Grandmother.

"Dear Grandmother," I said, while Rachael sat on the edge of my bed writing it down. "I miss you very much. Dad says we won't be able to see you now for a while. Today we had a fun time on the beach but I was bad and got into trouble. So I have been punished by not being able to play with Jennifer until the end of vacation. That's O.K. though because there are still plenty of other things to do. I can go out and meet other people on my walk on the path from Paraggi to Portofino.

"At night the path is beautiful. Sometimes we have taken long walks even at eleven o'clock at night right up to the top of the path by the wall where you can see Portofino's harbor.

"I wish you could be here with us. I hope your hips aren't giving you too much trouble. I'd love to meet you here and show you the walk we take. Love, Calvin."

When Rachael finished writing it all down she said, "You're a sweet boy to remember Grandmother, she'll love this letter."

"Well, thanks for helping me, now it'll be spelled right. I'll copy it, get a stamp, and send it." Rachael had always helped me like this when I couldn't write. Because of going to school in England now I could write better but I still couldn't spell anything so for something important like a letter to Grandmother she would still help me.

When Rachael left the room I took the letter I had dictated and put it out on the bed next to me, then took the pad of paper and held it on the bed next to the letter. I knelt down to write on the pad in front of me. This is how I copied the letter to Grandmother.

Dear Jennifer,

I miss you very much. Dad says I won't be able to see you now. Today we had fun but I got in trouble. So I have been punished and won't be able to see you. That's O.K. though because I can go out and meet you on the path from Paraggi to Portofino tonight at eleven o'clock right up on the top of the path by the wall.

Love,
Calvin

This way my letter to Jennifer was spelled right. So far the idea Mary gave me was working out fine.

Because I was not going to let laziness spoil my plan I copied out the real letter to Grandmother too in case Mom asked about it. And sure enough a few minutes later she came in and said, ''Rachael told me about how thoughtful you're being writing to dear Mother. That's wonderful, she'll be so blessed by it.'' I held out the letter and Mom said she'd get an envelope and stamps at the front desk and post it. Then she hugged me and said, ''I'm sorry all that unpleasantness happened today; perhaps your father was a little harsh. I'll speak to him about it.''

''You'd better not, Mom. Not in the mood he's in and all.''

She hugged me again and kissed my cheek and said, ''Thank you for understanding.''

Suddenly I was filled with love for her and hugged her back. ''I love you, Mom.'' When she stepped back to take the letter and go she had tears in her eyes and it made me get tears in mine because I knew it must not be easy being my mom. Dad was awful rough on her when he was in a Mood, especially a really bad one like he seemed to have been in on this whole vacation.

There was an hour before supper, which was plenty of time for a fast walk to Paraggi and back. It took about twenty minutes each way.

When I got to the Pensione Biea I could hear the sounds of clinking forks and knives and glasses of the dinner guests out on the terrace. They ate earlier at the Biea than we did at the Nazionale. It was perfect. Jennifer had always had the same room since we were little and since no one locked their doors at the pensione I slipped into Number Nine with no problem. I put my letter on Jennifer's pillow. But as I was leaving the room I thought, what if her mom comes in and sees it? So I put it under the pillow, then stopped because I thought she might just lie down and never feel it under there and it would lie there under her head getting wrinkled and get thrown out in the morning by Lucrezia when she made up the room.

Then I had an idea. I took Jennifer's hairbrush, which was next to the sink, and wrapped my note around the handle. I tied it tight with a black ribbon that was lying there that I had seen in Jennifer's hair. I slipped the brush with the letter attached to it under the sheets and blanket to where I knew she'd hit it with her foot.

As I ran back up the path toward Portofino I smiled when I thought how Jennifer would jump when her foot hit the bristles.

That night at dinner Mom seemed kind of anxious and strange. I took it to be that she was nervous that Dad would smash stuff again. But Dad was in a better mood; he even leaned over and kissed Mom and said she looked beautiful. Janet and Rachael and I all exchanged glances, and Janet nodded in satisfaction, as if to say that the second honeymoon idea was hers to begin with and see how well it was working.

The dinner was fine and the manager stopped hovering around when he saw Dad would not be throwing things that night. And even though the waiter tried to serve us all minestrone while Mom said grace, this worked out too because for some reason Mom's prayer was short that night so the soup didn't get cold. I casually asked what everybody's plans were for after dinner and to my relief Dad said, "Well it's been a long day. I think we'll get an early night. What do you say, Elsa?" Mom said fine and Janet looked at

Rachael and nodded like this meant something too but I didn't know what.

Then Rachael asked Dad, "May we take a walk out to the lighthouse?"

And Dad said, "Sure but be back in by ten."

I said, "I think I'll go to bed early too."

Mom said, "That's a good idea, darling."

So it had all worked out perfectly.

On the way up to my room I checked my watch against the ship's clock that hung over the front desk at the hotel to make sure my watch was right. It was. It was eight forty-seven, which meant I had about two hours to wait.

The path was different late at night. It was cool and dark. You heard little rustling noises in the plants that hung over the wall but there was nothing to be seen. The smells were different too. They were dreamier, harder to pin down.

I had left my room and gone down the backstairs through the hotel laundry room and out into the alley at a quarter to eleven. Before that I had lain under my covers, with my clothes on, ready to go, but in bed nevertheless in case Mom came in to kiss me good night. That night she didn't come in to say good night so I got hot lying there under the covers for nothing.

When I got to the high point of the path to Paraggi I expected Jennifer to already be there waiting. She was always the first to do anything or get anywhere. But she wasn't there. So I walked farther up the path to see if I could meet her.

Then I got to worrying that I might meet someone else and that he would recognize me and say something later in front of Mom and Dad about having seen me. So I turned around and went back to the high point on the path, slipped over the wall, and sat on the rock ledge below where no one would see me if someone came along.

A lot of the lights on the yachts were still on. I could even hear a little music coming over the water from one of them where they were probably having a party or, as Mom would say, they were in "a drunken stupor pretending to have fun all the while hurting inside because they are lost."

I heard light footsteps approach the top of the wall and stop. I peeked cautiously over the wall. There in the moonlight Jennifer was standing in her nightgown and bare feet. She didn't see me so I just looked for a minute before I spoke because she was so beautiful. She didn't have her hair tied back in her usual ponytail but had let it out. It made her look older and prettier the way it framed her face and hung down her back. I suddenly got very nervous and wished I hadn't come out to meet her at all because I had no idea what to say or why I wanted to see her so much. Then she turned her head and saw me and said, "What are you goggling at, you silly boy?"

I climbed over the wall and she walked toward me and I said, "How are you?"

"Do I look ill to you?"

"No, I was just asking."

"Whatever did you shove my hairbrush down my bed for?"

I tried to explain but she was still talking and said, "I'll get you back for that, you feebleminded child." Now I wasn't so nervous because Jennifer was acting rude like she always did.

"How come you came out in your nightgown instead of getting dressed?"

Then I got nervous again because Jennifer turned

all around but fast like a ballet dancer. As she spun around on her toes she said, "Why? Don't you like my nightie?"

"Yes, I do."

And then she made it worse and said, "Do you think I'm beautiful?"

I seemed to be swallowing my throat. Something was stuck in my chest, sort of blocking it up. I was trying to think what to say when Jennifer stepped up to me and kissed me for the second time that day, only this time it was on the lips. I could smell her breath and it smelled like the hay did when it was fresh-cut up in the mountains where we lived. I just about died, but then came to enough to know that if I didn't kiss her back I'd never forgive myself as long as I lived. So I kissed her back a lot.

Then Jennifer pushed me away and said, "There. I suppose that's what you wanted."

And before I could stop myself I said *out loud* what I was thinking, which was, "Jennifer, I love you."

For the first time since we were three years old Jennifer didn't say anything back at all. She only smiled and I felt like I had just won a prize because her smile was a real smile not a cute or sarcastic or funny smile but just plain and sweet.

So we stood there and she kept smiling at me in a slow sort of way and took my hand in hers and still didn't say anything but led me back toward Paraggi. We walked for a while holding hands and I could hear the blood in my ears as if I was underwater and I prayed my hand would not get all sweaty the way it does when you're waiting to get strapped.

When we got to the Pensione Biea Jennifer said, "I'm going to my room now, you silly boy. But if you swim out to the rocks under the castle tomorrow morning at about ten I'll be there.''

Then she gave me another kiss but only on the cheek this time. I said good night, but she was already gone though I could still smell the scent of fresh-cut hay.

24

I RAN ALL the way back up the path toward Portofino singing in my head, ''Jennifer, Jennifer, Jennifer,'' over and over again. When I got to the top of the path I stopped for a minute to look at the place we had been standing when Jennifer had kissed me in the moonlight. I stood there wishing she would appear again and trying to remember how it was when we kissed.

By now the music from the yachts had stopped. It was very quiet and you could hear all the little night noises very clearly. From the harbor came the distant sound of the slap of the lapping waves on the sides of the yachts and the clink of their anchor chains as they moved up and down on the gentle swells of water.

I decided not to go back to the hotel right away but sit for a moment and watch the wide silver path of moonlight on the water of the bay. I climbed over the wall to the same spot on the ledge where I had hidden when I was waiting for Jennifer to come out to me. As I sat there looking at the water, it occurred to me that I had never doubted that Jennifer would come to meet me. I knew she would. She always kept up her side of our bargains, she always had. The wind made the ferns growing out of the wall rustle and sway and I heard a cat someplace yowling as I thought about how fortunate I was to have Jennifer for a friend.

Then I heard voices on the path; they were very close. Right above me. Whoever they were, they must have walked silently up to my spot and only started talking when they got there.

"You know what I feel for you. How could I help coming to you!"

It was a man's voice; he sounded very upset and tense, like he was in the middle of an argument. I sort of recognized his voice but couldn't exactly place it right away.

Then a woman's voice answered him. "Oh, Jonathan, things are terrible between Ralph and me right now. I wish I could think."

I had to grab the ferns to keep from falling because I *did* recognize the woman's voice. It was Mom's!

The man said, "I have prayed and begged for the Lord's guidance and I can honestly say that the Spirit has led me to you and that somehow in some wonderful way our meeting tonight was foreordained and the blessing of the Lord is on it."

Now I knew who it was who was talking! It was Jonathan Edwards! He was supposed to be back at the mission in Switzerland tilling the vineyard of the Lord as Dad would say, along with the Keegans', until Dad got back to do the tilling himself. I remembered what Janet had told me on the train and I got all hot all over and my face went red right there in the dark with no one to see. I hung on to the ferns and thought I'd fall for sure and each second was the longest I'd ever been through, even worse than the time I got caned at boarding school when I had to bend over and recite the Lord's Prayer while I was hit with the cane at the end of each line. Even worse than when I had to lie on the snow waiting for the stretcher sled when I broke my leg.

"Oh, Jonathan," Mom said. And then I couldn't believe my ears because I heard kissing! He was kissing my mom! Jonathan was a lot younger than Mom; in fact, he had been a student of Dad's when Dad taught Summer Bible School when Jonathan had been sixteen. Dad had led him to the Lord! Now he was kissing my mom! I heard it and it sounded a lot longer and wetter than the kiss I had given Jennifer, which had been a lot more respectful by the sounds of it. Then I heard Mom all panting and breathless say, "Jonathan, this is wrong! We can't!"

"Oh, Elsa," he said, and I heard him sort of sniff and cry a little.

"I feel the same way," Mom said, and she started to sniff, then I heard a lot of shuffling around and once in a while I heard muffled sniffing and a sob or two but I couldn't tell which one was doing the crying because it was all muffled up. So I guessed they were hugging and crying like Mom always did when someone was leaving for a very long trip and we sang, "We shall meet again on that bright distant shore." But this time Mom didn't sing any hymns.

After a while Jonathan Edwards said, "Elsa! Come with me!" and Mom said, "To where?"

"Back home. We can start over."

"Jonathan, I feel for you, very deeply. I feel more

for you than I have ever felt for anyone but I cannot give in to this temptation. It's wrong, and I think you know this, too."

"Elsa, I can't live without you! Not even a day! That's why I followed you here and called you up at the hotel this morning!"

That answered one question of mine because I was wondering if he had put a note in Mom's bed and how he could have been sure she would get it and not Dad. Now I knew why Mom had seemed so nervous all day and especially at supper. She knew! I looked at my watch and I saw it was ten minutes after 12 A.M. So I figured he had said, meet me at midnight someplace and Mom had said let's meet on the path to Paraggi. And had probably explained to him about how to get there. Then I wondered where he was staying and as if he knew what I was thinking he said, "At least come back to the Pensione Biea with me tonight."

"I can't, Jonathan. I can't!"

"I love you!"

"Oh how I wish I could!"

I heard more kissing and some groaning. Then Mom said, "But I really *cannot*!"

I knew that tone of voice and I could have told Jonathan Edwards it was no use to ask again but he didn't know Mom as well as I did so he kept on trying anyway. "Please, Elsa, I beg you! Please! I need you! Just this once! You're driving me crazy!" But Mom just kept saying no between more kisses. Then she shouted, "Jonathan we *cannot*! In fact I don't think we should ever meet like this again!"

"Then there's no point my going on living!" Jonathan said. And before I could even realize what was happening he came flying over the wall as Mom screamed, ''No!''

He sort of went by in a blur and as he jumped he yelled, ''Forgive me, Lord!'' He fell about fifteen feet into all the prickly pear cactus and fig trees that grew on the bank below the wall.

Above me Mom rushed to the edge of the wall and screamed, ''Jonathan!'' And she looked down and I couldn't help looking up. She was leaning right over me and her face was almost touching mine. ''Hi, Mom,'' I said.

Then my mom leaped backward like I was a snake and she screamed something, not anything in particular, just a long wail kind of thing. Since now she knew I was there I climbed off the ledge and back over the wall onto the path and saw she was sitting on the path looking scared with her mouth open.

We stared at each other but before we said anything we heard Jonathan Edwards call out, ''Help me!''

So we both went back to the wall and looked over and the moonlight didn't help any because down in the thicket of figs and cactus it was all dark. Jonathan began to groan and call out, ''Oh, please! Please!''

''He's hurt,'' Mom said.

''Probably not very badly,'' I said. ''It's not very far down.''

Mom called out, ''Jonathan, are you hurt?''

And after some more groaning he said, ''Yes.''

Then Mom said, ''How bad is it?''

''I think I've broken my leg and— Ow! I can't move because I'm stuck in something,'' said Jonathan. Then he cried out in pain. I whispered to Mom, ''That would be the cactus.''

Mom whispered to me, ''What shall we do?''

I wanted to say, ''I'll go get Dad,'' but I didn't

because Mom already looked scared enough.

So I called out to Jonathan Edwards, "Climb down to the road, it's just below you."

There was a long silence. Finally Jonathan Edwards said, "Who's that?"

So Mom said, "It's Calvin."

Then there was such a long silence I thought maybe he had gone unconscious. And Mom said, "Jonathan, are you all right?"

And then there was more groaning and finally he said, "Elsa, why is he here?"

Mom looked at me, a sort of question.

So I lied.

"I felt sick and got up to go down the hall to the toilet and I saw you leaving your room when I came back and I followed you because I was worried about you and didn't want you to be alone if you were in some kind of trouble or Dad was being mean or something."

Mom hugged me and said, "I wish you hadn't, but it's not your fault."

Jonathan called out again, "I said, *why's* he here?" And this time there was an edge to his voice like the tone Dad used to Mom when he asked her a question he knew the answer to but asked anyway just to make Mom admit something. Like when he'd say, "Excuse me but what time do *you* say it is?" when Mom was late.

Suddenly Mom got mad, real mad, and she yelled at Jonathan Edwards, "Because he's my dear son! That's why! Because he has every right to be! He's a good and faithful boy! Because he loves his mother! Because he trusts me! Because we have family! That's why!"

Mom burst into tears and since Rachael and Janet

weren't there I had to comfort her. She put her face on my neck and got it all wet with her tears while Jonathan Edwards groaned and finally shouted out, "God damn it! Won't someone help me!"

Mom sniffed and wiped her tears and called back, "I will not have that sort of language used in my presence or in my child's presence!" From the way she was talking I figured she would not be kissing Jonathan Edwards much from now on.

Mom said to me, "I'm going to have to do some explaining to you about all this. I realize that. And if you hate me for what I've done I won't blame you. But will you help me just this once?"

"I don't hate you, Mom," I said. I should have waited till later to say this because I made her cry all over on me even more than before and in the meantime Jonathan was yelling out louder and louder, "Oh, the pain! Oh, the pain! Why won't *someone help me!*"

Then Mom said, "Can you climb down and see if you can help him to the road while I run back to the hotel and call a taxi?"

"I think I can," I said.

Mom stood watching me as I climbed down the wall holding onto all the vines and ferns that grew out of it. When I was safely down I called up to say I was fine and Mom said, "Wait on the road," and I heard her running off down the path toward Portofino.

I picked my way through the cactus to where I could see Jonathan Edwards lying. When he saw me he turned his face away and groaned. But even if he didn't want to look at me he let me untangle his shirt from the brambles. I found his glasses lying next to him and I put them on his face. Then I helped him get up on one leg and hop a little to the bank above the road. I said, "You'll have to sit and slide down the bank. It's just dirt."

He said, "My leg!" But he sat down anyway and slid with me guiding him and we got to the road where I helped him to hop across it and sat him down on the wall above the water to wait. We could hear the waves below. And I suddenly thought, "If he jumps from here, he really will kill himself," and I worried he'd try again so I held on to the sleeve of his torn shirt. But he wasn't thinking about committing suicide now because he said, "Are you going to tell?"

"No," I said. Then I thought about Dad and I thought about how he was when we hiked together and about the spear gun he gave me on my eleventh birthday so I said, "On one condition."

"What?"

"By the time we get home next week you have to be gone."

"How will I do that?"

"You figure it out."

We sat silent for a while. The moon was beginning to sink down below the horizon so it was getting really dark now. He said, "O.K. That's how it'll be."

"O.K."

He started to sort of sigh and sniff and breathe deeply and finally he said, "I'll write a letter of resignation from the mission and go back to Westminster Seminary to complete my Master of Divinity degree in youth ministry. It's my only option."

"Fine," I said.

"My future will be in your hands," he said with a sort of sob.

"I won't tell, don't worry."

After a while the taxi came around the corner of

the empty road with Mom in it and it stopped. In the headlights we could see that Jonathan was pretty cut up by the fall. He had cactus pins stuck in his shoulder and cheek and his leg was bent the wrong way.

On the way back from the emergency room at the hospital in Santa Margherita Mom and I sat in the back of the cab holding hands and we never said a word until we reached the communal parking lot at Portofino. Mom paid the driver and we walked back to the Hotel Nazionale. About halfway there I looked at Mom and could see her face in the pale light of the street lamp. She looked worried sick.

"Mom, I will never tell. You can count on that."

Mom was too embarrassed to look at me because now we had gotten Jonathan Edwards to the hospital I guess it was all sort of sinking into Mom's head what this must look like to me. So she didn't turn her head to look at me but just bit her lip hard and her chin quivered. Then she said real quiet and small, "Thank you."

25

• • • • •

I DIDN'T WAKE up until late the next morning. When I did finally open my eyes I lay in my bed staring at the cracks in the plaster of my ceiling and listening to the strange sounds echoing in the air shaft coming from other people's toilets.

Suddenly I sat bolt upright. Jennifer! She was going to wait out on the rocks and I was in bed! I was late; it was already ten-fifteen. She was waiting and I wasn't even up yet!

I pulled on my swimming trunks, grabbed a T-shirt, my goggles, snorkel, and flippers, and raced out the door, down the hall, and out of the hotel.

When I got to the high point on the path I couldn't help stopping to look over in the light of day to see if I could tell where Jonathan Edwards had fallen when he had jumped last night. Sure enough, a fig tree branch was broken about halfway down and the arm of a prickly pear cactus was torn off and lying on the ground. Then I looked at the spot where I had been sitting on the ledge and I noticed that the fern growing out of the wall was all wilted from my squeezing it so tight.

Jennifer had waited. When I swam out to the rocks I was in a panic because I was sure she wouldn't be there. But when I climbed out of the water I saw she had waited for me because I saw her goggles were lying on a rock near the water.

Jennifer stood up from behind a rock and said, "I thought that at least they knew how to keep time in Switzerland!"

"Hi," I said. "Sorry I'm late."

"Why do you Yanks always say 'Hi'?"

"I don't know; why do you say 'Hello'?"

"Because we speak English!"

Since I had lost this argument before, in fact lost every argument we ever had, I changed the subject. "Did you see any fish when you came out? I didn't."

"Why were you so late?"

I told her I had woken up late and she said, "What were you up to last night to make you so tired?"

"You know, you were there."

Then Jennifer pretended she didn't know what I was talking about and she made me tell her the whole thing over again. That made me sort of embarrassed because out here in the sun on the rocks it didn't seem the same as last night. When I finished telling how I ran back to the hotel after I left her at the pensione (of course I left out the part about Mom and Jonathan Edwards) I stopped talking and Jennifer said, "What are you gawking at?" Because I was looking at her thinking how I would like to kiss her some more.

"I wasn't; I was just thinking."

"Who taught you to do that?"

"Very funny," I said.

We put on our snorkeling stuff and jumped into the water and started to look for fish. We hardly saw any at all. But I didn't mind because I swam behind Jennifer and watched her ponytail fan out in the water and the way the bubbles streamed off her back when she dived and how strong her legs were. When she came back up from one dive I noticed how tight her bathing suit was under the water and how it was almost as if she had nothing on at all.

Then I had a problem because my Little Thing went hard. In fact it had been doing this quite a lot lately—one of the "marvelous changes" in my developing body.

Because I had on the Italian kind of swimming trunks, more like the tight kind of underpants instead of boxer-style American trunks, I was afraid Jennifer would notice what my Little Thing had done. So I swam in front of her from then on and didn't do any diving and when she was below me I'd tread water so if she looked up she would only see flippers and bubbles and not my Little Thing sticking out of the top of my swimming trunks.

I waited for it to go down again, but maybe because of Jennifer's tight bathing suit or because I was embarrassed, it stayed up. I started to worry about what I'd do when we stopped swimming around and I had to climb out on the rocks. We didn't have towels with us so I had nothing to wrap around me. I couldn't very well flop down on a jagged rock because Jennifer would know it was weird and would want to know what I was doing since it hurt even to sit on those rocks let alone lie on them.

Jennifer got out of the water and watching her climb out I was worried and at the same time kind of fascinated because as she climbed out her bathing suit slipped up between the cheeks of her bottom. When she stood up she reached back and straightened it so it covered her bottom properly again. She didn't even bother to turn around when she did this but only laughed and called out to me, "Did you get a nice look at me bum?"

I turned away but it was too late because she had seen me push up my goggles to watch her. Being embarrassed and all I got even harder and I knew as long as I thought about it or wanted it to go down it never would.

Jennifer said, "Come out and climb up to the castle with me."

"I want to swim more," I said.

"If you think I came all the way out here for the pleasure of watching you paddle about, you're sadly mistaken, you twit!"

"In a minute, I'll get out."

"In a minute, I shall swim back to shore and find some nice Italian boy who will be *properly* attentive."

She was joking but I could hear the argument sort of sound coming into her voice. I knew if I fooled around much longer she'd start to get mad at me. And I couldn't think what to do so I tried to squeeze my nuts, or as Mom would call them, my "testicles." It hurt a lot but it still didn't make my Little Thing go down. Jennifer was watching me and said, "What on *earth* are you doing?"

"Nothing, just pulling up my swimming trunks."

"Are you coming out? Yes or no?"

"Why don't you get back in and we'll swim across the bay to the other side."

"What on earth for?"

"It's better over there. More fish."

"There's only sewage over there. You know that. Are you really going mad? What's gone wrong with you?"

I wondered how Jennifer could tell something was wrong and if maybe she knew!

"I'll count to ten," Jennifer said, and she started counting.

"*One*, if you don't get out you'll not see me again this holiday. *Two*, I shall know you do not love me whatever you say in the moonlight. *Three*, I shall tell your father you have disobeyed him and he shall beat you as you deserve. *Four*, if you did get out I might let you kiss me again but why I should I don't know. *Five*, you look very stupid just now with your silly goggles pushed up on your forehead and your hair all standing up. *Six*, you're not even trying to get out so perhaps I shall make you!"

She dove off the rock and grabbed me before I had a chance. We wrestled around and my mask was knocked over my eyes so I couldn't see very well and I pushed her away but she was laughing at me and grabbed me around the middle. While she was trying to pull me toward the shore she felt it! For a second she didn't know what it was so she didn't move her hand right away. Suddenly she realized. Then she was the one who acted like she had been bitten. She pulled her hand away and her face got a little red. She giggled suddenly and splashed water in my face and laughed at me and started saying over and over again, "All is explained! All is revealed! All is explained! All is revealed!"

I got mad and embarrassed all at once and shouted, "Shut up!"

She laughed even more and said, "Poor thing. Do

we want to take It for a walk? Does It want to go out?''

I couldn't believe she would talk like this. So I just stared at her dumbfounded.

Then I realized that it had at last gone down. I swam over to the rocks and climbed out and Jennifer climbed out after me and didn't say any more about it. I guess she understood that I didn't think it was very funny. We both pretended nothing had happened and after a while I said, ''I think I'd better get back to the beach before the rest of the family wonders where I am.'' We agreed I'd go first, then she'd wait about ten minutes so we wouldn't be seen together in case Dad or Janet had the binoculars out today.

By the time I got back to the beach I had decided I'd never wear the small tight Italian kind of swimming trunks again. As I walked up the sand to where I saw our family spread out around the deck chair I wondered how Mom was. And if Dad knew about Jonathan Edwards. But everything seemed normal and everyone just looked up at me, then went back to reading their books.

Mom smiled at me and the way she smiled was sorrowful, not her usual cheerful way.

I asked, ''When's lunch?''

''Whenever you want,'' Mom said.

Dad said, without even looking up from the book he was reading: *Karl Barth—The Heretic*, ''I've changed my mind about Jennifer. You can play with her but no more practical jokes. Understand?''

I said, ''Thank you,'' and ''Yes, I understand.''

Then Janet said, ''You're spoiling him rotten.''

But Mom said, ''That's enough, Janet. And another thing, you're not to pull his ears anymore like you did yesterday. Do *you* understand, young lady?''

Janet just nodded and looked angry at being called "young lady," since she was eighteen now, but didn't say anything back.

"Call me when lunch is ready," I said, and I walked over to where the Banini was standing arguing with a man about something that the man had left in one of the rowboats yesterday. He said the Banini had stolen it because he couldn't find it now. The Banini turned and winked at me, then turned back to the man and started shouting again.

As I stood there I thought about how this vacation was not going as planned and how it was better and worse at the same time. And I thought about what I should say to Mom now she knew I knew about her and Jonathan Edwards, and if Dad would ever find out, and what would happen then. But I wondered most about how to act in front of Jennifer now she had discovered the truth about my Little Thing and what it did.

26

ON THE WALK back to Portofino Mom touched my hand and motioned with her head which was to say that we should fall behind the others so we could talk.

I slowed down and let Janet and Rachael pass us. Dad was already out of sight, way ahead of us all. By the pace he was setting we knew he was in a Mood. My stomach sort of tightened up. I hoped he wouldn't do anything too embarrassing at dinner or someplace else in public.

Rachael and Janet went around the corner up ahead of us. Then Mom stopped walking so I did too.

"Calvin," she said, "I thought you'd like to know he's back in Switzerland."

"What about his leg?"

"It's in a cast and will be fine. But the big news is he'll be gone before we get back."

"How do you know?"

"Because he called the hotel from the station in Milano on his way back and told me." There was a little bit of a quiver in her voice but she looked pretty determined when she said, "I won't ever see him or speak to him again. I thought you'd like to know that."

"That's all right, Mom."

"The Lord has given me a second chance and a wonderful son. More than I deserve." Now her voice was really all trembly and since I didn't want her to cry on me again I changed the subject.

"Mom, how much do Janet and Rachael know?"

"I guess they know a little but not about the other night."

"And Dad?"

"I don't know what to tell him. You know your father. It's not as if I could talk to him without—or confess about it, you know."

"Yes, Mom, I know."

Mom looked at me real hard and said, "You won't—?"

"No, I promise."

She nodded and hugged me and said, "You're a blessing to me. I know I can trust you."

On the way back to Portofino Mom and I stopped and sat on a bench overlooking the town. We sat silently. I looked at the wall next to the path and saw a huge lizard run along it then dive into a crack in the sun-baked bricks. I wondered why Mom never asked me what I was doing on the ledge hiding that night or how I got there since the lie I had told didn't explain that part. I guess she was worried enough about her own secrets not to ask me about mine.

When we got to the Hotel Nazionale the manager was waiting for us in the lobby in front of the *Ricev-*

imento desk. He was wringing his hands and looking very upset.

As we came through the front door, which had a ship's steering wheel stenciled on it in gold leaf, and stepped inside he rushed forward and said, "Mrs. Becker, there ees a deesasster things! Queeck! *Sono malato!* Coma weetha mea!"

He grabbed her by the arm and pulled her up the stairs as I followed. Mom kept saying,. "What is it?"

And the manager kept saying, "Coma weetha mea! *Faccia presto!*"

When we got up to the hall he hurried us to Mom and Dad's room and, without knocking, barged in. I heard him say, "I finda youa wife!"

I heard Dad's voice bark, "Where have *you* been? If you had been here when you were supposed to be this wouldn't have happened!"

When I stepped into the room I saw Dad sitting up on the bed. He was on the bed, but dressed. I noticed his shirt. It had lots of blood on it. Then I saw his head was bandaged and there was blood on the bandage too. There was the doctor sitting on the edge of his bed taking Dad's blood pressure. He had on a stethoscope and was listening to Dad's heartbeat with the listening part under the blood pressure cuff. He said, "Sshh . . . I can no 'eeara nossing for the *pressione del sangue*, if you speaks!" So we all waited quietly until he had finished. Then he looked up and said, "*Perfetto!* One 'undreds and twenty-fives over eighties! Youa likea a younga boys! Wonderful! You will leeve to be onea 'undreda yearsa olds! *Meraviglioso!*"

"Oh, Ralph! What happened?" Mom said.

The manager said, "It falla ona 'eem!"

"What fell?" Mom asked.

''The toilet tank,'' Dad said.

I looked through the open door of their bathroom and, sure enough, the big porcelain toilet flush tank, which was supposed to be bolted up in the wall above the toilet, so when you pulled the chain it flushed, was lying broken in half on the tile floor. There was about an inch of water on the floor and blood splattered around. The pipe was wrenched off the wall and bent where the falling tank had pulled it down.

Mom looked too, and said the wrong thing. ''Oh, Ralph, how did you do *that*?''

And the manager chipped in. ''Eet never 'appena before. Whata deeda youa dos?''

Dad was so mad at Mom for saying ''How did you do that?'' that he ignored the manager and shouted, ''Don't 'Oh, Ralph' me! You bring us to some fool place instead of our usual pensione! What did you expect!''

''But the pounding music kept you awake over there,'' said Mom.

''And you think this is better?!''

''I never expected something like this.''

''You and your fool ideas!''

''Calma! Calma!'' said the doctor. ''You musts composing youraselfs!''

I didn't say anything but I bet I knew what had happened. I bet that Dad had been in a Mood and pulled the chain the same way he slams doors at home when he's in a Mood. I bet he yanked that thing with all his might and it all came down on his head. And I bet Mom knew this and I bet the manager did too, because he had seen Dad at our table on the dining terrace breaking stuff.

I thought about saying as how we were better off at the Biea since the rooms had no toilets, only showers, so Dad had been safer. But of course I didn't since I could see well enough how a remark like that would strike Dad.

Mom turned to the manager and said, "We're *very* sorry this happened. I hope you will be able to fix it."

Dad yelled, "What about my head?"

The doctor tried to get Dad to lie down and kept saying, "Calma, calma!"

Dad yelled, "I'll 'calma' you." And he shoved the doctor so hard the doctor staggered back from the bed. Then the doctor got all dignified and put away his stethoscope and his blood pressure stuff and turned to go.

Mom said to the doctor, "I'm so sorry he's in a Mood."

The doctor said, "I shalla proscribe *sedativos*." He started to write down a prescription.

The manager said to Mom, "We weell 'avea to adda the costa ofa repairings to youra beell."

"I understand," Mom said.

"Elsa, if you pay one penny of the cost of that toilet tank I'll leave you!" Dad shouted.

Then the manager wrang his hands and looked from one person to another and Mom said, "But, Ralph—"

"In America you'd be sued for having such dangerous sanitary arrangements!" Dad yelled at the manager.

The doctor handed Mom the prescription and said, "Twicea a days and eef he 'asa troubles in thee nights to sleepings takea twoa mores."

Mom shook his hand and said, "Thank you so much. How will we pay you?"

The manager stepped forward and said, "We weel pays for the medicals treatments!"

Mom said, "Thank you so much."

But Dad said, "What about the toilet?"

"*Youa* musta bear the costa of thees," the manager said.

He bowed and left the room with the doctor just as a maid came in with a bucket to clear up the water from the broken tank.

"Oh my head," Dad bellowed and leaned back on his pillow.

"Is it bad?" Mom said.

"What's it look like to you, Sherlock? I had ten stitches. Why didn't you walk home with me so this wouldn't happen?"

Mom took his hand and held it and said, "I'm sorry, I should have." Dad grunted, closed his eyes, and lay still. I tiptoed out and went to my room.

At supper it was just Rachael, Janet, and I who were there. Mom stayed in Dad's room with him to feed him some minestrone.

Janet said, "I'm thankful this has happened."

"Why?" Rachael asked.

Janet answered, "Because adversity has a way of drawing people together. This is God's way of helping Mom and Dad come closer to each other again."

"I don't know. It doesn't seem like Dad needed the toilet to fall on him to make him love Mom more," Rachael said.

"Toilet *tank*, Rachael, not *toilet*. When you get a little older you'll understand some things better," said Janet.

I said, "Anyway 'All things work together for the good of those that love Him,' don't they?"

"I hope you mean that because if you're just saying it flippantly, it's blasphemy,'' said Janet.

''Janet, why are you always so suspicious?'' Rachael asked. ''Of course he means it. Calvin wouldn't joke about the sovereignty of God!'' And she looked at me and I said, ''Of course not.'' Then Janet said, ''I *hope* that's true for your sake!''

Mom came out on the terrace when we were eating our dessert of stewed pears in chocolate sauce and Janet said, ''How is he?''

''He's asleep,'' Mom answered. ''Whatever the doctor prescribed sure is strong. It knocked him right out.''

Rachael asked, ''Can we stay and finish our vacation or do we have to go home?''

''Of course we'll finish the vacation,'' Mom said. ''Anyway the doctor said he's got to rest quietly for a week in case he has a concussion.''

I said, ''That toilet tank must have hit him pretty hard.''

''I bet it was a big shock,'' added Rachael. Rachael tried not to but she started to giggle.

Janet looked shocked and said, ''Rachael! It's not funny! Your father was seriously injured!'' But Mom started to smile and then she laughed out loud. Then I laughed and finally even Janet's mouth started twitching. Then we all howled with laughter so long and hard that tears ran down our cheeks and we started choking like we'd throw up.

The other guests were staring at our table again. The manager stood nearby wringing his hands. That made us laugh even harder because Rachael gasped out, ''I . . . bet . . . *he* wishes we were still at . . . the pensione . . . !''

We all screamed with laughter and I slid out of my chair onto the floor and almost wet my pants. Just as we were beginning to calm down and I got back into my chair Janet said, " 'Vengeance is mine, saith the Lord,' " and that struck us all as very funny so even though Mom said, "Janet!" we all laughed again so hard some people stood up at their tables to watch us better.

27

THAT SUNDAY WE had church in Mom and Dad's room. Janet and Rachael sat on Mom's side of the bed, Mom sat on the chair by the dressing table. I got to sit on the windowsill, which was great because that way I could watch what was going on in the square and harbor during the service and still look like I was paying attention. Dad was propped up in bed with extra pillows from Rachael's room that Mom had sent her to get so Dad could sit up to preach.

The toilet tank still wasn't fixed so the manager had sent up a red plastic bucket. When you wanted to flush you filled the bucket in the bathtub then poured it down the toilet. Mom told us when we came in to church, "If you need to use the bathroom, please go to the one at the end of the hall."

I said, "Why?"

"Ours still has its problem. It's a little unseemly," Mom said.

Dad gave me an angry look so I didn't say any more. His angry look was scary because his left eye was almost swollen shut. With the bandages like a blood-soaked turban, and because he hadn't shaved for four days since the accident, he looked more crazy and dangerous than usual.

At the beginning of church Mom said, "Dear, shall I do the Bible reading?"

Dad said, "I can still do my pastoral duties, thank you!" He snatched his Bible back from Mom, who had just picked it up off his bedside table. "I've prepared a sermon and there is no need to think that just because of my accident I can't lead the service."

I sighed because I had hoped that with Dad hurt we wouldn't have any church. At least I thought that it might be a short service. Now I saw that Dad was determined to do the whole thing no matter what.

Janet had asked the manager if he wanted to join us at worship but he hadn't wanted to. Rachael had put up a notice on the hotel bulletin board, right next to the bus schedule and the poster for "The Pretty Boys" quartet, which was playing at La Busola in Paraggi. It read:

Reformed Evangelical Protestant Worship Service
(PCCCCUSA)
To be held in Room 36 at 10 A.M. Sunday
Rev. Ralph Becker, D.D., Minister, presiding
Are you hungry for the Word????

After dinner the night before, while the others went for a walk in the square, I had stood against the bulletin board for at least a half an hour so I'd block people's view of Rachael's notice. I hadn't dared to take it down, but I didn't want the other guests to see it either. Not that I thought any would come but because I knew they all thought we were strange enough and this would just be one more thing. So I stood there until most of them were done eating and had gone up to their rooms or out for a walk.

Dad had started the service. ''Elsa, pass out the hymnbooks, please.'' He asked us to open to page 208 and sing ''Just As I Am,'' which we did. We all sat down again, except Dad, who hadn't stood up, and Dad opened his Bible up and read the part where Jesus is telling the parable of the ''Wheat and the Tares.'' Then we sang ''In the Sweet By and By.''

Dad asked Janet, whom he called ''Deaconess Janet,'' to lead us in prayer. Janet prayed a long prayer and in it she started preaching to Mom and Dad about love and forgiveness. She even quoted a line from the Lord's Prayer: ''Forgive us our trespasses as we forgive those who trespass against us.''

It annoyed Dad and I saw him start squirming around in his bed. Janet kept praying and said how thankful she was that the Lord forgave us all for what we did, ''even when we have sinned against Thee, o Lord, even if we have been angry, despondent, or wrathful and have forgotten Thy mercies and have fought with our neighbors or loved ones or not been reconciled to those Thou hast given us to care for.'' Janet sounded like Mom did when she was using her prayers to get even with Dad because she knew Dad wouldn't dare answer back during a prayer or say bad things about Mom taking her needs to the Lord.

This was the first time *Janet* had ever used prayer to preach to Dad about his temper and I could see he was getting very restless. He cleared his throat pretty loudly a couple of times. Janet prayed, ''Lord we just come to You on Thine own day, this Thy Sabbath, and we ask for Thy forgiveness for all our sins during the week. Especially for the sin of anger. We thank Thee that Thou chastiseth those whom Thou lovest and we pray that we will *all* harken to Thy voice.''

Dad was staring straight at Mom and the way he looked at her must have gotten through to her somehow because she opened her eyes and looked at him. I could see them both because I was only pretending to have my eyes shut. Dad mouthed the words to Mom, ''*Shut her up.*'' Mom looked shocked but then Dad clenched his fist and shook it a little to show he meant it. He thought Mom was the only one who saw him but I was looking through my eyelashes and saw him do it.

Mom touched Janet on the arm. Janet faltered in her prayer and opened her eyes a little and looked at Mom. Since this had never happened before, someone getting a prayer stopped, we all exchanged glances, except Dad, who wouldn't look at anyone. Rachael, who still had her eyes closed and was waiting for the prayer to end, turned bright red, blushing with embarrassment at the silence.

Then Dad cut off Janet's prayer before she could start up again. He said, ''Amen.'' That made Rachael open her eyes and look a question at Mom, who shook her head just enough to let Rachael know not to say anything.

Dad sat up straighter and started to preach his sermon with his Bible open on his knees and his sermon notes on the bed next to him. He looked up once in a while and glanced at each of us the same way he would do at home when we had church in the living room. He preached in a loud voice as if there were hundreds of us there. He preached for an hour and a half about how God was a loving God but a just God nevertheless, so he had chosen some to be saved and some to be "Vessels of Wrath," lost since before the beginning of the world. And how the Elect who believed could never be lost again no matter what and those predestined to perish, the Unregenerate, could never be saved no matter what.

Then he said that some people called our Calvinist doctrine of predestination "cruel" because of the part about people being chosen by God to be lost, and the part about The Total Inability of Totally Depraved men to come to God, unless He forced them to by His Irresistible Grace.

Dad preached how the Elect were so secure nothing could take them out of the hand of God. And how Calvin had shown us that man's so-called free will was fallen and depraved along with everything else so there was no way we could really choose to do anything because only God in His Sovereignty really had choice anymore. "This is because of the doctrine of Total Depravity—man's total inability to contribute to his own salvation in any way because he is deaf, blind and dead in his sins." Then he said how some people thought this doctrine of the Sovereignty of God, our intellect being fallen and all so we couldn't think or choose because of our Total Depravity, was not biblical because there were so many passages about how we were supposed to choose to do the right thing and Jesus *seemed* to say in some verses you could be lost again if you made the wrong choices, like when He said that "Many will come to me on that day and say Lord, Lord," and Jesus would say, "Depart from me I never knew you." But, Dad explained, what this really meant was that these people were not of the Elect in the first place so even though they *thought* they were Regenerate, they weren't because God hadn't predestined them to be saved from before the creation of the world but to be Vessels of Wrath. Dad explained how in the Bible where it said that God desired all men to be saved it just meant that God desired all the people He had *chosen* to be the *Elect* to be saved.

Then Dad said how we were not bound by dead, man-made tradition like the Eastern Orthodox or Roman Catholics, who believed in free will and other heresies, and how if everyone followed the teaching of Calvin and the other great Reformed theologians like Zwingli, they would understand what the Bible *really meant* because Calvin was right about it so we didn't need traditions to follow because we had Calvin and the PCCCCUSA.

Dad closed in prayer and we sang two more hymns, "I Will Make You Fishers of Men" and "Wide, Wide as the Ocean." Then Dad said we could go.

Outside it was a perfect day. All the Sunday tourists had arrived on the tour boats from Santa Margherita and were taking pictures of each other with the yachts anchored in the background. I saw Gino with his little movie camera following two young priests, filming them as they bought pistachio ice cream cones at the Gelateria. Gino saw me and stopped filming and beckoned me over to him. I ran across the square, past all the Italian families with their perfectly dressed children out for their Sunday after Mass stroll. Gino said, "I go 'ave lunch wees my friend on 'ees boat. You wanta to come?"

"Yes, thank you very much."

"We go at one a serty."

"Which boat?"

When he said the *Esther Oratta* I got that very

excited feeling you get when something great happens because the *Esther Oratta* was the biggest and most beautiful yacht in the whole harbor. It had been docked in Portofino every year since we had been coming here. Mom had always wondered aloud who the owner was and now *I* was going to have lunch on it!

At one-thirty Gino came walking toward where I was waiting on the dock. He had changed out of his usual dungarees and was now wearing a light blue summer suit with a yellow silk shirt and a red cravat. He also had on a white straw hat. By the way he walked I could tell he had had some drinks while he was getting ready for lunch. He was choosing where he put his feet pretty carefully.

When we stepped on to the yacht a crewman in uniform saluted us while another took our arms to help us off the gangplank onto the teak deck.

Ropes lay coiled in perfect circles on the deck. The brass fittings were polished up to where they glittered white hot in the sun. Everything was starched and ironed-looking. From the crew's white pants and T-shirts with the name of the boat on them to the cushions on the wicker chairs that were in a semicircle on the back deck, every item was fresh, new, perfect. We followed the sailor into a big lounge. It had a real fireplace in it and over the fireplace a painting of a ballerina, which was in a huge gold frame. Gino pointed to the painting and whispered to me, "Degas."

The sailor led us down a hall to another lounge in the front of the boat. This one had a dining room table in it. It was made of chrome-plated steel and had a glass top that was so thick the edges looked like blue ice. In the middle of the table was a huge silver bowl of roses that must have had at least two hundred big coral pink rosebuds in it.

A man in a white suit and sunglasses stood up and stretched out his arms in a welcoming gesture to us when we came in. He looked about seventy years old and walked with a limp like one leg was way shorter than the other.

"*Maestro*!" he said as he hugged Gino and kissed him on both cheeks. Then he shook my hand as Gino introduced us. "Don Andriotti, thees ees my younga friend Calvin, Calvin, Don Andriotti." I shook hands and Mr. Andriotti said, "I 'ope you likea my boat." I said I did.

A sailor came over to us with a tray full of glasses of champagne. We each took a glass and followed Mr. Andriotti out to the front deck where a very tall woman in a black bathing suit was lying in the sun. We all sat down under a pink awning in the shade and sipped champagne while the woman got a sailor to rub suntan oil on the back of her legs.

I tried not to look like I had never had champagne before. I looked to see if you were supposed to drink it fast or slow. I copied Gino and took a sip whenever he did. Pretty soon we finished the first glass. The sailor gave us more so we sipped that too.

Then a ship's bell rang and we all went back to the dining room. I noticed that Gino and I had drunk a lot of champagne. I was having trouble walking but no one seemed to mind.

At lunch we had smoked salmon that the lunch-time sailor cut right off a whole fish that was on a silver fish-shaped platter. Another sailor stood behind our chairs and kept pouring white wine in our glasses and serving us capers and chopped hardboiled egg and onion to go with the fish.

Gino saw how I was fumbling with my fork and he put his hand over my glass when the sailor was about to pour more wine and shook his head. The sailor bowed and stepped back and didn't give me any more after that.

Gino and Mr. Andriotti both were talking about painting and about a new gallery that Gino was thinking of having represent him. Mr. Andriotti was very polite. Every couple of minutes he'd stop speaking Italian and turn to me and repeat what they were saying in English so I could follow along, which I thought was very nice of him. I wanted to tell him how very, very nice I thought he was but I had trouble thinking about the words. When I tried to say, "I think you're . . ." I started to laugh for some reason so I stopped and watched the horizon go up and down through the porthole instead of talking.

When lunch was over we went to the back part of the deck next to the dock. Mr. Andriotti smoked a cigar and Gino smoked his cigarettes. Mr. Andriotti offered me a cigar but I said, "No thank you." As he put the silver cigar box back on the coffee table he said, "These are the besta—Monte Christo, Cuban. If youa change you mind, 'elp yourself."

A sailor brought out some coffee and I had an espresso. While I was drinking it I looked up and saw Mom and Rachael and Janet all staring at me from the dock. They were whispering and looking thrilled and mad all at once. I didn't know what to do, whether to wave or pretend they weren't related to me.

Mr. Andriotti saw me looking over his shoulder and he turned to see what I was staring at. Then he turned back to me and said, "Ees that youa charming mosser?"

I said, ''Yes.''

He stood up and bowed to Mom and said, ''I 'ope eet ees all right I have borrowed your charming boy to 'ave luncha weeth us?''

''Oh that's fine. Thank you,'' said Mom.

Mr. Andriotti said, ''Woulda you come join us for coffee?''

''I'm sure Calvin is doing well by himself.''

I saw Janet and Rachael both give Mom a look because no one had ever invited them onto a yacht before and I could see that they were dying to come on board. But Mom took them by the arm and smiled at us, then turned and kept walking to where the steps cut in the rock go up to the path to the lighthouse. They kept going up the steps till they disappeared. Janet looked over her shoulder once but they didn't come back.

I was saying to myself, ''Thank you, Mom,'' the way sometimes I heard Mom say, ''Thank you, Jesus.'' Mr. Andriotti turned to me and said, ''You 'ave a charming mosser.'' I said, ''Thank you, so do you.'' Later I thought about it and decided I had not said exactly the right thing just then but at the time it seemed O.K. and Mr. Andriotti and Gino didn't mind.

Mr. Andriotti asked one of the sailors to show me around his yacht and the sailor did. I couldn't believe it. How big it was inside and how in one bathroom there was a real marble tub with Roman statues in niches in the wall. And in the big bedroom the walls were paneled and the white carpet was the thickest I had ever felt. The sailor showed me the engine room and explained how it had twin diesel engines. And he showed me how the radar worked. He explained how the boat had a crew of twelve men on board and could cross the Atlantic Ocean in four and a half days from the Strait of Gibraltar to the island of Bermuda.

But when I asked him about Mr. Andriotti, who he was and what he did, I knew Mom would want to know, he didn't say much. Then we went back and Mr. Andriotti shook my hand and hugged Gino. We left the yacht and he called ''*Arrivederci*!'' after us and we turned and waved as he went back into the lounge.

As we walked away from the yacht tourists watched us to figure out if we were famous. One lady pointed us out to her husband and got him to take a picture. All because we had gotten off the biggest yacht in Portofino. I tried to look rich and important but I was having trouble doing that because I still felt as if I was on the boat, what with the ground going up and down.

''What does Mr. Andriotti do?'' I asked Gino.

Gino laughed and said, ''Do? 'ees the beeggest creeminal in Italia!''

Then I said, ''No, really, what does he do?''

''Why you noa beelievea me? I tella you 'ees a capo. Very powerful creeminal.''

''Then why do you have him for a friend?'' Gino just laughed. But I still didn't really believe him because Mr. Andriotti seemed like one of the nicest people I had ever met. I decided if Mom asked me I'd tell her he owned an airline.

28

• • • • •

I MADE A big mistake. I guess I was still a little drunk from my lunch on Mr. Andriotti's yacht. I told Rachael about how it was on the yacht. I met her in front of the hotel and she asked me why I was not able to walk very well. I had never told her or anyone else how Gino gave me whiskey and water because I knew I'd get into trouble and never be allowed to see him again. But it had been such a big day and I had had so much champagne and wine that I got carried away and started telling the truth.

Before I told Rachael the alcohol part I made her promise not to tell Dad. But I forgot to make her promise not to tell Mom. She behaved like a Pharisee. She kept the letter of the Law but not its spirit. While I talked she was all interested and didn't act shocked but asked lots of questions. But in her heart she was plotting my destruction.

Sometimes Rachael was worse than Janet, who was

at least straightforward about your destruction. Janet probably would have given me a choice between her telling on me and me letting her be the instrument of chastisement. Like the time she found me in Mom and Dad's bedroom, when I had opened Mom's private drawer in the dresser and was showing Mom's underwear to Jacky Keegan and Janet caught us and sent Jacky home then gave me a choice of punishments. I took Janet's punishment but probably should have let her tell Dad because she made me stand with my arms straight in front of me holding Dad's huge thick *Strong's Exhaustive Bible Concordance*. If my arms started to waver she'd hit my legs with a coat hanger. She made me do this for an hour until I just couldn't anymore then she let me go and change into long pants to hide the hanger marks.

But at least you knew where you were with Janet. I trusted Rachael, that was my big mistake. Later when she came to my room and cried and said she was sorry and how she didn't know I'd be punished so hard, it was too late. The next day I told her I forgave her but in my heart I kept saying "Liar," even while she hugged me and we made up.

I babbled to her about the Moët Chandon champagne and about the Orvieto wine at lunch and she listened to it all and when I was done she said, "Of course I'm going to have to tell Mother."

I shouted out, "Rachael! You promised!"

Rachael said, "Not to tell *Dad*. But I never said anything about Mom. This is *really serious*. You're clearly intoxicated! You have alcoholic tendencies. I have to tell Mom for your own good, it's my Christian duty. You'll thank me later." But I never did.

"Calvin," said Mom, "I'm so disappointed."

"I'm sorry, Mom."

"This is very serious."

"I know."

"This is not some little boy thing, but a serious adult sin. In fact it's all too common. According to *Time* magazine, juvenile alcoholism is on the rise and is the principal cause of juvenile delinquency."

"I won't do it again, Mom. I promise."

"I'm so sorry, darling, but I'm afraid this is so serious that I will have to tell your father about it. He has the right to know about your drinking problem."

"But, Mom! I won't do it again. I probably won't ever get invited onto a yacht again in my life."

"You'll find other places to drink."

"No, I won't."

"I wish I could believe you but the first casualty of alcoholism is the truth. Alcoholics are liars."

"But, Mom! I promise!"

"I know after what happened the other . . . night and . . . how sweet you were, not telling and all, that this might seem unfair but it's for your own good. I cannot live the rest of my life knowing that I have allowed you to be ruined by alcohol because of my own sin."

Mom got all teary-eyed and hugged me. Then she led me into Dad's room.

Dad's bandage was off now. He had a green and yellow bruise around his eye and a scab with black stitches in it where the cut was on his forehead. The light still hurt his eyes so in the daytime he stayed in the room with the shutters pulled to. He only came out of his room for dinner on the terrace and a walk around the square at night.

Dad was sitting on his bed reading his Bible and making notes in the margin for his next sermon.

"Ralph," Mom said, "Calvin has something to tell you."

Dad didn't look up. He said, "Elsa, I wish you wouldn't interrupt my quiet time with the Lord."

I looked at Mom and took a step back toward the open door since I agreed with Dad. But Mom took a step forward and closed the door behind her and said, "Ralph, this is serious."

Then Dad looked up from his Bible and said, "What's he done now?"

Mom said, "Tell your father. And tell him *all* of it."

So I did. At least not how I had trouble walking but that I had had two glasses of an alcoholic beverage.

Then Mom chipped in and said, "He told Rachael he had four glasses and became intoxicated! She says he was actually stumbling!"

Dad said, "Is this true, boy?"

I almost said, "No, of course not. I just want to be strapped so I decided to lie and pretend I had violated the temple of the Holy Spirit for the fun of it."

But instead I nodded and tried to look really sorrowfully repentant like I had already learned my lesson so I didn't need any more punishing. I looked as downcast as I could and hoped Dad would be reminded of the Prodigal Son and how the father in that story had welcomed him back and all. But Dad stood up in a real determined way. I got that wobbly feeling in my legs and my hands started to sweat and I felt like somebody had a hand over my mouth. I couldn't breathe very well.

Dad said, "Leave us, Elsa."

Mom gave me a real sorry look. I knew she wanted me to nod or something to show I understood she had only been doing her duty but I wouldn't do it and just stared away from her. Then she left and closed the door so softly I had to turn around to see if she was really gone.

"Young man, this is serious. In the Scriptures we read that the Israelites would take incorrigible youths outside the city gates where they would be stoned to death."

"But, Dad, I . . ."

Dad didn't stop to listen to me. He continued and his voice became louder like when he preached in our living room to us.

"Do you know why they did that?"

"No, Dad."

"Because there is nothing worse, *nothing more hopeless*, nothing God hates more than a hardened young heart. A lying heart. A deceitful heart."

"Yes, Dad."

"And because once a young person becomes incorrigible and begins to give himself over to the pleasures of the world and forgets the ways of his father and mother it is better he should die than spend a miserable life in depravity."

"Yes, Dad, but I'm really sorry and . . ."

"Today our customs have changed and we the spiritual Hebrews no longer are living in a theocracy so we use other methods of discipline for incorrigible youth who grieve their parents."

I tried to change the subject.

"Dad, what's a theocracy?"

"You know perfectly well, and you know that you are going to have to pay a severe penalty for what you have done because there is a difference between naughtiness and real sin. This is real sin of the worst kind." He stepped forward and took me by the back of my neck and led me around to the foot of the bed. "Take down your pants and bend over the bed and wait."

"Dad, how many am I going to get?"

"You'll soon know. Don't stand up or move or cover up with your hands or I'll just give you more. Understand?"

"Yes, Dad."

I waited and my legs shook a little but I didn't move or cover up. I heard Dad open the cupboard and I knew he was getting out his belt of braided black leather he had been given as a "thank-you" for heading the Evangelical Men's Bible Fellowship Study at the annual Reformed PCCCCUSA conference at Berchtesgaden in Germany. It had "John 3:16" inscribed on its silver buckle.

I heard Dad step up behind me and I heard him take a practice swing with the belt. It whistled a little because of how the air funneled through the thick ropes of braided leather.

"I'm afraid adult sin must suffer adult punishment." This sounded bad and it was. "Please believe me that I am grieved and that I will be suffering with you," Dad said.

I thought that he wouldn't be suffering as much as I would and I was right because when the first hit landed I knew I was in real trouble. It was so hard I saw white light.

I started to study the bedspread, which had pictures of Venice on it. Now whenever I see pictures of the Rialto Bridge I still get a sweaty feeling on my hands and sort of choke a little. I counted the people on the bridge on the bedspread, people in carnival masks. The ladies wore long dresses and I noticed how you could see almost the whole of their breasts they were pushed up so far. Under the bridge was a gondola with a man and woman kissing in the stern.

Then he hit me again and it was right on the first strap welt so it burned more than the first one and the pain went up to my neck. I wondered what part of the picture I had peed on since the picture was printed all over the bedspread. I dug my hands into the bedspread and made one of the Rialto Bridges crinkle up so it looked as if the people in the masks were a lot shorter and the gondola disappeared.

Then he hit me again. This one came in a lot higher and got me on my lower back and the tip of the belt whipped around my side and stung me on the really sensitive skin on the side of my waist. I felt that hit more than any so far. The Rialto Bridge got fuzzy looking because I was looking at it through tears. It was raining in Venice.

Then he hit me again and this one landed lower down on the back of my legs.

I thought about the belt. How heavy it was and how it was so long that Dad needed to loop the end right around his side almost to his back. He had said you couldn't cut the end or the braid would unravel. He must have adjusted the belt in his hand because the next hit hurt me so much I knew I had been hit with John 3:16. Only the buckle could hurt that much.

"Sorry, I didn't mean to get you with the buckle," Dad said.

Since my legs had sort of crumpled he paused while I straightened up and bent over again. I was having trouble staying in one place because my hands and legs had gotten so wobbly. I crawled on the bed so I wouldn't slide down to the floor. I laid my face on the Rialto and Dad finished my strapping. He hit me a total of nine times. I kept count.

Then he said, "You may get dressed now."

I tried but my hands wouldn't work right. Dad had to help me pull my pants up but before he did he said, "Wait, let me get a Band-Aid first." This was to cover the place the buckle had cut.

When my pants were up Dad said, "Let's shake hands like gentlemen."

When I got back to my room Mom and Rachael laid cold cloths on my welts and even Janet asked if I was O.K. I said, "Yes," but I wouldn't speak to Rachael.

29

MY WICKEDNESS BROUGHT the family back together. When we gathered for dinner that night everyone was united in being nice to me because I had been strapped so hard. Rachael and Janet gave me a lot of sweet pitying smiles and Mom acted like I was a wounded soldier or something and kept hovering around. Dad was nicer to all of us than he had been the whole vacation. He gave me one hundred lire to buy an ice cream cone after dinner. When I asked what time I had to be back from walking around the square that night, he said, "Eleven o'clock will be fine."

Mom and Dad seemed to be getting on better too. Dad's head wasn't hurting very much now and Mom had gotten the manager to agree not to charge us for the toilet tank Dad had pulled down. Dad joked about how Mom could talk anyone into anything.

And everybody laughed, even Mom, when I said, "Especially if she threatens to use the Gospel Walnut on them."

"Oh, Calvin, how can you be so levitous?" The way Mom said it really meant that she thought I was pretty clever and was glad that with the welts and the buckle cut I was still joking around. When we were done eating and were waiting for the fruit bowl to be brought over by the waiter, Dad said, "How're you feeling now, boy?"

"Fine," I said.

"Sitting okay?"

"It's a little sore."

Then he reached out and gave me a quick pat and said, "Well, you were brave, I'll say that!"

Janet and Rachael, who had seen my welts, both nodded in agreement. Janet told me that my strapping was the family record for sure.

Mom said, all cheery to change the subject, "Has Jennifer opened up at all this year?"

Rachael said, "Yes, I've been praying that you'd have the opportunity to witness to her this vacation."

"Your prayers have been answered," I said. "We've had some good talks about the Lord."

I don't know why I lied but I guess it was because I wanted to keep the mood happy.

"Praise the Lord," Mom said.

"That's a *real* answer to prayer," Rachael said. "Thank you for sharing it with us."

Even Janet smiled, though I don't think she really believed me.

"We'll invite her to church this Sunday," Mom said. "Shall I ask her or do you want to?"

"I will," I said.

"I brought some tracts with me," Janet said. "You can give her one."

"Thanks," I said.

I knew I'd never invite Jennifer to church or give her the Great News Publishers tract Janet handed me from her purse.

The front of the tract had a picture of a man's face on it. He had his hand under his chin to show he was thinking. There was a big question mark over his head and over that was written, "Which Way? Life or Eternal Death?" Behind the man was a door with a staircase leading from it with arrows by the staircase. One arrow pointed up and was marked "Eternal Life" and the other arrow pointed down and was marked "The Unbelievers' Judgment."

Mom had once read this tract to us at family prayers. It was about a man who had been raised in a godly home but who never made a personal profession of faith in Jesus. When he grew up he strayed far from the Lord and was filling up his empty life with the pleasures of the world: drinking, dancing, smoking, and even worse things the tract called "The fleeting pleasures of the flesh." Then he had a serious accident. After the accident a godly nurse told him he should trust Jesus for his recovery, physical and spiritual. Then the story sort of split into two parts. Like two answers you could choose between to solve a problem on a test. In one the man got bitter because of his accident and turned his face away from the godly nurse who was sharing a Scripture with him about "He whom the Lord loveth He chastiseth." The man finally got well without the Lord's help even though Jesus was standing knocking at his unregenerate vile heart. A year later he was drunk and he stepped in front of a freight train. He had had his chance with the godly nurse but it was too late now and he went weeping before the Awesome Judgment Seat of the Lord in a state of Original Sin and Total Depravity. He was judged to be a goat—a Vessel of Wrath—predestined to damnation, not an Elect sheep, and got sent to the Left Hand of the Lord, where there was gnashing of teeth. He wished he had listened to the godly nurse and invited Jesus into his heart when he had had the chance. His last thought in the tract before he went into the Lake of Fire was "If only . . ." After that the story stopped and they didn't say what he was saying or thinking to himself in the Lake of Fire even though he had plenty of time to say a lot because he was there for all eternity.

But in the other story, the man chose the right way and listened to the godly nurse and the "Good News was like refreshing waters on a parched land" to him. He prayed the Sinner's Prayer right there in his hospital bed and got better and gave his life to the Lord, gave up his career as a nightclub singer and started to work in a mission for alcoholics. And the desire for alcohol, tobacco, singing worldly songs and swearing left him entirely, "for he was filled up with something far, far better!" He didn't get hit by anything so you didn't get to see what happened when he stood before the Lord but it was pretty clear he was an Elect sheep and would get to go in at the Right Hand and hear the blessed words, "Well done my good and faithful servant. Come into the joy of the Lord," or something like that.

But I figured he still had problems because of the fact that if he *wasn't* one of the Elect, "predestined before the foundation of the world'' to be saved from Utter Total Depravity, then he might live his whole life like he should, maybe even marry the godly nurse and go to be missionaries with her in Liberia and hold Negro babies while she vaccinated them against polio, but it still might not work out. The Lord might say, ''I never knew you,'' and the man would say, ''But I invited you into my heart,'' and the Lord would say, ''Maybe, but I never came in, see. You are a goat. Once a goat, always a goat. You were never one of the Elect.'' Then the man would get mad and say, ''What the hell are you talking about! Nurse Jane here never said anything about this!'' Then the Lord would say, ''Too bad she didn't study Calvin's *Institutes* more, then she would have known.'' And the man would shout, ''Known what?!'' Then the Lord would say, ''About Reformed theology, that's what, pal!''

Then in my head the story got weird because I imagined the Lord saying, ''But you'll be able to study all about it now,'' and the man said, ''Where?'' And the Lord said, ''In the Lake of Fire of course.'' And the man said real sarcastically, ''How's that?'' And the Lord said, ''Because Calvin's there too.'' Then the man said, ''I thought he was a great and godly man and explained everything about God and all to everybody so we could be real Christians instead of Eastern Orthodox, Roman Catholics or Baptists!'' Then the Lord said, ''Yeah, but he's not one of the Elect, his mind was unregenerated, he is the *original* Vessel of Wrath.''

''Calvin,'' Mom said, ''what are you daydreaming about, darling?''

''Calvin and Jesus.''

Then Mom and Dad exchanged pleased looks like they had just won a prize. And I could see that Dad thought my correction had been timely and was helping me a lot.

Gino covered up his eyes very dramatically and said, ''Don'ta tempta mia!''

I was showing him my welts and had pulled down my pants so he could see how bad my injuries were.

I pulled up my pants and Gino uncovered his eyes. He said, ''Leta me tella you a lesson to learn. *Never* pulla your pantsa down and benda over in front of an olda queena likea mia!''

I laughed and he did too, then I asked him if he had ever seen welts like these before and he said once on his sister, when his mother had whipped her with a rope all over her body. I asked him why had she been whipped. Then suddenly he stopped smiling and poured out more whiskey and drank it for a while and I thought I'd never hear the story. But in the end he told me.

''It was een 'forty-four,'' he said. ''We were leeving een Modena and the Germans where steella therea before the Americans arrived. There was a German boy my seester loved. She loved 'eem too mush because she beegin to tella 'eem to be careful because my oldest brosser was in a partisans who were to blow up the truck. And because she tella the German to be careful they catch some partisano only two days before they leave and shoot them. Then my seester cry and tella my mother, who take a rope and she beat my *sorella* so much my *sorella* faint and is seeck in bed for more than a week. After the war my *sorella* go to Hamburga to meet the German boy and they marring. But my mother never speaks 'er again and my brosser say if 'ee ever seeing 'er again 'ee keell 'er. So I never see 'er again or see 'er children.''

PORTOFINO

• • • • •

I wished I hadn't asked Gino to tell me his story. Gino kept drinking when he told me. When he was done he cried and sat quietly watching the ash on the end of his cigarette.

30

• • • • •

I WORE MY shorts to the beach so Jennifer wouldn't see the belt marks. Also because of the problem I had had the day I couldn't get my Little Thing to go down. I'd asked Mom if I could get a new pair of swimming trunks but she had said, "Why? The ones you've got are brand new."

I didn't want to explain so I just said, "They're a little tight but that's O.K., never mind."

So I wore my khaki shorts with my swimming trunks underneath and no one in the family asked why because they had seen the marks on the top of my legs so they could guess.

Jennifer said, "I've got a new Lielo we can use to bathe from."

A Lielo was a kind of English air mattress. Mr. Bazlinton blew it up with a foot pump. He showed us that it had three air chambers for safety. One in the pillow part and the other two divided between the six round tubular floats. The Lielo was made of blue canvas with a rubber coating on the inside. When you put it in the water it got much darker-colored. When you lay on it face down you could smell the rubber and the water would pour over the edges when you moved and make your stomach feel cold even though the seawater was really very warm. That was because the water trapped between the crevices where the round tubes met would get really hot in the sun and so the new water felt cold by contrast.

Jennifer and I loaded our snorkels and masks onto the air mattress and asked Mr. Bazlinton if we could go right around the point of our bay, beyond the castle, and snorkel out of sight of the beach.

He said, "Very well, but you mustn't be more than twenty yards or so from the shore, old chap. If you are you will run the considerable risk of one of the motor launches running you down. Stay together."

We set off and I asked Mr. Bazlinton to tell Mom which way we were going so she wouldn't worry when she looked up and couldn't see us in the bay anymore. Also because that way I knew it would be too late for her to say no and later I could say Mr. Bazlinton had thought it was all right so I thought she would agree. How could Mom disagree then? Mr. Bazlinton was English and had been to Cambridge University and spoke with a really "refined accent" like she said.

Jennifer lay on the air mattress with her head hanging over the end looking down through her mask at the sandy sea floor sliding by under us.

Since I had the flippers I paddled us from behind

by half lying on the mattress with my legs in the water kicking.

"Can't you do better than that?" Jennifer said. "We're hardly moving at all!"

"So why don't you help with your arms?" I said.

Jennifer didn't answer me but stuck her head back under the water and kept on watching. I tried to kick harder.

"You're splashing me all over," said Jennifer. "Mind out, will you?"

"You said you wanted to go faster."

"You needn't splash like that. What's the use of being on a Lielo if you're being soaked all the time by freezing water?" Then Jennifer put her face back in the water so there was no use me arguing because she couldn't hear what I said.

I tried to kick deeper under the water. To do that I had to slide most of the way off the Lielo. This made the Lielo tip up at the front end.

"How am I supposed to be able to see the fish?" Jennifer said. "You've gone and made the Lielo bend right back, out of the water. I can't keep my head under now, you great gormless twit!"

I climbed back up on the Lielo so Jennifer could hang over the end again. Now my chin was resting on her thigh. When I kicked I guess my chin sort of pushed up and down. Jennifer took off her mask and looked at me.

"What do you think you're doing, you nasty child?" she said.

"What do you mean, 'what am I doing'?"

"Don't tell me you are unaware of the fact that you're rubbing your face on my thigh!"

"Where am I supposed to be? How can I paddle if I don't hang on like this?"

"You needn't get stroppy. And get off my leg. You're as bad as Winston!"

I knew what she meant and it made me mad. Her mom had a cocker spaniel named Winston that would stand up, hold on to your leg with its front paws, and then rub itself on you as if it were mating with your foot. If you were alone with it that was O.K.; you just pushed it away. But if it did it to you when someone else was watching, especially Mr. or Mrs. Bazlinton, then you didn't know whether to push it away or pretend you didn't notice what it was doing because it was really embarrassing. So I knew what she meant and I hadn't been doing anything like that. But I couldn't think what to say back so I just tipped over the air mattress and held Jennifer under the water for a few seconds. When I let her up she shouted, "Look what you've done, you twit! My mask's gone to the bottom!"

I said, "I'll dive for it."

"I jolly well hope so!"

I put on my mask and dove but I couldn't reach her mask before I ran out of air. We were too far out in the bay and the water was really deep.

When I came back up, Jennifer said, "You're so bloody feeble! Anyone could get that."

I said, "Oh yeah. Why don't you try?" Jennifer put on my mask and dove down. She didn't have flippers on so I knew she couldn't do it.

When she came back up about a minute later she had the mask in her hand. And after she had gasped in some air, she said, "So much for the Yanks! That's one for the jolly old U.K., boyso!" Then she tossed my mask back to me and put on her own.

I wished I had stayed in Portofino that morning or that a speedboat would hit us or something because how was I supposed to get Jennifer to love me if I couldn't even dive as deep as her?

Then she said, ''Does the poor little infant feel terribly small?''

That's when I got really furious and jumped onto her air mattress and kicked as hard as I could and paddled with my hands and headed straight out toward the horizon. Jennifer called out to me to stop but I just kept on going. ''That's my Lielo you've got there. You bring it back this instant!'' she yelled. I kept going. After about five minutes I cooled down and turned the air mattress around and started to slowly paddle back into our bay. Each time a gentle swell of water would roll under me it would lift the Lielo a little and I'd sit up and scan the water but I couldn't see Jennifer.

Then my heart started to pound and I looked around and realized that I had left her in the mouth of the bay a lot farther out than we ever went. I got really scared and started to call out her name. I started to yell it at the top of my lungs and paddle at the same time back to where I had left her.

I remembered that I had been about opposite the really big cypress tree on the hill when we had been diving for her mask. When I got there I put on my mask and swam all over looking at the sandy bottom. And I prayed, ''Dear Heavenly Father, *please* help me to find Jennifer. Forgive me for leaving her. *Please* have her be fine. *Please* forgive me for drinking alcohol on the yacht and for drinking at Gino's. I won't ever do it again. *Please* don't punish Jennifer because of me. *Please* have Jennifer be O.K.''

All I could see was sand. I began to wonder if a speedboat had hit her because a couple of water skiers were nearby. How would they have seen her in the middle of the bay? "Oh, please, Jesus, help me. Help Jennifer. Oh, Jennifer. What will Mr. Bazlinton say? What will I say? What lie can I tell? Sorry, Lord, I won't tell a lie I'll tell the truth, but please make her be all right so I won't have to lie or tell the truth because she'll be fine, Lord!"

I started to get choky and I felt like crying and maybe I did but since I was in saltwater if I cried tears I couldn't tell because my face was wet anyway.

Then I remembered that if you found a drowned person soon enough you could revive them. Janet had told me this. I was wasting precious seconds. I must get help. So I started for the beach and yelled out, "Mr. Bazlinton! Help!" But we had come out way too far for my voice to be heard.

"Help!" I yelled. Then I thought that it would be quicker to swim to the rocks, climb out, go up to the road, and run back to the beach. So I started off for the rocks. But I kept calling, "Help!" And praying, "Oh, Jesus, please, please!" And I was saying, "Oh, Jesus, please help me find her!" when somebody said, "No problem, laddie, here she is!"

Jennifer stood up from behind a large rock and laughed at me till she almost got sick and every time I tried to get a word in edgewise she'd scream out, "Help me, Jesus!" and laugh some more. I paddled toward her as hard as I could because I had decided to kill her right there and then even if she was a girl and even if I did love her.

It took me about a minute to reach the rocks. And when I did, Jennifer started to climb over them to get away from me. I took off after her. I slipped and hit my shin really hard and it hurt a lot but I was so mad I didn't care how much it hurt as long as I could catch her and kill her. Then I heard her yell out, "Ow! I'm hurt!"

And I yelled back, "Good, I hope you die!"

But she didn't answer. When I got to her she was sitting holding her foot and bleeding a lot from the arch because she had stepped on a broken wine bottle and was cut horribly deeply. She looked up at me and tears were streaming down her cheeks.

I said, "I'm sorry, it's my fault."

"Don't be an ass, it's my silly fault. Oh my foot!" she said. Then she started to cry even harder because it hurt her so much and, I think, because she was scared: it was really bleeding hard, not like a regular cut but like a picture in *Life* magazine of an accident or a dying soldier. There was a puddle of blood under her foot. "What *are* we to *do?*" Jennifer wailed.

All of a sudden I remembered the first aid things Janet had taught me.

I jumped over the rocks to where I had dropped my mask. As I ran back to Jennifer I pulled off the rubber strap that holds the mask on. I told Jennifer to let go of her foot and hold out her leg. Jennifer did what I said, and I loved her more than ever for trusting me. I found the pressure point behind her knee. I picked up a big mussel shell that was lying next to where her pool of blood was, and I told her to hold the shell round side down in the hollow behind her knee. Then I tied the rubber strap around her knee and it pressed the round part of the shell into the back of her leg. I looked at her foot and sure enough, the blood was only oozing now, not pouring out as if it was water from a tap.

I stood up and pulled off my shorts, and ripped them up the side where the seam was on both sides, and I wrapped them tight around her foot. I took the strap from her mask, which was back behind the rock she had hidden behind, and I used it to tie my torn khaki shorts tight around her foot. No blood soaked through.

Then I put my arm around Jennifer. I wanted to stroke her hair but my hands were bloody so I didn't. She lay her head against my chest and we sat still for a second or two and she said, "Thank you!" And I didn't know what to say, so I said, "It's my fault for chasing you. Forgive me."

"Don't keep talking nonsense. I was the one who made you. I'm sorry. And I'm sorry I behaved in such a beastly way before."

It was so unusual for her to be so polite now I really couldn't think what to say. I helped her up and she held on to me while she hopped back to the air mattress. I got in the water and held it against the rock while Jennifer lowered herself onto it. She was very brave; she winced in pain but never said a thing. Even though her hair was all plastered around her face and she had blood smeared on her nose and mouth and cheek and her eyes were red from crying, she looked even more beautiful than she had in the moonlight and I felt a sort of flopping around in my stomach and chest and I wished I could die for her because I loved her so much it hurt.

She lay on the air mattress and I swam behind and paddled but I was careful not to upset it by going too fast. When we got near the beach Mr. Bazlinton waded out to meet us because he had seen us coming back and saw that something was wrong.

He didn't panic or yell or anything but just said, "Looks as if you've had a spot of trouble, eh?" And he picked Jennifer up and I followed them to the pensione. Mrs. Bazlinton got the pensione owner to call the doctor. In the meanwhile we all sat in Jennifer's room and waited.

No one asked what had happened. After Mr. Bazlinton took my shorts off her foot, Mrs. Bazlinton went faint and had to sit down because the cut was a lot worse than she'd imagined. It gaped open and the edges were all blue and when they undid the strap a little from around her knee the blood welled out so they tied it tight again. And Mr. Bazlinton said, "Nasty business, eh?"

No one really noticed me. I just sat on the edge of the bed and waited. Jennifer said it hurt. Mr. Bazlinton said, "That's my girl," and held her hand.

The doctor arrived and when he saw the cut he said, "*Mama mia*! 'Ow deed thees 'appen?"

Jennifer said, "I trod on a bottle on the rocks."

The doctor said, "You could 'ave been bleeding to death. Eet ees a very deepa." He spread out his stitching things and Jennifer got very pale and closed her eyes.

"I'm afraid I can't watch this, dear," Mrs. Bazlinton said. "Your father will stay with you." And she walked to the door. Then she turned to me, "You'd better come along as well," she said. So I got up to go. But Jennifer opened her eyes and said, "Please, Mum, can he stay? I'd feel better."

When she said that, it was like a firework went off in my head and I could have done a cartwheel but I didn't, of course.

Mrs. Bazlinton said, "Certainly, dear." And she went out.

Then the doctor put Jennifer's foot to sleep with some shots. The first one hurt and Jennifer cried out a little in pain. But after that her foot was numb.

While the doctor threaded up his needle and waited for her foot to numb up completely, he said, ''Who deed thees?'' And he pointed to the rubber strap and the shell tourniquet.

Jennifer said, ''He did,'' and looked at me and smiled.

Then the doctor said, ''You 'ave saved thees young lady's life. You should be a *dottore*.''

''We're frightfully grateful, old chap,'' Mr. Bazlinton said.

''That's O.K.,'' I said.

Jennifer smiled at me and the doctor put in the first stitch.

31

SITTING ON THE beach eating our picnic, I watched Mom and Dad. They seemed happier together today than they had been for a while. Dad was leaning back against Mom's knees; he had one arm draped over her leg while he held a prosciutto sandwich in his other hand. Mom was reading out loud to us from *Robinson Crusoe*, the original story that is, not the one that was edited by atheists who had cut out all the original Bible-believing Christian content to make it "more marketable to an unbelieving world," as Mom put it. My welts were fading so I had on my bathing suit today. Mom was very pleased when Mr. Bazlinton came over to say that he was sorry about my ruined shorts but that they had probably saved Jennifer's life. Janet had even been nice to me because I had said in front of Mr. Bazlinton that it was Janet who taught me the first aid. He had thanked her and shaken her hand and said, "Well done."

Janet said afterward how inspiring the British were, just like Winston Churchill. Dad said he was proud of both of us. So for once Janet and I were on the same side. Only one bad thing happened out of all this and that was that when Mr. Bazlinton had come over and thanked me, Mom said, "Mr. Bazlinton, the Lord certainly was present in preserving dear Jennifer, wasn't He?"

Mr. Bazlinton looked a little surprised but not too surprised, because of all the years he had watched us say grace at the pensione. He said, "Certainly, certainly." Then he turned to go but Mom laid her hand on his arm and said, "Would you care to join us in a moment of thanksgiving?"

"I'd love to but I really must be getting back to . . ."

But Mom just started praying anyhow. And because she had her hand on Mr. Bazlinton's arm, he couldn't escape without yanking his arm away from Mom. So he stood there looking down at his feet and he kept clearing his throat.

"Dear Heavenly Father," Mom prayed, "we just come before Thy heavenly throne this day in thanksgiving for dear Jennifer and Calvin, who You preserved for Your own marvelous purposes yesterday. And we just ask that You will just stretch out Thy gentle hand and just touch little Jennifer that her foot may be made whole once again. We pray now especially that in her hour of need Thou wilt touch Jennifer's dear heart with Thy love and just let her feel Thy dear presence with her that she wilt come to Thee, Lord, and accept Thee as her personal savior. And we just ask that Thou wilt also so touch Mr. and

Mrs. Bazlinton with Thy sovereign love so that they will know the joy of Thy love for eternity. And we just thank Thee that Thou hast sent Thine only begotten Son that whosoever shalt believe in Him shall have eternal life and not perish. So Lord, draw near to the Bazlintons in this hour of testing; heal Jennifer and reveal Thyself to the Bazlintons that like Elisha their eyes mayest be opened. In Jesus' sweet precious name we pray, Amen.''

While Mom had been praying I watched Mr. Bazlinton's feet. He stood on one foot and began to dig a pretty deep hole in the sand with the other. When Mom was done Mr. Bazlinton looked a little dazed, then he glanced around and noticed a couple of people watching us all praying. He said, ''I'm much obliged, now I really *must* get along,'' and he backed away and walked up the beach pretty fast without looking around once.

''Mom,'' I said, ''I wish you wouldn't.''

''Wouldn't what?''

''Pray like that.''

Mom and the girls looked shocked and Mom said, ''Calvin, we are *never* to be ashamed of our Lord!''

I said I wasn't ashamed but somehow it seemed kind of rude to make somebody suddenly pray with you when he wasn't expecting it.

''Mr. Bazlinton was grateful we cared enough to bring Jennifer to the Lord. Anyway it was an opportunity to share the gospel with him while his heart was tender for Eternal Things.''

''But isn't that sort of unfair?''

''What do you mean?''

''Well, you know: to preach at someone through your prayers when you're pretending to be praying to

God but you're really using your prayers to preach or something.''

Then I was really surprised because all of a sudden Dad said, ''I must say I agree with Calvin. I'm not comfortable manipulating The Things of the Lord even for evangelization.''

Now I was sorry I had said anything because Janet and Rachael both gave me looks to say, now see what you've done! You've started a fight!

But instead of fighting, Dad just said, ''Well never mind, we all come to the Lord in our own way.'' And he sounded so reasonable and all that it was like I was part of the wrong family because Dad was never reasonable. Mom wanted to say more things. She always did. But I guess we all looked so relieved that Dad was being reasonable that she just said, ''Shall I read another chapter?''

And we all said, ''Yes.''

Mom sat back in the deck chair and we all sat on the towels and listened to the story about the footprint in the sand and how Robinson Crusoe got his man Friday.

When the chapter was done I walked up to the Pensione Biea to see Jennifer. She was lying on her bed all propped up on pillows. Next to her was a bowl of fruit and a bottle of San Pellegrino mineral water. Her foot was bandaged and was up on a pillow. Jennifer had on the same white nightgown she had been wearing on the path above Portofino when we met in the moonlight. Her mom and dad were on the beach so we were alone. ''How are you?'' I said.

Jennifer answered by holding out a bunch of grapes and saying, ''Have one.''

I sat down on the chair next to her bed and said, ''When are you going to be able to come out again?''

"I'm not. We're leaving two days early since there's no point me sitting in bed here."

"You mean you're leaving today?"

"No. Tomorrow morning."

Then we sat awhile and ate some grapes and I swallowed all the seeds because I didn't want to spit them out in front of Jennifer. She spit her seeds out right into the wastepaper basket like it was a game.

"What am I supposed to do with you gone?" I said.

Jennifer spit some more seeds, then said, "I suppose you'll have to amuse yourself for a change!" And she spit a seed at me and winked.

"Well, I don't think it's funny. I'll miss you, a lot."

"You're very sweet. By the way, is your mum off her onion?"

"Why?"

"Because," Jennifer said, "she stands on beaches and prays for an hour or two with people's fathers and these people's fathers come into their daughters' room and say they've met a religious lunatic."

I couldn't think of what to answer so I ate some more grapes and swallowed more seeds.

"Jennifer, will you give me your address so I can write to see how your foot is?"

Jennifer spit out another seed and said, "Is that all you want to know?"

"Well, what's wrong with that?"

"You're not thinking of visiting us in England on your school hol's are you?"

"Why, wouldn't you be glad to see me?"

"Don't be silly, of course I'd be glad to see you if you can refrain from chasing me onto broken bottles!" And she spit another seed at me and laughed.

Then Mrs. Bazlinton came into Jennifer's room. I stood up to go, but she said, "You may stay as long as you wish to keep Jennifer company."

Jennifer said, "Mummy, will you write out our address and telephone number for Calvin so he can visit us during school break?"

Mrs. Bazlinton didn't look very pleased but she wrote it out anyway and said, "*Do* write to us and let us know how you are." But the way she said it I could tell she didn't really want me to visit them. I could guess why. They knew we were strange people. Mom's prayer had proved it once and for all. I figured that on vacation they let Jennifer play with me because they couldn't help it but they didn't want Reformed missionaries showing up at home who were only vacation friends. Vacations were different than regular life—there were different rules.

I said, "Thank you," and folded up the piece of paper.

Jennifer said to me, "Could you hand me my hairbrush please?"

I did and when I was handing it to her she winked. I took the wink to be a message about the hairbrush and how I had used it before and how she knew I knew her mom didn't want me to visit but we could find a way maybe.

Then I went back to the beach.

Only Rachael was there. Mom and Janet had gone shopping in Santa Margherita and Dad had walked back to Portofino early. Rachael said, "I want to say how sorry I am I told on you. I didn't know how hard you'd get punished."

This was the second time Rachael had apologized so I just said, "I already said it's O.K."

"Are you still mad at me?"

"No. . . . Our family's strange."

"What do you mean, strange?"

"Come on, you know what I mean. What kind of people live in Switzerland and are missionaries to Roman Catholic youth? What sort of mothers pray all the time at people so they don't like me? How many people have dads that pull down toilet flush boxes and smash dishes? That's what I mean!"

"Well maybe we're a little different from other people. But what's wrong with that?"

"I'll tell you what's wrong! I'm sick and tired of it, that's what! I hate this family, that's what! I hate Mom's talks about our bodies and how they're changing, that's what! And I hate Dad's church services! And I hate Janet and I hate the Gospel Walnut and I hate being missionaries! That's what!"

Rachael stood up and said, "*Oh, Calvin!*"

And I yelled at her, "You sound just like Mom!"

Rachael yelled back, "I take that as a compliment! Mother is a wonderful woman of God! We are supposed to *honor* our parents!"

"That's a laugh! Mom's not a woman of God, she's a scarlet woman, that's what!"

Rachael really got mad and she screamed, "You cannot speak in that way, you are a . . . a . . ." and she started to cry but I didn't care.

I shouted, "I saw her *kissing* Jonathan Edwards!"

Then Rachael put her hands over her ears and said, "I won't listen to these things! You are a wicked boy!" And she ran off the beach and left all her stuff lying there. I sat down and I felt bad because I hadn't meant to tell on Mom but it sort of slipped out.

Rachael didn't come back so I picked up her towels and her Bible she always carried with her, and I walked back to Portofino. I was feeling sad so I didn't even stop to try and catch the lizards on the wall but went straight back to the Hotel Nazionale where I put Rachael's stuff outside her room.

Then I walked up to the church and knelt down in front of Mary. I prayed and I remembered I had never said thank you to her for the miracle of Jennifer in the moonlight. So I prayed, "Hail Mary, full of Grace, thank you for the idea on how to meet Jennifer. And thank you that she came out to meet me. And please help me to see her more when I go back to school in England because I love her."

I took fifty of the hundred lire Dad had given me and I bought a candle and lit it in front of Mary and crossed myself.

32

MOM CAME INTO the room where I was getting dressed for supper and said, "Why?"

"Why what?"

"Why did you betray me?"

It hit me what she was talking about and it hit me too that in a way Rachael was worse than Janet because Rachael had a conscience. She was very good and pious and she was a tattletale.

"Mom, I'm sorry."

"How *could* you? What are you trying to do to me?"

"We were arguing about something else and it just slipped out."

"You've probably ruined my marriage."

I saw she was really upset so I didn't say anything about how *I* might have told, but it was *her* that had done the kissing.

"Will she tell Dad?"

"She says she won't. I hope I can believe her. But you know Rachael."

Again I thought things but didn't say them. I thought how it was Mom who had given Rachael all those speeches about how your conscience was like a tender new plant and you had to care for it night and day and how you should always heed its still small voice and do what it said, which was like letting sunlight into a dark room so the tender little plant could grow. Well, Rachael's conscience had grown all right, like the vine in "Jack and the Beanstalk." And if Rachael heard or saw or even thought anything bad she told or admitted it and seemed to actually enjoy the punishment she got. Her conscience had had a lot of water and sunlight. It was so healthy it made Rachael a menace. If you could get some kind of weed-killer for consciences I would have poured it on Rachael's head—or her chest, if consciences are in your heart. I'd probably have poured it on both places.

Mom stood there a second, then said, "I hope you're satisfied!" She turned and walked out and shut the door behind her very quietly.

That night at supper Dad seemed fine, he even joked a little about the toilet tank hitting him and said how he liked being right in Portofino after all and how the Hotel Nazionale was quieter at night, even counting the sound of people in the square, that anything was better than listening to the pounding of music from the night club La Busola in Paraggi.

The manager came over to our table and handed Dad a letter. "Thees lettera camea for youa today."

Dad looked at it and put it down next to his bread sticks face up. I glanced over. It was marked "*Personal and Confidential*" in red letters. It had a Swiss stamp on it. I wondered what it was. Then I looked up at Mom because she had made a gasping choking gurgling noise in her throat. I saw her staring at the letter.

Dad finished his plate of ripe figs and prosciutto and picked up the letter and said, "I wonder what Jonathan Edwards wants?" as he slit it open with his table knife. Mom made some little hissing noises and Janet sort of sighed and Rachael actually squeaked like a mouse. I don't know if I made any frightened noises or not but my heart pounded pretty hard. Dad got the letter out and started to read it out loud even though it was marked "Confidential."

" 'Dear Ralph,' " he began. " 'It is with Christian sorrow and pain of conscience that I write to you to inform you that I am returning to the United States immediately.' " Dad looked up and said, "Somebody must have died," then kept on reading out loud. " 'At first I considered prevaricating to you about the cause of my sudden departure from the field of the Lord in which we have been co-laborers for the Kingdom. But the Lord has spoken to me and I feel that to not tell you the truth will only compound the wrong I have done.' " This sounded bad. It sounded like Jonathan Edwards was letting plenty of light into his conscience and was about to water it a lot. And that we were about to have a lot of trouble because the Lord had spoken to Jonathan. Dad looked up at us and said, "This is very odd, what *can* he mean?"

Dad looked back down and kept on reading. " 'I have committed the sin of King David who looked upon Bathsheba and coveted her. I have looked upon your wi . . .' " Then Dad trailed off and stopped reading out loud and started to read to himself. As he read I watched him and I saw his face go bright red and the big vein in the side of his neck started to bulge out. He slowly stood up while reading. Mom started to stand up too. She began to edge around the end of the table so as not to be right next to him. The waiter came over to ask if we were done with the first course but no one answered because Dad's face was going purple and Mom was taking more steps away from him into the potted palms. Several guests turned their heads to see what was going on. Dad stopped reading and whispered, "This is the end." He turned and walked to the door of the terrace and went inside and from inside he yelled, "Elsa, come up to the room! Now!"

Mom stood frozen. She was all white and she held onto the back of a chair to steady herself; she said, "Good-bye, children," and turned to follow Dad. Then we all said at once, "No, Mom, don't go with him!" because we knew he was really angry. Worse than ever before and it was probably dangerous and we loved Mom and didn't want her killed on vacation.

Mom said, "I must!"

We all stood up and said loudly, "No, Mom!"

The waiter came over and said, "What ees the problema weeth the prosciutto?"

But we ignored him and Janet grabbed Mom's arm and said very impassioned, "He'll kill you!"

Everyone in the restaurant looked at us even more because Janet had shrieked this out pretty dramatically.

Mom followed Dad anyway. We all stood looking at each other horrified then we all ran after her.

We arrived at the top of the landing of the hallway outside their door just as Mom went into the room. We stood in the hall holding on to each other. Rachael kept saying, "Please, Lord Jesus," and Janet would say to her, "Just shut up," every time Rachael said, "Please, Lord Jesus!"

I didn't say anything. But I thought that if it took my whole life I'd hunt down Jonathan Edwards and kill him for telling. He had promised me he'd leave and not make any more trouble.

We all listened and kept waiting for screaming and yelling sounds and the sound of Dad smashing stuff or throwing things at Mom, but it was deadly silent in their room.

Janet said, "He's strangling her. That's why we can't hear anything! He's killing your mother!" And she looked at Rachael and me like we weren't taking this seriously enough. Rachael burst into tears and Janet slapped her and said, "Get a hold of yourself." We waited some more and then suddenly the door opened and Dad stomped out into the hall. He had his suitcase in his hand. And from behind him we could hear Mom saying, "No, please, Ralph, no!" But Dad kept on going anyway. He walked right past us without speaking a word. We stepped back to let him pass by us in the narrow hall. He walked down the stairs and disappeared without ever looking at us even though he had had to squeeze by us in the hallway.

We all ran into the room to see what he had done to Mother. She was fine except she was crying. Nothing was broken or even turned over in their room. Rachael blurted out, "Where's he going?"

"I don't know," Mom said. She blew her nose and said, "It's entirely my fault. I have destroyed our family and now you've lost your father. Can you ever forgive me?" She started to cry very hard and we all hugged her and cried, too.

When we were done crying we asked her more

about it. Mom told us how Dad never said a word. Just finished reading the letter, dropped it on the floor, pulled down his suitcase from the top of the cupboard, swept all his stuff into it, and marched out. Mom went over to the place where the letter was lying and she picked it up and read it to herself and her hand shook. "He told him everything!" she said. I thought about how when I found Jonathan Edwards I'd make him suffer before I actually killed him.

I wanted to know what was in the letter but I didn't ask and Mom wasn't saying. She put the letter into her pocket and that was that.

None of us knew what to do next. So we sat there awhile. Then Mom said, "We'll go home tomorrow morning on the first train. Maybe he's going home."

That meant our vacation was going to be cut short by three days. Now it began to sink in how terrible this really was. Janet said, "I suppose we'll be going back to America?"

Mom said, "Of course there is no way we will be able to remain in the Lord's work under these conditions."

Mom got up and started to pack all her things up to be ready for the morning. And she found a few clothes of Dad's he had missed when he swept all his stuff into his suitcase. Every time she came across a pair of socks or his pajama bottoms, she would burst into tears and say, "Oh, Ralph, what have I done?" and hug the sock or whatever and rock back and forth.

Rachael and Janet would exchange glances and nod their heads like they were agreeing with her about something. It made me mad to see how they were enjoying it all. So I said, "What about the rest of our vacation?"

"I'm terribly sorry, dear," Mom said.

Janet dug her fingernails into my arm and whispered, ''I think we have enough problems without *you* adding to them.'' And she dug extra specially deep when she said, ''*You*.''

''Ow!'' I said.

''Don't take it out on him, Janet!'' yelled Rachael.

Mom didn't say for Janet to stop hurting me, she only kept moaning to herself, ''Oh, Ralph. Oh, Ralph, what have I done?'' and pressing his swimming trunks, which she had found on the floor, to her face.

Suddenly the door burst open and we all jumped. Dad was standing there and he dropped his suitcase and said, ''Elsa, I have been a fool!'' We all froze because Dad crashed down on his knees and half shouted, half cried, ''Elsa, I have driven you from me! Forgive me!'' And he started to sob, and then Mom rushed over to him and crashed down on her knees too and they hugged and wailed and sobbed on each other's shoulders.

Janet grabbed me by the hair and whispered, ''Come on, let's get out of here.'' She pulled me and Rachael toward the door. But Dad stood up choking and sniffing and said, ''Stay, children! There's no point you going. What was hidden has been revealed!'' So we stayed but didn't know where to look because this was the most embarrassing thing in the world.

Dad and Mom hugged and kissed some more and came over and sat on the bed. Dad turned to us and said, ''Never forget what has happened tonight.'' He was speaking in his preaching voice. I knew *I* certainly wouldn't forget. Then he said, ''Your mother and I have both been behaving foolishly. I because I have not been paying proper attention to your mother and loving her the way Christ loves the Church, of which marriage is a picture. And your mother because she has done a foolish sinful thing. But I want you all to see that the love of Christ is bigger than us both.''

Mom turned to us and said, ''Yes. Oh yes, Lord Jesus.''

Dad said, ''We both beg you, our children's forgiveness.'' We mumbled that it was fine and got up to go. This time Dad let us leave and we all went to our rooms without saying anything to each other. It was sort of like a dream because it had ended so well. We all felt happy and like Rachael said the next day, it was like the second coming of Christ had happened and we had been raptured and met Him in the air just as the Anti-Christ was closing in.

33

THE LAST DAY in Portofino I went around to say good-bye, and see you next year, to all my vacation friends. The last day was always a sad day and now I was at a boarding school in England it was also a day when I started getting that sick, going-back-to-school feeling, in my stomach. It was the same feeling of hollow anxiety I had all year in school. After a while it got so I didn't even notice it except when it got especially bad the day before tests or before punishments and at other times like when they served liver and Matron would make me sit at my place until I ate it all, even if it was hours later.

Once she had served me the same piece of cold liver for two days running. At every meal it looked worse, especially at breakfast. At lunch on the second day I had finally eaten the whole thing without chewing any of it. After that I asked to be excused from the table and ran out to the toilets where I threw it all up.

Besides that sort of thing, there was the hard lump of homesickness in my chest which only got worse when letters and things arrived from home because I wasn't there. Even though I hated being at home, compared to being in Italy, I hated boarding school even worse. I had gotten used to being years behind everyone else in my schoolwork and to lying about most things since I couldn't do them the way I was supposed to. But I never got used to the last day of our summer vacation in Italy.

Gino told me to keep up my drawing at school so I could become an artist like him. Then he laughed and said, "But maybe you no wanna to be likea mia!"

I said, "Of course I'd like to be like you." And that was true, too. Gino got to stay in Portofino all year except when he went back to Modena to visit his mother and brother.

The bartender at the bar on the dock said, "Senda me a posta card for the bar." I said I would. I said that every year and I always forgot to send one for him to put under the glass on the bar top along with hundreds of other postcards, some from very famous people. The ones from the famous people he put face down under the glass so you could see the names on them. I guessed the ones that were face up where you saw the pictures were from people who weren't famous. The bartender stood drying glasses like he did all day and night and said, "*Ciao*, Calvino, seea you nexta year!" when I left.

I went up to the church but didn't go in since there was a wedding going on. I looked in the side door across at Mary in her faded blue gown. I nodded to her and wished she would nod back or cry or something like the false pagan superstitious Roman Catholic ''simple people who are sadly deluded,'' as Dad said, swore they saw her do sometimes.

Then I walked over to Paraggi to say good-bye to the Banini. Jennifer had already gone home to England so I didn't hurry along the path. I picked an almost ripe fig and ate it on the way and when I got down to the road I decided to swim from the rocks below the road to the beach since this would be my last chance to swim before we got on the bus to the Santa Margherita station at noon.

I left my T-shirt and sandals on the rocks and dove in and swam underwater as far as I could, then turned over and swam on my back almost the whole way to the beach. I stared up at the little clouds in the pale blue August sky and wondered why sky and clouds looked so different from one place to the next. This was an Italian sky for sure. You'd never see the sky looking like this in Switzerland or England.

Gino said that the English never produced any truly great painters because they didn't have good light. Italy had the best light, he said, and that was why they had the greatest painters. I had asked Gino, ''What about Holland and Rembrandt and all?'' and Gino said, ''Eet ees all tooa small! All too interior! Portraits yes, families seetting at table, yes, but Botticelli? Never! 'Ow could Venus be born out of the gray Northa Sea een a rainstorm on a colda day?!'' And he would turn back to his easel and say, ''No, no, Italia ees where you musta paint! Painta Life! Germany for cars and beer, America for preetty girls and beesineess, but Italia ees where you paint!''

It was true. The light *was* different in Italy. It made things glow.

Janet said that was just my imagination and light was light wherever it was but she was wrong. When I told Gino what she had said, he said, "That'sa why 'alf the world cannot understanda art, they don'ta know 'ow to look! Your seester would make a good German!"

When I reached the beach I got out of the water as slowly as I could because this was my last swim of the year in the Mediterranean. Every step I took out of the water I felt more like crying. I went up to the Pensione Biea and asked Lucrezia if I could shower off since I was going to be riding trains for the rest of the day. Lucrezia acted like I was still a guest in the Pensione and handed me the key to one of the unoccupied rooms that had a shower. She even got a towel out of the hall cupboard for me. I asked her how her parents were and she started to cry because her mother had some kind of cancer and was at a clinic somewhere near Milano. Then Lucrezia said that we can only hope and pray about such things and she crossed herself. If I had been my mom I would have taken this as a sign from the Lord that Lucrezia's heart was open to God's Word and witnessed to her about how only Jesus could help her and how she must believe in Him and not the Pope and how she should lead her mother to the Lord before it was too late. But I was not Mom so Lucrezia never did hear the Good News from me because all I did was to cross myself too and say, "I hope she gets better." Then I went to take my shower and the water was like it had always been, lukewarm, but at least the sea salt wouldn't make me itch for the whole train trip.

I walked back down to the beach and I found the Banini having an espresso at the beach bar. He was reading a copy of *La Stampa*, which he put down when he saw me. ''Why youa no comea to 'elpa me today?''

''This is our last day and I had to pack this morning. We're leaving at noon.''

''So soon! Youa only stay a few days. Whya you no stay longer?''

''I wish we could. I wish I lived here.''

''No, no, Italia noa good to leeve een. No good work, no good money. You are lucky een America.''

''But I don't live in America, I live in Switzerland.''

''Svizzera the same. Gooda money, gooda job. You noa wanta to leeve een Italia!''

We argued a little more and I told him that Italy was the best place on earth and he laughed and said something to the fat lady behind the bar about what I had said and they both laughed, but not at me I don't think, but about Italy. Then he pinched my cheek and told me to come back soon to help him with the boats.

All this time I was getting sicker and sicker and sadder and sadder feeling because the clock was saying ten to eleven and I knew I had to start back to Portofino, get changed, and be ready to leave the hotel at twelve sharp. I ran down the beach to see if there was anyone else to say good-bye to. The Italian family asked me to have lunch with them and I said I couldn't because I was leaving and they all shouted out, ''*Buon, viaggio!*'' I cut through the Pensione Biea to get out to the road and for no particular reason I ran up the back stairs to Jennifer's room and tried the door. The door was unlocked and the room was empty and the bed was stripped down to the mattress. But I could still smell the Pears soap Jennifer used and the smell made it like she was right there and made my chest ache.

Then I noticed something sticking out from under some folded towels on the dresser and I picked it up. It was Jennifer's hairbrush. It had a couple of long pale blond hairs of hers stuck in it. I reached out and touched one of the hairs and ran it through my fingers and thought about Jennifer and the only picture I could get of her in my mind was of her face next to mine with blood on it, all pale and hurt and tears on her cheeks when she cut her foot. I turned and left her room as quietly as I could and held her hairbrush under the towel Lucrezia had lent me so no one would see me with it.

I ran out the back door and up the road and as I ran I wondered if Jennifer had left the brush on purpose for me to find.